WHEN RED MIST RISES

AILEEN & CALLAN MURDER MYSTERIES
BOOK FOUR

SHANA FROST

Copyright © 2021 by Shanaya Wagh

All rights reserved. No part of this publication may be reproduced, distributed, or transmitted in any form or by any means, including photocopying, recording, or other electronic or mechanical methods, without the prior written permission of the author, except in the case of brief quotations embodied in critical reviews and certain other non-commercial uses permitted by copyright law. For permission requests, write to author@shanafrost.com

This is a work of fiction. Similarities to real people, places, businesses, or events are entirely coincidental.

Website: https://shanafrost.com

WHEN RED MIST RISES

First Edition.

ISBN: 978-93-5526-843-3

Written By: Shanaya Wagh as Shana Frost

Copyedited by Laura Kincaid

Proofread by Charlotte Kane

Image on the cover by RitaE and Peter H

Print Cover designed by Germancreative

For my dear Reader Friends.

Your love inspires me to write.

BOOKS BY SHANA

You can find an entire (latest) catalogue on the website:
www.shanafrost.com/books

But here's what you can read next…

Aileen and Callan Murder Mysteries

When Murder Comes Home

When Eyes Don't Lie

When Birds Fall Silent

When Red Mist Rises

When Old Fires Ignite

Banerjee and Muller Mystery Series

Smokes of Death Beer

SCOTTISH GLOSSARY

Banlaoch- Female Warrior
Bairn- Child/Toddler
Bampot- Crazy
Boke- Vomit
Feartie- Coward
Eejit- Idiot
Wee- Little
Shinty- A team game played with sticks & a ball

This book is written in English (UK)

PROLOGUE

Loch Fuar, 3 p.m.

DD,

I am so naïve. My thoughts swing like a pendulum, never steady, never still.

Even fools see the light, and I didn't.

It's all about to end now – today. I have toiled in thought and judgement must happen.

I have done nothing but suffered. Suffered such pain and agony.

It all ends today.

Such satisfaction it gives me to say that.

Aye, it will end now. And there will be peace.

Loch Fuar, 8.30 p.m.

DD,

I thought agony was past me and now I'm blindsided again. I never had many expectations of her. Flighty little thing – so cruel, so manipulative.

To run away, to leave and to break apart a family. It comes to her like breathing. She set a curtain on fire; set a home on fire.

All is lost again. In mere days, peace has been shattered, and now there's only silence.

Silent screams threaten to tear me apart. I can't see, can't hear, can't taste, can't touch. I can only smell. Smell the devastation.

Loch Fuar, 8 p.m.

DD,

You've been my one faithful friend, my rock, the only one who understands. We burn together; we rise together. Not like a phoenix, oh no, but like a metal burned and shaped, scraped until smooth.

Today my world pivoted again. Unlike Pompeii, the destruction, as I look back on it, unravelled like an unwanted Christmas gift. Something that sits in your loft until it festers and stains.

And now it's all splintered. But once again, the earth is peaceful. For once, I let myself feel. This time I can't see, can't hear, can't touch, can't smell, but I can taste the tears on my tongue.

CHAPTER ONE

Finding your best friend was the hardest job ever. He knew Blaine lay six feet under, but where was the body?

Squish.

He doubled over as the mud sucked at his Wellingtons.

Autumn in Scotland meant rain, the least ideal weather for treading through the peatlands.

On a freezing, rainy morning, all Detective Inspector Callan Cameron wanted was to stay warm, snuggled next to his girlfriend. But the job came before comfort.

His watch indicated the tenth hour, yet the sky didn't agree. Grey clouds hovered threateningly, blocking out all the sunlight.

Callan ducked to enter the tent and tuned into the crackle of the radio.

This vast peatland hadn't seen another soul for decades and now scrub-wearing officials littered the virgin land. Police constables from the other town, a team of forensic anthropologists and pathologists, and Callan all huddled under the tent. A few poor police constables stood guard outside, dripping from head to toe, teeth almost chattering, as they flanked the white-and-blue police tape.

'Dr Brown.'

The scrub-wearing pathologist turned to him, her face grim. He'd known her for years but had never called her anything but 'doctor'. The new Callan let people in.

She crooked a finger. 'Detective, follow me.'

Callan huffed. Guess he was in for a shower too. He bundled into the scrubs and set off behind the doctor.

Goosebumps-inducing drops of rain smacked against his numb face.

His heart contracted.

How could he be so desperate to find Blaine's body yet not want to find him?

Aileen Mackinnon had suggested that finding Blaine would put a lid on the past. It would make Callan acknowledge the end of hope he'd held on to for fifteen years.

Dr Brown entered a barricaded area where brownish-red mud lay in a heap, along with bright yellow markers cautioning them to tread steadily. The smell of fresh earth entrapped them.

Callan drew in his wet lip and sucked on it like an ice lolly. He took a moment, bracing himself for what lay in that ditch.

His best friend.

Dressed in all black, his soot-coloured hair in a military cut, Callan fit in with the roiling clouds. A lone figure amongst the flashing red and blue lights.

Callan squished his way beside the doctor and crouched.

She carefully folded back the sheet covering the ditch. 'The bloody rain's slowing us down. We need to remove him now. It would damage the body otherwise.'

Callan grunted, unable to form words, craning his neck to see the corpse.

Fifteen years it might've been, but the peat never let anything rot away. Blaine Macgregor would look the same, all these years later, like Sleeping Beauty – unaged.

Fists clenched until his knuckles turned white, jaw clamped so hard he worried his teeth might splinter, Callan dared a peek.

A body lay, clothes covered in granules of mud. Baggy jeans and a red sweatshirt contrasted with the grey light. Curls of short strawberry-blond hair tickled his forehead. And the face…

Cold tingles zinged through Callan. The rain, coupled with the breeze, had nothing to do with it.

This couldn't be.

'That's… that's *not* Blaine, Dr Brown.'

Dr Brown swivelled towards Callan. She'd narrowed her bottle-green eyes, and the faint wrinkles beside them stretched into tight lines. 'I thought as much. Those baggy jeans are typical 1980s. My mum loved those.'

Callan ran a hand through his hair, displacing a few raindrops.

Oh crap! If this wasn't Blaine, they had a new body on their hands.

'Do we ken who it is?'

Dr Brown sighed. 'I called you as soon as we cleared out the peat. I got some preliminary pictures before you arrived, but I'll need time to examine him to give you any information.'

This man needed to be in the system already for his fingerprints to tell them anything.

The temperature dropped a notch, making Callan want to draw his arms in.

Not Blaine. He still hadn't found Blaine.

Who was this man?

Callan did a quick calculation. 'How long do ye think he's been here?'

'Judging by his clothes, he's from the late seventies or eighties – unless he liked vintage styles.'

Callan raised his blue-grey eyes to the landscape around them. 'And no sign of Blaine Macgregor?'

Dr Brown pursed her lips. 'Sorry.'

'Maybe we need to get the metal detectors out again.'

Nodding, the doctor replaced the sheet over the ditch. 'I'll try to get the results to you as soon as I can.'

Callan dug his toes into the ground and stood up. 'Could ye email us a picture of the body? I'll cross-check it with older missing-person cases.'

A nod was all he received as the doctor got to work on removing the man from his burial place.

Callan walked out of the tent, scrub-free, and into the thrashing rain, letting it wash over him. He needed to contact his boss. After all, they had a new case to investigate.

HUDDLED IN THE WARM AROMA OF COFFEE, DRY IN HIS fresh pair of all-black clothes, Callan ran his boss, Detective Chief Inspector Rory Macdonald, through what had transpired at the peatland.

'Goodness, Callan, another bog body?'

Callan sipped at the bitter sludge in his cup, savouring the burn on his tongue. The warmth sent his frozen fingers and lips tingling. 'What did the peatland look like thirty to forty years ago?'

Rory stared into his own mug. 'Ye would've been a wee thing then. No one ventured in those cursed lands, especially on misty days. It's easy to lose yer way or slip into a ditch.'

Callan contemplated what he'd seen, his photographic memory replaying the scene.

The scents and frigid water droplets came to life, igniting his skin with goosebumps.

The corpse in the ditch lay on his side, as if sleeping. His left hand lay limp, squashed under his body, the right carelessly resting on his torso, his denim-clad legs in a tangle.

He wouldn't have gone to *sleep* if he'd fallen in that ditch, would he? He'd have tried to get out.

Callan leaned a hip on the reception desk of the silent police station. 'I reckon he never tried to get out – couldn't. If I wanted to jump to conclusions, I'd say he was dead *before* he got in.'

Rory sat his mug on the table with a thud. 'Don't leap before ye think. Has Dr Brown found any evidence to suggest it was murder? We don't need to raise public alarm. People will question how many bodies the peatland has swallowed. Maybe they'll think every missing person's buried there. Let's wait until the pathologist confirms there's foul play involved.'

Callan nodded. It made sense. Until a few months ago, murder had never painted the Highlands of Loch Fuar in blood.

And now they'd had a few too many. Bloody hell!

Rory tugged at a tuft of his candy-floss-like white hair, and Callan noticed it was unusually ragged.

'Don't.' He glared at Callan. 'Suzie thought it would be good to give my hair a trim while I napped.'

With his grandchildren, this burly detective turned to mush, a doting grandfather. He'd let his grandchildren get away with murder for sure.

Rory had once come to the office with painted nails and glitter stuck to his collar, calling it his penance for fathering three children. Now he had another eagerly awaited grandwean on the way.

Callan couldn't wrap his head around the entire circus. Why give birth to little devils?

'I'll dig into the missing person files from the 1970s and '80s.' He swivelled right when his stomach let out an audible roar.

Aye, he'd forgotten breakfast again.

Ever since that brief respite at the beginning of October, the last couple of weeks had been a grind. He'd barely seen Aileen, usually had to wrangle the two minutes to brush his teeth and the circles beneath his bleary eyes now matched the dark shade of his hair.

Rory chuckled. 'Maybe snag some snacks at Isla's.'

He'd eat sand at this point. The divine snacks at Isla's Bakery would be akin to eating ambrosia.

And it would hopefully help him find the dead man sooner. A murdered man, his gut was sure.

COLD RAINDROPS SPLATTERED HER MAROON COAT, AND SHE shivered when the wind kissed the exposed skin on her neck. A breeze from the underworld.

Everything sat in darkness, her vision tunnelled to focus on the only light flickering above a door.

A white hand reached for the doorknob. Her other ghoulish hand touched the wooden door, and it eased open. The groan sent a shudder through her, the light overhead heating her scalp.

Aileen set one trembling foot in the doorway. Her

breath hitched at the strong stench of freshly polished wood and musk.

The air inside this place didn't move, as if petrified by Medusa. Dust particles froze under the light beam and then – then something tightened a noose around her neck.

It tightened and tightened. Aileen gasped, fought, and flailed her arms.

Oxygen, Oxygen…

Someone forced her hands back and the grip on her throat squeezed until tears leaked out of her eyes.

Oxygen.

'Ah!' Aileen shot up, gasping. She'd worked herself into a frenzy again, her legs wrapped in the bed sheets.

Aileen's hand caressed her throat, her parched throat.

Just a nightmare – like the one she had every night.

Doubling over, she pushed her head between her folded knees, her heart still slamming against her chest.

Her shirt stuck to her armpits, damp and stinky. She needed a shower.

Aileen peeked at the bedside clock.

'Ten! Breakfa—'

No, she didn't have to make breakfast for her guests.

Now her eyes dampened with hurtful tears. She didn't have any guests and wouldn't for the foreseeable future.

Aileen tugged the laptop which rested on the other side of the bed.

People who crunched numbers until the wee hours of the morning – especially when those numbers held no hope of salvaging a business without taking on a huge debt – slept in.

Aye, the smart accountant from the city had burned through the cash from her severance pay. She'd led with her heart and landed in a ditch.

Aileen gnawed on her lip, pushing the prickle in her throat down.

If Dachaigh failed, her gran's hard-earned money and reputation would sink faster than the Titanic and it would be Aileen's fault.

She should have known this, predicted it, and worked harder. Aileen covered her face. This meant the end of her adventurous dreams.

With such dismal business, Dachaigh would run out of money in three months. Then winter would descend with a vengeance. A season where most tourists would head for warmer countries.

She'd have to leave all this behind: the scenery, the freedom of being her own boss, her new friendships and Callan, her new *boyfriend*.

Failure. The great forensic accountant had finally landed on her face.

What would they say?

I told you so.

Aileen pushed herself out of bed. Even if she had no guests, she had an inn. At least she could keep it clean and then grab a chocolate eclair or two from Isla. Some chocolate eclairs and her worries would vanish.

AT TWO IN THE AFTERNOON, AILEEN WOUND HER WAY TO Isla's Bakery.

Her friend's wild red hair stood out like a flame in the dreary woods through the glass windows. The rain beat down on Aileen's back as she dashed into the bakery's calorie-filled warmth.

Aileen braced for the rib-crushing hug Isla greeted her with every day. But to her astonishment, Isla remained behind the counter, dealing with the long line of customers who wanted the chicken-stuffed pastries she served after noon.

If only Aileen had a booming business like Isla's.

She excused her way to the counter, shrugging off scowls and glares sent her way by the queuing crowd.

Where was Isla's nephew? The teenaged Andrew helped out at the bakery. He worked from dawn till 9 a.m. and after he finished his classes for the day.

'Hey, Isla, where's Andrew?' Aileen called out over the buzz of gossip.

Isla's feet didn't bounce as she worked, and dark circles ringed her eyes. Aileen had never seen her best friend this low on energy.

Thinking on her feet, Aileen grabbed an apron from the hook and jostled towards Isla. 'How can I help?'

'Man the till!'

And so they worked, falling into a surprisingly easy rhythm, the queue moving along quicker until it dwindled then fizzled out when the counters emptied.

Only then did Isla push her hair off her face and groaned. Aileen led her to a chair, wanting to put up her own feet. How did Isla manage this for eight hours?

Isla sank into the chair, shoulders drooping. 'I've been on my feet since 5 a.m.'

Golly! Returning to the coffee machine, Aileen bit her lip as she contemplated which button to press. She finally settled on one and the machine screeched to life, spitting out a dark brew. The smell mingled with the sugary aroma of pastries, easing the tension from Aileen's spasming muscles.

She placed the warm mug and the last remaining scone in front of Isla. 'You need the energy.'

Without a word, Isla gobbled it up. Every silent bite

mushroomed Aileen's worry until it bloomed as big as an elephant.

'Where's Carly?'

'With Daniel.'

'How is she? Are her new teeth causing her trouble? How's Daniel?'

'Good.'

Aileen sighed. She placed a hand on Isla's shoulder. 'What is it, dearie? What's wrong?'

Isla tugged at the tissue paper until it tore in two. 'What's with you and Callan asking these questions!'

Callan had come to the bakery? The sod hadn't called her in four days. They hadn't even communicated except for a few brief messages in the morning.

Aileen tempered down her worries about their relationship. 'Tell me, Isla. I can see it in your face.'

Isla still didn't look Aileen in the eye. 'Nothing. I-I'm worried about Andrew. He didn't show up today, and he isn't answering my calls. Maybe he just let loose last night with his friends – he is still a teenager after all. Or maybe he worked late on that assignment he was complaining about.'

Skipping work because he partied the night before? Unlikely – he wasn't the type.

Aileen squeezed Isla's hand. 'Why don't you give me his address and I'll check up on him? And perhaps you can pull some strings and get someone here to help you out? I'm sure many people from Loch Fuar would be happy to help.'

Isla nodded, yet didn't move.

'I'll call Daniel and we'll arrange it. Don't work yourself ragged.'

Aileen made arrangements for the evening rush, asking Barbara, the owner of the tea room for help. They needed reinforcements when the last batch of the day hit the shelves at five, and Barbara happily stepped in.

After a long while, Aileen slid into the car, programmed Andrew's address into her GPS and rolled out of the car park.

What was going on with Andrew Mackay? Why had he skipped out on work?

CHAPTER TWO

Callan blew a raspberry at the state of his desk.

A couple of months ago, he'd taken it upon himself to clean his office and rid it of the mounting papers. And then Aileen had happened.

Now the mountain had piled again thanks to Mrs Douglas's relentless cat and its mud baths in Lieutenant General Warren's vegetable patch.

But the furry feline wasn't the only lawbreaker in Loch Fuar now.

A shiver of apprehension zinged through his back.

'Ye'll meet the shredder one day, I promise ye,' he warned the papers.

If only he could become comfortable with technology.

Aileen teased his poor tech skills often, saying her ninety-year-old gran, Siobhan, had more of a techie thumb than him.

He still hadn't called her. Callan rolled his eyes, then smirked. He might not know much, but he now knew how to track a device using another connected to it via the cloud.

And he was damn proud of himself for that. Next time his girlfriend decided to go and get herself almost killed, he'd track her and lock her in a cell. If he let her continue on her trouble-strewn path, he'd age faster than Siobhan.

Callan refocused his attention on the computer humming in front of him. He'd put in a search for anyone who'd gone missing thirty to forty years ago.

Of course, no one might have reported this man missing, or his name might've got lost when the police digitalised their databases, but perusing the records was a start.

The computer spat out a list of names.

He worked through the list, eliminating all women and then anyone under the age of twenty-five.

His heart ached for the families of these people more so now that he knew how they felt. Would he ever find Blaine's body in that vast peatland? Would he ever get to say a proper goodbye?

Half an hour later, he'd narrowed down his search to only five people who matched the description.

Then he clicked on the email the pathologist had sent him with the pictures.

His computer screen froze. 'Damn it! No wonder I cannae use technology.'

He smacked the machine. 'Bampot!'

A droning of a fan emitted through the thing before it heated up.

'I dinnae want to cook omelette on ye, ye eejit!'

'Hasn't Aileen taught ye something about using machines?'

Rory leaned on the open door, hands in his biscuit-coloured trousers.

Callan hit print without a thought, lest the thing broke down. The only person who could repair this monstrosity lived an hour away.

The printer in the corner screeched to life.

'Ah, Callan, I need to get Robert to take yer printer away. The next time I come here ye might be under the paper.'

'I ken!' Callan stalked to the printer as it spat out the pictures.

Rory dared to step in, gingerly manoeuvring around the mess on the floor.

Callan stacked the warm sheets together, letting the fresh smell of ink wash over him. Using magnets, he pinned them to the murder board.

Rory rested against Callan's desk. 'That's the bog body?'

'Aye, I'm checking the pictures against the missing person records.'

Rory hummed. 'Baggy jeans and a loud jumper screams 1980s.'

'So Dr Brown said.' Callan held up the papers he'd printed off. 'I reckon the sooner we find him, the sooner we can inform the family. I dinnae want them to find out from town gossip.'

Rory leafed through the missing-person files, then snapped them closed. 'It's hard to remember cases from that long ago. I would be a... let me think... sergeant then. Aye. And we had a fair share of missing people.' He pointed to the map of Loch Fuar on Callan's desk. 'Found the lot, living in a lone cave by the loch, high as kites. Ten eejits.'

'Ye hauled their arses in?'

'You bet I did.' Rory grinned. 'A day after, my wife gave birth to our eldest. I took it as a good omen.'

Callan picked up the rest of the files and started going through the pictures.

Wrong hair colour, too old, too short, too tall.

Callan flipped them over.

'What happened to the rest of these people?' he wondered out loud.

Rory held up his hands. 'I dinnae ken. My take is this man here' – he pointed to a stout older man – 'ran away. I heard his wife wasn't the most cordial woman. According to gossip, he's settled down in another town. Found a friendly woman and is happily coupled up.'

'And his case is still open?'

'If ye were hiding from an overbearing spouse, do ye want the police to find ye?'

'Well, our bog body doesn't match anyone from these…' He trailed off when his eyes landed on the last file. 'Rory, I think we found him. Lucas Fraser, aged thirty-one, was reported missing on 20th May 1981 by his parents. The police deduced no one had seen him for a week by that point. He had a brother who studied in the states, a Logan Fraser.'

Rory peered at the file. 'Is there an address for the parents? They might be deceased now, but perhaps the neighbours know where the brother is?'

Callan stubbed a finger. 'Aye, there is an address.'

THE ROAD WOUND AROUND TREES AND THE RIVER. CALLAN sped down the curves, his car's tyres gripping the tar perfectly. Within a couple of minutes, he parked his SUV by the kerb next to a modest house. Someone lived here for sure.

The earthy fragrance in the air and the height of the lawn meant someone had recently mowed it. The plants in the small garden swayed in the breeze, diamond-like water droplets resting on the leaves.

A car sat in the driveway and the door held a wreath with a nameplate in the centre: 'Fraser'.

Callan frowned as he knocked on the door.

The door opened to reveal a stout woman with salt-and-pepper hair. She had an apron tied around her wide hips and a scent of sweet cinnamon emanated from her.

'Oh, I'm sorry!' She wiped the flour off her face. 'Ye caught me in the middle of baking a batch.'

Callan held up his badge. 'I'm DI Callan Cameron. I'm looking for Logan Fraser.'

Her eyes rounded to match her gaping lips. 'What has he done? He just wanted those leaves to experiment, I swear. It was harmless. I keep telling him he can't pluck flowers and leaves from our neighbour's garden, but his passion for botany gets the better of him. He's absent-minded sometimes.'

Callan waited for her to stop rambling. 'I'm not here about the leaves, Mrs…?'

'Oh!' She dusted her hands on the apron. 'I'm Lottie. Charlotte Fraser. Logan's my man.'

'I'm here about his brother, Lucas Fraser.'

Charlotte pressed her fingers to her lips. 'You better come in,' came the muffled invite.

The Frasers' home reflected Logan's love of botany, the walls painted in light green, the upholstery a darker shade. In the living room, one wall was papered with a recurring leaf design, its verdant colours drawing the eye, and numerous plants sat on the windowsill or next to the furniture.

The different shades of green in the living room, along with a subtle hint of slate grey, gave the area an earthy, calm feel, and wafts of cinnamon enticed Callan's taste buds.

'Log! Come out here.' The holler assaulted Callan's

ears, but the green pillows propped up on the sofas – a lady's touch – soaked up the vibrations.

A door somewhere in the house creaked and shut. 'What is it, Lottie? I told ye, high decibels upset the babies.'

Babies?

'Yer plants will do with a bit of noise,' Charlotte harrumphed, planting her hands on her hips as a balding man with a rotund belly waddled into the room.

'Who are ye?' he asked without greetings.

Callan flashed his badge. 'DI Callan Cameron. I'm here about yer brother.'

And with that, Callan watched the colour drain from the Frasers' faces. He hated this.

He waited while Charlotte placed warm cinnamon buns and home-made cookies next to three steaming cups of tea. She seemed to want to keep busy, but he didn't complain, knowing her fussing gave her husband time to settle.

A couple of minutes in, he had to push on.

'We've found yer brother, Mr Fraser.'

Logan Fraser closed his eyes, intertwining his fingers with his wife's. 'During yer recent excavation at the peatland?' His voice cracked at the end.

'Aye and because of the peat we could identify him, but we'd appreciate it if ye'd head to the hospital and identify him formally.' A heaviness had settled in his throat. He'd moved boulders to say those words.

How would he react when they found Blaine?

Logan's knuckles turned white as they gripped the sofa cushion. 'I-I…'

Callan sighed. 'Believe it or not, Mr Fraser, I can sympathise with ye.'

Eyes glassy with tears, Logan said, 'He was the elder

one, prettier too. He looked like our maw – tall and handsome. Girls swooned when he walked by.'

Charlotte squeezed his thigh. 'Ye're dashing too, my love.'

He shook his head. 'Ye never met him. He wore the charm like a bespoke jacket.' Looking Callan in the eyes, Logan added, 'He never brought any of them home – well, none lasted long enough. We were four years apart and never really hung out.'

Callan reached for a cookie, placing the tea aside. 'Ye didn't see eye to eye?'

Logan chuckled at his question. 'Oh no, I adored my big brother. I looked like a slug next to him and it cramped his style. I liked my books, just like our paw.'

Their conversation entered a lull as Logan disappeared down memory lane, a small smile on his face. Bittersweet memories.

Callan scribbled all he'd learned about Lucas Fraser, his heart going out to the family. If or when he found Blaine, it would be like losing him all over again.

Charlotte slurped her tea, perhaps trying to swallow the tears pooling in her eyes. Tears for a man she'd never met but who was her brother-in-law.

Shoving another cookie in his mouth, Callan asked, 'When did ye last see yer brother?'

Logan massaged his forehead with his fingers. 'Oh, I've thought about it several times. I saw him a month before he went missing. He waved me off as I left this driveway.' He pointed to the one outside the house. 'We'd had dinner with our parents like we did every Friday. I made my way to uni to start my PhD in the US that weekend. It was the last time I saw him.'

When he reached for another cookie, Callan knew he

was addicted. Charlotte could bake. 'Did ye keep in touch?'

'Sure, but technology back then wasn't like it is now, so it wasn't frequent. I remember his big smile and his bubbly personality – friendly but a little mysterious. He kept his cards hidden.'

Callan munched on a cinnamon bun, letting the spice flower on his tongue. 'Ye didnae share secrets, then?'

'No, he wasn't the sort to have a heart-to-heart with anyone. He just got on with things.'

Going through his notes again, Callan nodded. 'And yer parents reported him missing when he didn't turn up for one of those Friday night dinners?'

'Aye, he'd never missed those. Our mum was the best cook. As good as my Lottie.'

Charlotte sent an adoring glance at her husband and shuffled closer to him. 'He told me all about Lucas when we met. We met a couple of his friends too.'

Friends?

Callan shuffled ahead, placing his elbows on his knees. 'And who were his friends?'

THE GPS GUIDED AILEEN INTO A NARROW LANE.

Stone cottages lined either side of it, their chimneys dormant. The sky faded into dark pink as the light in the sky extinguished.

Autumn meant shorter days. And after autumn…

But she didn't want to think about winter now.

It had taken her half an hour to get here. She'd left the main town of Loch Fuar a while ago, wondering if she'd taken a wrong turn.

But she'd followed the route her GPS had taken her,

and for a while hers had been the only car on the road as woods with tall trees passed her by.

Finally, hints of civilisation had peeked from between trees – a chimney here and a fleeting glance at a stone cottage there.

Aileen found a parking space right in front of the house she'd been searching for. It sat silent, its driveway empty, unlike the neighbouring cottage, where the steady beat of music made the door shudder.

Bracing herself against the cold, Aileen jogged over to the front door and rapped it with her knuckles.

No one answered.

She hopped on her feet to keep the chill at bay and tried again.

When she'd made up her mind to retreat to her car, footsteps sounded from within. Locks clicked, the door cracked open, and a face peeked out.

Aileen frowned.

Magenta streaks framed a delicate face. A nose ring glistened in the dim light and dark brows rose up until alarmed eyes met hers.

'Aye?' The voice sounded stuck between childhood and womanhood.

'Hi. I'm Aileen Mackinnon. I'm looking for Andrew – Andrew Mackay.' Her teeth would start chattering at any moment. She didn't like chatting to strangers, and the chill breeze froze her words in her throat.

The girl shook her head. 'He went off to the library an hour ago. Don't expect him back for another two.'

Relief washed over Aileen. 'He's okay then?'

Andrew's housemate studied Aileen's trembling shoulders and bouncy feet. Showing mercy, she opened the door.

Aileen took it as an invitation to enter.

She is not a suspect. It's okay.

Aileen had to repeat her new mantra a few times for it to register in her mind.

The living area was chaos. The cushions on the sofa didn't match, and each wall was painted a different colour: yellow, green and blue.

Bags, pens and notebooks lay all over the place and – Aileen shuddered – so did the dust. They needed a cleaning lady, for sure. If Andrew's housemates were half as busy as he was, they'd need someone to look after their place.

Most teens couldn't afford cleaners, though.

Aileen sat down on the cleanest side of the sofa, closest to the heater, and shivered at the blast of warmth.

Shoot!

The slender girl chewed on her lip. Her T-shirt had a skull in the centre with a knife stuck in its head. She wore leopard-print shorts in fluorescent yellow. 'How do you know him?'

'Andrew?'

The housemate nodded.

Aileen explained, 'He's Isla McIntyre's nephew. Isla's a friend. He works at her bakery. Andrew didn't turn up for work today and he isn't answering her calls. She's worried.'

Flicking her magenta hair, the girl said, 'He went out last night. Had a banging headache.'

Aileen intertwined her fingers. She hadn't met this girl before, but if she lived with Andrew, she had to care for him. Aileen had promised Isla she'd find Andrew, hadn't she?

Should she take the girl's word for it?

'What's your name?'

'Zay. Call me Zay.'

Aileen bobbed her head. She could talk to strangers. The old Aileen hadn't been able to. Now she'd learned.

'Did you see Andrew leave with your own eyes?'

'Maybe.'

Aileen didn't appreciate her non-committal response.

She wrenched open her mouth to ask more questions when Zay dusted her palms over her thighs. 'If you're done, I've got to get back to studying. Got a maths test tomorrow.' She stuck out her tongue in annoyance.

Aileen stood. 'Sure. Thank you.'

Outside, Aileen turned to Zay. 'Where's the library?'

Zay mumbled the directions and shut the door in Aileen's face.

Brat!

Aileen followed Zay's instructions and took a right turn. This road looked the same as the one she'd left behind.

These houses were a part of the college's student accommodations. The local college was forty-five minutes from the main town. Only students and professors lived here, right on the border between the towns of Loch Fuar and Loch Heaven.

The library should be easy to find. Zay had said she'd reach it in ten minutes.

When the road tapered off to the left, Aileen followed, her pants puffing out like smoke, her nose numb from the cold. She prayed it wouldn't start raining again.

Soon, the cottages fell away and trees lined the path.

Must be the park between the houses and campus.

She took a step and something rustled. Aileen froze.

What was that?

The sun had sunk further into the horizon, and darkness propelled by the foliage descended over the park.

Fumbling in her pockets, she switched on the phone's torch. She'd left her proper torch behind in the car.

Another wrong move.

Aileen bit her lower lip hard and pushed on. Five more minutes and the foliage thickened, as did the inkiness.

She couldn't see a soul now.

Shining her torch behind her, she realised she'd left the houses behind.

How far had she come? Wouldn't the campus have its own lighting? Was she lost?

She took another step and her torch caught something: a pole.

No, a signpost!

Relieved she was still within civilisation, she hurried to the post. Here the path forked, one route to the right and another straight ahead.

The straight road led to the college classrooms and the other to the library.

The path to the right narrowed and darkened until it misted in the distance. She couldn't linger in the cold, could she?

Aileen shrugged. With no other choice, she made her way down the path.

Another five minutes and Aileen swore she'd lost her way. She'd been walking far longer than Zay had said she'd need to – or so it felt, anyway.

She'd stuck to the path just as the signpost indicated, though weeds and grass had swallowed the cobbles.

And the darkness was winning over her torch's meek light.

Crack!

'Oh!' Aileen swivelled her torch but couldn't find where the sound had come from.

She gasped, heart thundering as images floated through her mind – horror-inducing pictures.

In the middle of nowhere, with only silent barren trees for company, dried leaves and branches under her feet, and the full moon looming over her, Aileen remembered Marley. Lost, cold and terrified.

A thick mist settled around her, smudging the moon like a dot scribbled with white chalk.

Another trembling step and Aileen's foot caught on a branch, and she stumbled.

'Oomph!' she cried, her phone flying out of her hand, head ready to bang against the ground. Most wouldn't call her fall graceful.

Her knee collided with the mud, then her right cheek, making her see stars.

Leaves, twigs and living organisms under her body crunched and died.

The forest settled then, shrouded in a silent veil.

Aileen didn't move, as if plastered to the ground.

A stray thought entered her mind: maybe the mud had moulded to her form. She'd fallen in a spread-eagled position, lying there like a murdered corpse.

After a long minute, her fingers twitched.

'Shit!' The puff of breath leaving her mouth disturbed the mud on the leaves. Something tickled her nose, and she sneezed, startling a poor bird.

Even those self-defence sessions with Callan hadn't been this bad!

Like a banshee woken up from its slumber by a gong, Aileen stretched her right hand and patted the leaves.

Where had her phone fallen?

If she'd broken a bone, she needed help.

At that point, her mind had gone into shock, not registering any pain yet.

Her hands wrapped around a lukewarm metallic object. Ah, her beacon of hope.

She lifted the thing and groaned.

Her Humpty-Dumpty fall had cracked the screen of her phone, which, in true Highland fashion, had no reception.

'Bloody hell!'

So far gone she was, she didn't even reprimand herself for the curse.

Pressing her stinging palms to the ground, Aileen pushed up.

'Ouch!'

She'd scraped her palms raw. Even her elbows stung.

Spitting mud from her mouth, Aileen tugged at her hair.

A few twigs and leaves came loose, the rest stuck into her dark brown locks.

When she tried to stand, both her knees protested. Hell, Siobhan had less creaky knees!

Holding on to a branch, biting her lips when her palm smarted, she righted herself.

One foot in front of the other.

'One, two, three, four, fi—Ouch!'

She made her way through the mist, stumbling like a drunkard.

Eerie moonbeams penetrated the mist, guiding her forward. She didn't dare use her phone. It had already been low on power, and she might need it later.

'Forty-six, forty-seven, forty-eight—'

She looked towards the sky and blinked.

The trees abruptly broke off here, opening up to a huge field.

Not a field. Aileen eyed the goalposts at either end of the grass. A shinty pitch.

Tall trees loomed on three other sides. The foliage thinned to the right. Aileen swore she could see a light over the trees.

Was she at the damn library?

She could've been in Australia, she didn't care. As long as she saw people again.

Aileen stumbled to the right, still taking the support of the trees.

A few trees in and she heard a sniffle.

Eyes wide in alarm, she peered behind the trunk and had to squint.

Was that a person?

Hope bloomed in her heart. She shone her torch into the darkness and her heart sang.

'Thank you for answering my prayers.'

She hopped towards the head her torch illuminated.

'Hey! I…'

Aileen faltered then, the scene registering in her addled brain.

A boy lay in the foliage, face tilted to the side. Her torch caught something glossy matting his hair. And the boy's eyes? They stared at the trees, unblinking.

Glassy *dead* eyes.

And next to him, the red-haired lad…

Aileen's eyes widened. 'Andrew!'

CHAPTER THREE

Aileen stared at her phone screen with pursed lips. Why wasn't Callan answering her calls? Didn't he know about the murder yet?

She shuddered, thinking about the scene.

Sitting on the stairs of an ambulance, draped in a blanket that didn't keep the cold at bay, Aileen wanted someone to speak to. The people around kept her tears in check and her back ramrod straight.

Callan would be on his way here. Of course! No wonder he hadn't answered her call.

As much as she'd hate to say it, she needed him. The walk through the woods had been terrifying and running into another body?

She'd barely been coherent when she'd called 999 and asked for an ambulance and the police – her phone mercifully getting a signal once more.

When she'd seen the blood matting the boy's hair, she'd known she couldn't save him. And his unfocused eyes…

Andrew had been next to him, on his knees, his red hair matching the spots on his white T-shirt. She'd been too scared to ask who'd done this. Especially since Andrew held a curved shinty stick in his hand and hadn't responded to her being there, just staring dumbly at the dead lad.

Blood, along with strands of hair and brain matter, had covered the dead leaves.

Bile rose in her throat, making her tongue taste bitter. She hurriedly dumped water into her mouth, swirling it around. The cold perspiration on the bottle soothed her smarting palms.

As far as she knew, they hadn't found any injuries on Andrew.

Why had he been unresponsive? Was it shock? How long had he slumped there with just a shirt on his back?

He'd tucked his jacket around the lad's shoulders, as if he might be cold.

Who was the lad?

Aileen rubbed her palms over her shivering arms and winced when the open wounds stung.

A police cruiser came to a halt behind the police tape.

The door to the right opened and out stepped a tall, dark man wearing a trench coat and hat.

With that get-up, she'd recognise this man anywhere: Detective Inspector Declan Walsh with the police department in Loch Heaven, the neighbouring town.

His razor-sharp eyes landed on her huddled form, lips pressing into a line. He strode over to her. 'Ms Mackinnon, I never thought we'd meet again under such circumstances.'

Aileen sighed. She hadn't hoped to find a body either, especially not such a gruesomely battered one.

Her insides roiled as if a tornado raged in her gut. 'Detective Walsh, I would say it's, uh, nice to see you but... why are you here?'

He pointed at the dark woods, red lights highlighting the verdant autumnal trees. 'This area falls under our jurisdiction. You'll know this by now, but we need a statement.'

Aileen swallowed and told the police all that she knew. 'What – what about Andrew?'

Snapping his notepad shut, the police officer Walsh had assigned to her shrugged. 'We need more information from him. Would you like someone to drop you home?'

Aye, she'd have liked Callan to respond to her. Bloody sod!

Aileen shook her head, voice trembling. 'I'll be fine.'

SHE WOKE WITH A LOUD MOAN, HER LIMBS WEIGHING DOWN on the mattress like concrete blocks. The gong banging in her head sent her brain rattling.

If the clanging didn't stop, she'd go off her rocker.

Aileen let a yawn slip as she groped for her phone. It crashed to the floor, eliciting a growl from the banshee on the bed.

Her fingers twisted around the battered thing.

'Hello?' She snorted it out like a snore.

'Aileen?' came an unsure questioning voice.

Concern registered somewhere in her brain.

Aileen struggled with the warm blankets, heavy muscles and eyelids refusing to comply. Sitting propped up on one elbow, she placed the voice. 'Daniel! What's happened?' Isla's worried eyes came to mind, and sleep vamoosed like a thief hearing sirens.

After driving back to Dachaigh, Aileen had barely plugged in her phone to charge before tumbling into bed with her muddy shoes on.

'I'm sorry to ask so early, but can ye come here, to the bakery? I need a hand.'

'Of course.' Aileen brushed her teeth, slipped on something that wasn't pyjamas, and rushed out the door in record time.

The sun's rays barely kissed the edges of the mountains, a blanket of silence draped around the Highlands; the birds still nestled cosily in their beds. Not a soul headed out into the cold autumn morning.

Her car jerked to a halt outside the bakery and she dashed inside, barely pausing to read the 'Closed' sign.

Did Isla know?

For the first time, no one loitered inside. The counters sat empty and so did the shop. Where was Isla?

'In here,' Daniel McIntyre called.

Aileen's footsteps echoed as they smacked against the tiles.

Isla's tiny office seemed to be the hub today.

Daniel's broad frame filled the room. Behind the desk sat Isla, her eyes worried and her red hair wilder than ever. Andrew, his gaze trained on the floor, sat in the visitor's chair. No one said a word.

Aileen froze in the doorway. 'Isla?'

Isla jumped from her seat and rushed towards Aileen, not a hint of a smile on her face. Aileen took Isla by the arm and pulled her aside.

'What is it, dearie?'

'You saw him last night, didn't you?' she sputtered, tears trickling down her cheek.

Her lips pursed, Aileen nodded.

'What happened last night? He came to us in a police cruiser early this morning, but he won't tell me what happened!'

Aileen rubbed Isla's arms. 'It's not my story to tell.' And she hadn't had time to process what she'd seen.

'Please – you have to tell me!' Isla sobbed, shoulders shaking in agony.

Andrew might've been a nephew, but Isla cared for him like her own.

'He won't talk, Aileen!'

Aileen let out a long sigh. 'Let me speak with him.'

Patting Isla's shoulder in reassurance, Aileen strode into the office. Isla followed her, not commenting on her bandaged palms.

Aileen whispered to the McIntyres, 'Privately please.'

Isla grumbled as Daniel led her to the front of the store.

Aileen sank into the chair Isla had occupied, letting the smell of yesterday's yeast and vanilla essence calm her. But the atmosphere in here didn't match the happy memories baked goods brought.

Placing her elbows on the cold desk, Aileen stared at Andrew's hair. It flamed like autumn leaves against his peaky skin.

He still stared at the floor, as if it might soothe the wrinkles on his forehead.

'Andrew.'

He still didn't look up.

She could state the obvious and say Isla was worried about him or she could surprise him.

'I hear you want to study forensic anthropology. Guess you would be interested in the dig. You know, the one at the peatland.'

Andrew raised unsure eyes. 'Yeah,' he said in a hoarse, meek voice.

'You'll need to be a keen observer to succeed in that profession.'

He gave her a typical teen response – a shrug.

'Why don't you tell me what you saw last night?'

Andrew looked away again, lips tight.

'Look, Andrew, we both know what we saw. I want to understand if what I think I saw is what happened.'

'I didn't murder him!' he yelled as tears pooled in his horrified eyes. 'I would never. He's… Anvit was a friend.'

Aileen hadn't known that. 'How did you find him?'

Andrew shook his head. 'I tried – I tried to save him but… but I got there too late.'

Aileen intertwined her fingers and gave her next question some thought. 'What made you want to touch the stick? You must know about compromising a crime scene?'

He bobbed his head once. 'I had gloves on.' Wiggling his fingers, he explained, 'My fingers get cold easily.'

She didn't interrupt when he slid into silence again.

The clock in the corner ticked by, egging Aileen's heart to beat faster.

'Look, I – I didn't understand what hurt him. But I saw the blood,' Andrew choked. 'Everywhere, blood, so much blood.' He buried his face in his palms and breathed heavily.

'I couldn't piece it together. What had hurt him? Who had hurt him? And the shinty pitch, the woods around it are hot spots to hang out, or…' He sighed, shaking his head. 'You know… It sees its fair share of activity.'

'So someone took a great risk killing Anvit where they did?'

'Aye.' He placed his hands on the desk, palms down, head still bowed. 'I knew I couldn't save him, so I looked around to see if whoever hurt him was loitering. His body was still warm when I touched him.'

Aileen wanted to ask him why he'd touched the lad, but she kept silent, letting him speak.

'Whoever had... There was no one around, but I found the stick discarded in the hedges. And I can't—'

He cut off as a commotion came from outside. The door to Isla's office flew open, smacking into the doorstopper.

Aileen pushed away from the table. 'What's happening? Detective Walsh?'

He tipped his hat. 'So you're determined to solve this one as well?'

Andrew's chair flew back as he stood too, his mouth hanging open. 'What—'

When PC Robert Davis approached him, Aileen protested. 'Robert, what's the meaning of this?'

Aileen rounded the desk, hips smacking into a corner. She halted beside Andrew.

'We want to take him to Loch Heaven for formal questioning,' Walsh explained.

Andrew visibly swallowed, his fingers trembling. He faced Aileen then, eyes wide in a face where freckles battled with a scruff of beard.

What she saw in them was pure innocence and a call for help. This young lad had tried to save his friend and was now a suspect because of it.

He dipped his head as Walsh touched his arm and led him down the corridor then outside, where a crowd had gathered, despite the early hour. Rumours soared up around them, yet Andrew didn't react. He slid into the police cruiser, staring at his intertwined fingers. When the car started, he turned his head and met Aileen's gaze once more.

Aileen watched, helpless as Andrew's stricken face disappeared down the road.

How could they do this to a grieving teenager? And

where the hell had Callan gone? She turned to a devastated Isla. These were his friends.

For the first time, she tamped down her instinct to call him. Instead, she helped Daniel usher his weeping wife back into the warmth. She locked the door of the bakery behind her and followed them to the concrete walls of Isla's office, away from watching eyes.

'Isla, I'm—'

Isla's shoulders shook. 'Oh, that wee bairn! He wouldn't hurt a fly,' she wailed.

Daniel drew her into his arms, face in a sombre frown. 'What was he doing in those woods?'

Aileen looked at the usually lovey-dovey pair, her heart breaking a little for the uphill struggle that lay ahead of them. Being a murder suspect was never easy, but how much harder would it be for a teenager?

Her mouth acted before her brain filtered her words. 'I'll save him. I'll save Andrew and get him back to you.'

CALLAN CARESSED HIS CHIN, A TELL FOR WHEN HIS MIND churned. He'd placed a list of names on his thigh, feet dangling over the desk. The rest of the papers crunched underneath his calf.

Lucas Fraser surely had an army of mates. And from what his brother had said, fifteen of them had been his pals right from school.

A social butterfly, if he could apply such a term here.

Out of the fifteen, twelve were alive and – Callan smiled – he had phone numbers for each of them. His smile turned to a grimace. Hell, the victim might've liked people, but Callan certainly didn't. Now he'd have to call them all.

Callan had been an arse not calling Aileen back, especially once he'd heard there'd been a murder in Loch Heaven. A murder that involved Isla's nephew. But not calling her was a good way to protect Andrew. The closer he stuck to the book, the better off they'd be.

But, Callan thought as he whipped out his phone and stared at Aileen's name in his call logs, he could message her. His good morning sat unanswered, and he knew why.

'I'm really sorry for not calling. How are you?' he thumped out, the pull of his heart like a magnet, urging him to go to Dachaigh and hold her.

No, he needed to stay away so no one could say he'd interfered in Andrew's case, which might cast doubt on his innocence again.

He took a deep breath and reached for Lucas Fraser's friends' phone numbers. Nothing like mind-numbing work to keep one occupied.

By the fifth call, Callan wanted to pull his hair out. He hated door-to-door interviews, but calling the friends of a man who'd been missing for decades was worse. They thought he was offering a therapy session to unveil their dirty laundry.

Goodness!

Lucas Fraser hadn't had any close friends – he'd just had a lot of acquaintances. Callan stared at the empty page where he'd made only one note, a name.

Isobel Murray.

Unbeknownst to his family, Lucas Fraser had a girlfriend. Four of Lucas's friends had attested to the fact that he had been in a relationship with a clingy girlfriend who got jealous easily, but they were in love.

He typed the name into the system and frowned.

The system showed one Murray around the 1980s: Leana Murray. And she'd had her share of conflicts with the law. A parking ticket, illegal drinking and driving charges, plus a vandalism charge that the victim had dropped.

Where was Isobel Murray?

Callan scratched his jaw, trying to figure out who'd know about her. His boss had gone off to a meeting at the local council and Isla, despite knowing everyone now, wouldn't have known Loch Fuar's residents forty years ago.

What was to say Isobel even lived in Loch Fuar? She could've come from the other town or been a student at the college.

Could Leana Murray and Isobel Murray be related? It seemed unlikely – Murray was a very common surname in these parts.

He typed 'Leana Murray' into the internet search engine and found a link almost at once. Someone had uploaded a scanned copy of an article from four decades ago.

It described the vandalism report against Leana and how the claims had been revoked, saying it had been a misunderstanding. Details about the place she'd broken into and what had been taken weren't mentioned; nor did the article have a photograph of the woman.

Callan toggled back to Leana's record and read through it again.

The vandalism charge intrigued him. He opened up the reports on that case.

High-value goods, including old vases, original snuff bottles from China and pieces of Queen Anne furniture, had all met their demise.

Callan plotted the address on a map – the property was situated up a wee hill where the views were as stunning as the property prices.

Why target a rich property to vandalise but not steal anything?

He read the full report. No stolen items and apparently the insurance company had paid the damages in full.

It must've cost them a fortune.

Callan toggled back to Leana Murray's record, scratching his jaw again as he gave it another glance.

She hadn't had another brush with the law since that vandalism charge. Either she'd turned over a new leaf or – a sinking feeling settled in Callan's gut – she'd disappeared.

Bloody hell!

Running a frustrated hand through his hair, Callan picked up his car keys. Best to ask someone with a long nose.

CALLAN REACHED THE NURSING HOME LATER THAT morning.

The person he'd come to see eyed him with disdain. 'Why are yer hands empty?'

She might be ninety, but Callan wouldn't let her kick him around. 'Ye ken what's happened, so ye ken Isla's Bakery is closed.'

Siobhan Mackinnon, Aileen's grandmother, never claimed to be the grandmotherly, ladylike sort. 'Ye could've got me whisky.'

'And get fined since I'm on duty.' He sniffed, smelling the malt in the air. 'And something tells me yer stash is full.'

She swatted her wrinkled but firm hands. 'Take yer badge off.' She pointed at his chest. 'And the rest of it for my grandwean. How many months does it take ye to make the next move?'

Of course, the news of Aileen's love life had reached this woman. But she wouldn't make it easy for him.

Callan shrugged. 'She's busy and so am I. We've gone on a couple of dates.'

'Get busy with each other!' Siobhan scoffed. 'Is it so difficult to do, lad? Do ye swing the other way?'

Golly! He was not here to speak about his love life with his angry girlfriend's grandmother.

'Isobel Murray. Who is she?'

Siobhan's wrinkled forehead crumpled further. 'Who?'

Callan sighed. Perhaps her memory wasn't as sharp as it used to be.

'We've found the body of a man called Lucas Fraser. His friends say he and Isobel Murray dated around the time he disappeared forty years ago.'

For the first time in a long time, Siobhan didn't snap a retort. She drew her eyebrows together in concentration. 'Do ye have a picture?'

'Just a name. I can't find her records. But' – Callan pulled out his phone – 'I found a woman named Leana Murray. Do you know her?'

Fixing her glasses over cerulean eyes, Siobhan squinted at the phone as she read the article. 'Ye need a new one, lad. What did ye do? Hurl the thing at the wall?'

Callan pointed at the phone. 'Leana Murray.'

Siobhan shook her head, letting her soft white hair bounce. 'I was busy getting the inn off the ground forty years ago.'

The TV crackled in the distance where she'd put on some horror show. Siobhan had several bunches of flowers, some with love notes attached to them.

Callan cracked a smile. She certainly kept busy.

So did her grandwean.

'No, I dinnae recognise her. Either she wasn't from

Loch Fuar or I never met her. Murray, ye say? I'll try to give that name a think. Where did ye say she stayed?'

'We don't have an exact address just that she vandalised a property called Violet's Rose.'

Siobhan narrowed her eyes. 'Violet's Rose, eh? I remember some controversy about the family who lived there. A nasty patriarch and scorned children. It's derelict now. Money makes people loony, and they were certainly wealthy.'

Callan nodded, noting down the scraps of information.

Perhaps Siobhan would recall something. Murray was a common name in Loch Fuar. Although, as far as Callan knew, none of the three Murray families had any family member named Isobel or Leana. And he'd done the calculations. The two women would be in their sixties or seventies now.

'Thanks.'

Siobhan waved him off. 'Ye can thank me by getting serious with Aileen.'

He managed a small smile as he walked away muttering to himself, 'I'd gladly ask her out again, but she'd rather spend time with a rodent.'

CHAPTER FOUR

Aileen twiddled her thumbs as she contemplated her options.

Number one: let Isla down. She took a shaky breath. That option didn't exist, although at the moment, it seemed like an outcome with a high possibility.

With your stupidity, there's about seventy percent chance of it happening.

Aileen cleared her throat. She could jump blindly into this with both feet or she could weigh her choices.

Her logic, or lack thereof, had led her to death's door just a few weeks ago. She'd also need to deal with Walsh without Callan. She didn't see eye to eye with him, and she wasn't the one with the handcuffs.

She had argued with Callan too, but she'd never contemplated being in his wrong books.

And now it felt like she wasn't a part of his book at all.

Aileen pushed away the wayward thought. She needed all the focus she could get.

Finding a middle ground could help her take a cautious step into this. She'd never solved a case alone, though not for lack of trying. Callan had just always been there. And if not him, Isla, gossip extraordinaire, would jump in to help.

Aileen tugged at a loose lock of hair.

Isla needed her. Why sit here contemplating options?

Daniel and Isla had headed off fifteen minutes before. She'd heard them arranging a lawyer for Andrew.

And here she sat, freezing her arse off in the car.

The engine rumbled to life, warming up the seats: a high-tech car for a high-tech accountant.

Aileen slid onto the road and traced the route she'd taken the previous evening.

The best way to ease into it would be to trace Andrew's movements last night. One thing she knew for sure: he definitely hadn't been at the library. She'd been lied to.

Zay inched open the door only to the point that Aileen could make out one eye staring at her.

Her intuition had her wedging her foot in the door. At least she wore boots, so the impact didn't crush her bones.

'Move!' Zay shrieked.

Aileen gritted her teeth. Her knee-jerk reaction told her to comply, but if she couldn't assert herself with a teenager, she had no hope.

'I want to know about Andrew.'

'Load of good that did!'

Aileen slammed her hand on the wooden door. The sound echoed through the narrow street, startling some birds. They cried, flapping their wings. A few orange leaves tumbled to the ground.

'I'm trying to help him.' Her reasoning fell on deaf ears. 'I— Ouch!'

Her hands flew to the back of her neck. Zay gave one push at the door, and Aileen lost her footing. The door rattled on its hinges and stayed shut.

She bounced on her feet. 'Oh God, oh God!' She wiggled, squealing, only to send the large ice cube, dripping freezing-cold rivulets, sliding lower until it lodged itself inside her shirt, right in the middle of her back.

To add salt to the wound, a cold breeze blew, freezing her fingers and nose.

Blast!

Aileen shut her eyes in agony, wriggling her torso, yet the ice remained pressed against her body.

Guffaws and a snort from behind the bushes caught her attention. A teenager filmed her from the window of the opposite house.

Trying her best to get the ice out, Aileen stumbled to where the laughter had come from.

Two other teens followed her with their phones out.

Bloody teenagers, technology and videos! And ice-catching bras!

'Hey!' she shouted. 'Who did that?'

They pointed at her, shutters clicking like she was a celebrity.

'We've got a viral meme, bro.'

They performed some elaborate handshake.

Aileen narrowed her eyes and thought about giving them grief. She'd never been this type of teenager. She'd been an observer, but since then she'd learned a thing or two about handling teenagers.

Aileen jerked her chin. 'Any of you friends of Andrew?'

The laughter died, and the phones disappeared, revealing faces with round cheeks and a smattering of facial hair.

They could've been twins with their matching hoodie-

and-jeans outfits and the blond streaks in their hair. The one on the right wore a maroon jumper and the other a green one.

As one, they jumped out of the bushes. 'Why do ye want to ken?' the green-jumpered one asked.

'He's a friend of mine.'

They snorted in unison. 'As if.' The red-jumpered one gave her a once-over.

Did she look that old?

Shuffling her feet, she tried another tack. 'The police took him in for questioning today.'

She saw the curtains drawing over their eyes. The red-jumpered one crossed his arms. 'So?'

'I can prove his innocence.'

The moment those words slipped past her mouth, Aileen grimaced.

Where the hell had that assertion come from? She didn't even know the situation or the dead lad.

The green-jumpered one mimicked his pal's pose, crossing his arms and shooting her a glare. 'How?'

A good question. How indeed.

She held out a hand. 'I'm Aileen Mackinnon.'

She'd only wanted to greet them, never expecting the reaction she got. Their jaws fell slack, almost slamming against the concrete under their feet. Eyes widened, star-struck, they watched Aileen.

A feminine voice squealed from behind her, '*The* Aileen Mackinnon?'

Huh? When had she become a celebrity?

Aileen frowned as Zay opened the door wide. She'd been listening to them.

'Come on in.'

Unsure, Aileen gave the three teens a look as she ventured inside the house.

Unlike the previous evening, Zay sat her in the middle of the couch. The teenagers all stared at her, their faces still slack-jawed.

The one with the green jumper broke the silence. 'Andrew never said he knew ye.' He saluted. 'My name's Leith.'

Aileen smiled. 'Hi.'

The other lad held up his fist. 'I'm Finlay.'

'Oh.' Awkwardly, she bumped her fist with his.

'We've heard all about ye.' Zay sat at the edge of her seat, eyes bright. 'All those cases ye've solved. Ye're cool.'

Never expecting praise, Aileen sat dumbstruck. They knew about her? Had they mistaken her for someone else?

'Aye, ye run Dachaigh and solved those murders. Wicked.'

'Thanks?' She cleared her throat. They needed to get to business, or she'd be here all day. 'Um, Andrew, where was he last night?'

Zay spoke. 'The library – I told ye.'

Aileen pulled out her yellow notepad, twirling the pencil in her hand. Not wanting to seem rude, she gave her next words some thought. 'That route to the library wasn't the quickest way, was it?'

The teenager straightened her shoulders. 'It's more picturesque.'

She hadn't seen any beauty in those misty, creepy surroundings. Aileen assumed she'd made her point and moved on.

'Who's the dead guy?'

Finlay licked his lips. 'Anvit Nair. Nerdy type – liked maths and science.' He paused, opening his mouth to say something, but shut it again.

'And?' Aileen drew out the 'N'.

Leith sat cross-legged on the floor and danced from

one butt cheek to the other, hands pressed against the bristled carpet.

'Ye shouldn't speak ill of the dead, but to be honest, he wasn't your typical nerd.'

Aileen narrowed her eyes. 'I'm going to need something more concrete than riddles.'

Finlay groaned. 'He knew how to smooth-talk the ladies, and the popular opinion is that he looks okay.'

'Handsome,' Zay cut in. 'Neat.'

Aileen's eyebrows rose.

'An in-demand arse,' Leith added. 'He loved a party, and where he went, ye knew the crowds would follow.'

'Especially the screaming girls.' Finlay pulled a face.

Zay rolled her eyes. 'Not true, although girls fluttered around him like a magnet. He liked the bottle too.'

All three of them nodded. 'Loved the pub,' Leith tutted.

Pubs and parties? How in the world did he get time to study? Aileen had barely had any after the hours she'd had to spend at the library.

Finlay described Anvit Nair. 'He had a lot of time on his hands. His parents and a scholarship paid for his education. So he didn't need to spend all his free time working late-night shifts at the burger place, if ye get what I mean. He had an internship, but it was only a few hours a week.'

'What about his friends? Any girlfriends? Boyfriends?'

Zay snorted. 'Half the female population and some males would've died to go out with him, but he had no one serious. Ye can find his following where *it* happened. Most people are laying flowers there.'

'You mean people are laying flowers at the crime scene?'

Leith drew in his knees. 'Aye, the detective came here

this morning after visiting the place. Hence we knew he'd been looking for Andy.'

'He didn't just come here looking for Andy, ye nitwit.' Zay waved her hand. 'He wanted to see Anvit's room.'

'Hold on.' Aileen looked them all in the eye. 'Anvit *lived* here? With you *and* Andrew?'

Zay shrugged. 'Aye.'

CALLAN ANSWERED THE CALL, ONE EYE ON THE DESERTED road. 'Hello?'

'Detective, it's Dr Brown. I'm done with the autopsy. Would you like to discuss it?'

A short while later, he parked and hiked his way towards her office, hoping for some evidence.

Dr Brown tugged at her hair, ruffling it. A mug of coffee sat on her desk, and judging by the brown stain on her shirt, she'd spilled some of it.

Gesturing for him to enter, she shoved all her papers aside. 'Excuse the mess – it's been mental here all day.'

An expected occurrence in their business.

Dr Brown smacked her palms on the desk and stared at him, unblinking. 'The Frasers are a decent sort.'

He'd thought so too, although those cookies had swayed his opinion. 'Aye.'

'He called me – Logan Fraser – last night. He and his wife came in today to identify the body. It was hard for him, but he did it.'

Callan swallowed the lump of emotion in his throat, imagining exactly how hard it would be. Hopefully, he'd give them closure by finding Lucas's killer.

One day he'd be doing the same thing for Blaine and with luck he'd have someone to hold on to then.

Fidgeting in his seat, Callan managed, 'What have you got?'

Dr Brown picked up a file. 'I've emailed you a copy, but I reckon you'll want to read my report now.'

Callan gave it a quick perusal.

The doctor intertwined her fingers. 'He had his last meal probably at a chippy. We found a wallet and handkerchief in his pockets. I've shipped his clothes and other belongings to forensics.'

Callan's breath hitched as he reached the most important lines on the report. 'Someone struck him from behind.'

'Looks like it. And there was a bit of a tussle. I found some woollen fibres, but unfortunately no DNA under his fingernails. The first stroke would've caught him unawares, probably stunning him. So he couldn't have fought his murderer with all his might. We're still looking for more evidence.'

Woollen fibres would be difficult to match all these years later, but DNA would do the job.

Callan ran a hand through his hair. 'So it's murder.'

Opening the file again, he ran through what it said. 'What sort of murder weapon do ye reckon it was?'

'We didn't find anything. No murder weapon, nor any discarded clothes that didn't belong to the victim. But we've yet to get a detailed forensic analysis of his belongings. As for the weapon used to do the dead, it's blunt, wooden. That's all I can say. As the report says, he died because of blunt force trauma to the head. The person struck him multiple times.'

Callan stilled as he thought it through. 'Would you say he was bludgeoned to death using a *stick*?'

She nodded. 'Aye, very much like that other lad, Anvit Nair.' She jerked her head towards the door. 'And I have to speak with the Loch Heaven detective about that. Nasty, nasty business.'

'But Lucas Fraser died forty years ago. Can the two murders be linked?'

Pushing an unwashed mug of coffee aside, Dr Brown reached for something else. 'Sorry? Oh, no I don't think that's possible. For one, why would the murderer stay silent for forty years?'

Callan thanked her for her efficiency and strode out the door, nearly smacking into a trench-coat wearing wall. 'Detective Walsh.'

DI Declan Walsh tipped his hat. 'Ah, I thought I'd run into you sooner. Ran into your girlfriend only this morning when I went to get that red-haired lad in for more questioning.'

Shit! Aileen would be furious. No wonder she still hadn't responded to his messages.

Callan stuffed his hands in his pockets. 'And? What's with that case?'

Walsh took off his hat, pushing the flattened hat-hair off his forehead. 'I wouldn't divulge details of a case to another detective who's so close to the prime suspect. But considering the case we solved last summer…'

He tipped his hat towards the row of empty waiting chairs in the banal corridor. 'Do you have fifteen minutes?'

Of course he did.

Their footsteps echoed into the silence as they smacked against the grey-tiled floor.

Callan lowered himself into a chair, mind sharp to absorb as much information as he could.

'Anvit Nair was no saint,' Walsh began. 'So at the moment, we have multiple people of interest. This lad, Andrew, says he wanted to help Anvit. They lived in the same accommodation. I asked him what he was doing in those woods. He said he was making his way home from the library.'

Callan tilted his head and pictured Andrew's freckled face and green eyes. 'That's likely. He's a sincere bloke.'

Walsh sighed. 'He didn't have any books with him – no computer or tablet. Just an empty backpack. We asked him about that. Taking his lawyer's advice, he clamped up. He won't tell us any more, and we've tried.'

Callan scratched his stubble, unable to believe Andrew doing anything criminal. 'What about other friends and acquaintances?'

'Alibied with evidence. The autopsy report Dr Brown sent me confirms death between 5.30 and 7.30 in the evening. It's a tight frame since his body had barely entered the algor mortis stage when the ME got there. We checked the alibis out. Two male friends he lived with were at a gaming party; another female friend was shopping for groceries. She's alibied by about ten people, has a bus ticket and shows up on the grocer's surveillance footage. Everyone's got an alibi except Andrew Mackay.'

Callan fisted his hands. Why was Andrew not telling them everything? 'What about the murder weapon? His devices? His calendar?'

'We're working on that. The murder weapon's been identified as belonging to a member of the college's shinty team. She'd reported it missing that afternoon. As for the devices, it would be simpler if we had them, but we checked his room and from what we have at this point, they are missing.'

Missing? What sort of information could Anvit Nair have on his devices? Information sensitive enough to kill for?

Callan leaned back in his chair. 'So Andrew's the only suspect ye have?'

Walsh sighed. 'There's a professor who confirms she was in that area but has given us references to check her alibi. Mr Nair's boss, under whom he interned, also has an alibi. We're yet to cross-check them though.'

'I don't work on instincts, Walsh, but Andrew Mackay isn't the sort to murder anyone. There's got to be an explanation.'

Walsh stood, affixing his hat on his head. 'I'm here for a word with Dr Brown. Hopefully she can shed some light on the report she's made, something that we're missing. I will be objective about this, but it would be so much easier if the lad talked.'

It could be easier for the police, but for Andrew? It could be incriminating. What had he done?

Callan ran a hand through his hair. Walsh was one of the good ones. At least that gave him some solace.

CHAPTER FIVE

Callan drew a line from Lucas Fraser's photo to where he'd scribbled 'handkerchief'. From there he scrawled 'DNA?'.

Then on the other side he listed 'Leana Murray', 'Isobel Murray', '20th May 1981' and 'Violet's Rose'.

He stood back and perused his less than legible murder board.

Then he drew a line from Isobel Murray to Lucas Fraser and wrote 'girlfriend' above it.

What other connections did he have?

He didn't know what connection Leana and Isobel had, if any. But he knew Leana had targeted Violet's Rose. Did that matter to the case?

Callan poured himself some coffee, sipping as he thought.

He'd checked out some old news articles about Lucas Fraser and his disappearance. None of them had mentioned a girlfriend, just like Logan Fraser had said.

Had he got the wrong name? After all, age robbed many of their memory.

His eyes fell on 'Violet's Rose'.

He had no other leads to follow.

Picking up the phone, he dialled.

'Lottie Fraser!' chirped a voice.

He could almost smell the cinnamon buns through the phone. She indeed excelled at baking. Smiling despite everything, Callan greeted her. 'Would you have Lucas's belongings?'

Many people would keep artefacts that reminded them of their loved ones, but others liked to purge in order to move on.

'Oh!' Shuffling sounds came down the line. 'Let me think. Log showed me a few pictures his parents kept. But could you give me a day or two to look in the loft? It's a mess in there and I don't really know what's where.'

Callan nodded. 'Sure, but if you don't find anything, would you mind letting us go through the pictures at least?'

'Er, of course! Is there anything we should know?'

'Why don't you search the loft and I'll come over then and explain?'

She sounded unsure, but relented saying it would be best for him to speak directly to Logan.

Callan thanked her and hoped she'd have something baking when he went over to pick up Lucas's belongings.

Staring out the window, Callan sighed at the damp afternoon.

But when did rain ever hold him back?

CALLAN FOCUSED ON THE ROAD, THOUGHTS OF AILEEN eating away at him. Aye, the sun should be overhead about now, and she still hadn't replied to his message.

And for good measure, he'd typed out another one

before leaving the station, asking if he could drop by that night.

It met the same fate as his previous missive: cold silence.

As Callan drove, he swore he saw Aileen's sedan pass him by, but he didn't stop. The last thing they needed was a public fight.

He gripped the steering wheel, chiding himself. What had he got himself into?

Dealing with another murder case where a brother grieved for his long-lost sibling, an angry girlfriend who wouldn't give him the time of day and hurting best friends, would drive Callan loony. To top it all off, he still hadn't found Blaine.

The road curved to the left and then swished to the right, round the base of the mountain, hugging the road with ease and making the detective behind the wheel proud. Aileen irritated him about his old ride, but as he loved to remind her: *old's gold.*

And there, she'd found a way back into the front of his mind.

Eventually, as the afternoon burned through the windows, the road evened out and Callan pushed the car into fourth gear.

If he wanted to reach somewhere and the road had no traffic, he'd choose to get to his destination faster.

Soon he was driving through an area where the houses sat far apart to enjoy the luxury of gardens and keep nosy neighbours at bay.

Counting the numbers on the road, he slowed his car, not wanting to miss the house he sought.

When he got to the top of the hill, where the road dissolved into a garden path, Callan found an entrance.

Violet's Rose.

The granite plaque was pressed into a concrete pole that held up one end of the wrought-iron gate. The bars reached over his head, tall enough to keep vandals and eager lads from climbing it.

Maybe the owners learned from the Leana Murray incident.

The house itself, Callan deduced after peering this way and that, had to hide behind the trees.

Creeping plants and cobwebs had wound their way through the iron bars, and the trees beyond stood tall, a tattoo against the sky where clouds crowded. No one had taken a saw to the branches to manicure them. The dense cover wove like a wild web, besieging the property.

A few weeds had found their way through the gravel and onto the tar.

He parked his car, pressing it into the hedges.

The area between the road and the gate once had gravel but was now littered with dead grass and plastic bottles.

Callan crouched to study the dirt.

No car tracks or footprints.

It meant no one frequented Violet's Rose. Could it be abandoned?

Tiptoeing around the mud to keep it undisturbed, he wrapped his hands around the rusting iron of the gate.

It was icy to his touch, showing signs of the seasons it had weathered.

Callan wondered what would happen if he tried opening it. The entire thing might crumble to dust.

He palmed the traditional lock still intact on the chain tied around the gate.

No more vandals, Callan noted.

He pulled out his notepad, penning his observations,

then stuck his face between the iron rods of the gate and squinted, hoping a spider didn't leap into his nostrils.

Some grey light found its way through the thick trees. Even in autumn, some leaves were green, the branches heavy with foliage.

A road had once cut through the trees. He saw remnants of it under the thinner weeds and saplings growing around the gravel.

Up ahead, the road curved to the right before it was swallowed up.

The rest of the gardens had fallen into disarray, choked with weeds and more of those creeping vines. Well and truly forgotten – and smelling it too.

What sort of family let a house located in a prime locality sit idle? Either they filled it with laughter and made it a home or they sold it to pocket the money.

Unless the property was embroiled in legal battles.

He stared at the sign – the embossed gold lettering fading into the black granite.

Violet's Rose.

He needed to ask around. Someone would know.

Crack. The sound of a twig snapping lured Callan's attention. Could it be an animal?

Frowning, he stepped back onto the road, the tiny pebbles crunching under his feet as he stuck to the edge.

A tall stone wall ran along the road, fencing off the property. Ivy, thick and unruly, draped over it.

The grey stones showed their age, and the upper blocks had crumbled to the ground, the debris perhaps contributing to the gravel under his feet.

A few feet away, the wall had collapsed under a fallen trunk.

Something in the distance rattled, disturbing the cobwebs on the leaves.

Callan narrowed his eyes and gave the ground a once-over. *Footsteps*, albeit small ones. He scrunched up his nose.

One hand on his gun, Callan ducked into the woods. He jumped over a few moss-covered stones and stuck to the mud; he didn't want to get his feet tangled in any of those vines.

Making as little disturbance as possible, Callan studied the area for the intruder.

A bird squawked, and something rustled in the shrubs.

Another step and Callan swatted at the invisible strands of the cobweb tickling his neck.

Blast!

Another scuttle sounded from behind the shrubs and Callan followed it.

Muddy earth coated the hem of his trousers. In his patent all black, it made little difference to him.

Aileen would be livid.

He bit the inside of his cheek to keep his focus.

Reaching a thick tree trunk, he hid behind it before standing to his full height. Callan took a breath of damp, mossy air and peered over his shoulder.

The tree's uneven bark dug into his jacket, some flakes falling loose where they rubbed against his back.

Callan focused on the distant outgrowth.

A chimney peeked out from between trees and Callan could see some shining object, perhaps a reflecting glass up ahead on its branches.

Was someone watching him?

Wanting to get closer, Callan lunged towards another tree, folding himself into the tall weeds. The chimney was still in sight, but the glass wasn't.

He calmed himself and stilled, ears perked up, listening for the slightest ruffle.

One minute ticked by and the entire wood held its breath. Nothing moved; Callan barely breathed.

Another half a minute passed and *snap!*

SHE IMAGINED PLOUGHING A FIST INTO CALLAN'S FACE. How could a man be so annoying yet striking? He'd sent her a couple of brief messages, as if that would do the trick. And he hadn't even contacted Daniel, his best friend. She'd gone to their house, after visiting Andrew's friends, to find an inconsolable Isla and a haggard-looking Daniel.

'Later, Aileen. We'll deal with that eejit later.'

Rage made her vision tunnel, and she almost drove past the florist. Her car screeched, drawing attention, but she'd be damned if she gave a flying fig.

She stalked towards the shop, still muttering.

Mrs Halliday ran the florist shop now. The inside of the shop was like the Royal Botanical Gardens in spring: lush, fragrant and cheerful, yet none of it rubbed off on Aileen.

Hands on her hips, she contemplated what sort of bouquet would be appropriate for the boy. Maybe she'd get one for Callan too – he'd be in the hospital after she was through with him.

She sniggered.

'Aileen.' Mrs Halliday greeted her from behind a counter. She'd cut her white hair into a bob and wore a lapis lazuli pendant around her wrinkled neck. Fingering the chain, she ambled over to Aileen. 'Looking for something?' A naughty light shone in her eyes.

Ah, another one who wanted Aileen and Callan together.

Aileen smiled despite the anger roiling behind her eyes

and snipped off the rumour before it could manifest. 'I heard about the dead teen and wanted to lay flowers for him.'

The smile withered from Mrs Halliday's lips. 'Oh, dearie. It's an awful situation. His mother loved to buy flowers here and, well, he did too.'

Sometimes the gossip mill paid off. Usually it would be Isla who'd find information, but now she had to venture off on her own. Aileen shuffled her feet, trying to loosen the tension she felt.

Speaking with people had never been her strength. She was still learning.

'What do you mean? He bought flowers here for his mother?'

Mrs Halliday cackled. 'You amuse me, lassie. A lad of eighteen buys his mother presents on Mother's Day. Those flowers weren't meant for mothers – they were meant for you know what.'

Aileen wanted to hear the words, so she played dumb.

Her eyes darted around the shop, latching on a few shoppers who stood still, ears perked up. Ah, Loch Fuar's trusted tattlers.

Grabbing Aileen by the arm, Mrs Halliday ushered her behind the counter. 'A lady's man he was, if I ever saw one. Rumour is he dipped into the older populace too.'

Aileen's eyes twitched; she wanted to grimace at that visual. Instead she hummed, nodding to hear more.

'Aye, I saw him with my own eyes, I did. Smooth talker as any. Well, can't speak ill of the dead.'

'Mm, an interesting young man. Who did you say this woman was?'

Surveying her shop for eavesdroppers, Mrs Halliday ducked closer to Aileen and whispered the name in her ears. 'Rosie Bailey.' Her breath tickled Aileen's hair. 'They had a thing going this month.'

This month? Fascinating man indeed.

Zay had texted her a bunch of names – female admirers. Rosie Bailey didn't star in the list, but the way things were headed, Aileen wondered if Anvit's murder might be the outcome of a jealous rage.

She bought a bouquet Mrs Halliday assured her would be appropriate for the occasion and made the forty-five-minute drive back to the crime scene.

The GPS took her along a more civilised route: cobbled thoroughfares sandwiched between stone buildings and then through a park whose muddy road had footprints littered all over it.

Grimacing at the sludge squishing under her feet, Aileen pulled up the hem of her trousers and found the solid stones, tiptoeing over them.

Annoying rain and a stupid killer. Why not choose a more civilised spot to kill?

Aileen blew a raspberry, reprimanding herself for her thoughts. She hadn't dared this mud path to study the theory of murder or motives. Her only aim in coming down here was to find out what kind of women Anvit saw.

Slowing down, Aileen eyed the blue police tape cordoning off the crime scene.

A string of flowers lay below the tape along with cards. A few sniffles echoed around her, mostly from girls and, Aileen noted, holding back an amused smile, women with greying hair.

A few guys loitered too, some lanky, some burly.

Was Anvit's killer here?

Leaves rustled when the wind blew, the scent making Aileen's red nose run.

She sniffled and almost lost her footing. 'Ouch!' Aileen

turned to face a willowy woman. Her hair – mostly white but with a few strands of black – was tucked in a hat, pearls glittered around her neck and a knitted sweater paired with black trousers gave her a chic appeal. A golden rimmed pair of spectacles hung around her neck on a matching chain.

'Pardon me, madam.' Her voice quivered. Placing a delicate hand on her rosy lips, she covered up a sniff.

Dark green veins protruded from her pale skin, but she'd manicured her nails. Only one had slightly chipped at the edges.

'Did you know him?'

Aileen's question brought her wide black eyes back to Aileen – they'd drifted to the police tape and the crime scene beyond.

She fluttered her eyelashes as if to keep the tears at bay. 'He was a student. The brightest.'

'I'm sorry for your loss.'

The professor shook her head. 'A loss for the entire computer science community. How did you know him?'

Deer caught in the headlights, Aileen fumbled.

She hadn't practised this, she didn't think she would be asked this question. She studied the bone-thin woman. Harmless, she judged, so she decided to stick with the truth.

'Oh, I didn't know him personally but, well, I have a friend about his age and the news of his death struck close to home.'

Light dawned in the other woman's eyes. 'I see. It's only natural for us to imagine ourselves in tragic situations. I'm glad you made it here.'

She touched Aileen's upper arm, her grip feather-like. 'It's kind of you to come and lay flowers. Compassion makes this world so much better.'

Aileen smiled and extended her hand. 'I'm Aileen Mackinnon.'

The professor's smile didn't meet her eyes, but she shook Aileen's proffered hand. 'Dr Moira Robertson. Mackinnon... Would you be the owner of Dachaigh?'

A small world. Aileen blushed. 'That's right.'

'Well, it must be nice being an innkeeper.'

It was – if the inn could survive the winter.

Aileen pointed to the gathered people. 'Aside from being a stellar student, he also made a lot of friends I see.'

Moira's eyes sharpened as they cut through the crowd. 'Yes. He wouldn't be employed by Gammit Inc if he weren't a team player. Now.' She cleared her throat. 'I need to hurry back before classes begin. No breaks, not for us.'

Aileen watched the woman leave, treading carefully in her pumps, then crouched to place the flowers and stood there for a while, solitary pain in her taut shoulders.

Anvit had to be a stellar student to affect a professor like that. Aileen huffed – her teachers had never cared one bit about her.

Finally, she made her way back to the car, mulling over what Moira had said about Gammit Inc. She had to look for that company.

CHAPTER SIX

Callan acted with haste. He swished, ready to strike yet not pulling out his police-issued handgun. For all he knew, it would be a harmless—

'Ouch!'

Something slapped him on the shoulder.

Ducking behind another tree, he gave his shoulder a fleeting glance and froze. What in the world?

A yellow splatter stung his black coat.

Was some eejit playing games?

Knowing this opponent wasn't carrying a real weapon, Callan uncurled and exposed himself.

Slap! Slap! Slap!

Three painful shots smacked against his gut.

'Bloody bastard!'

Callan fell to the ground, his stomach various shades of red, green, and blue. He didn't want to imagine the colour of his skin tomorrow.

Black and blue.

The shots eased, and Callan saw the bampot perched on a tree. A white shoe with untied laces dangled from a tree branch. His T-shirt, displaying characters from some popular cartoon, hung loosely around him, and his toothless grin was anything but innocent.

And he held a gun in his hand, the sort that shot paint bombs.

Hell!

He pointed it at Callan again and *smack*.

Callan wasn't an eejit, though. He rolled away, the shot just missing his shoulder as it splattered purple on the ground.

Another smash followed in its wake, but Callan, knowing where the little brat was, sought refuge behind a thick tree trunk.

A ball of blue splashed against the brown trunk. 'Who are ye?'

'I'm Detective Inspector Callan Cameron.'

This time, green splatter spritzed against his boot.

Bloody children!

Callan gritted his teeth. 'Get down here before I arrest ye!'

Cackles of laughter filled the sultry air. 'I'm in the tree.'

'And ye're bound to get hungry.'

A long silence followed. 'Am not!'

Callan felt a smile tickle his lips. Frustrating they were, but he had handled his share of six-year-olds.

'Sure will.'

'I've got chocolate.'

He peered around the truck and caught the boy's eye. The toothless grin had disappeared into a frown. 'Won't yer mum be worried?'

'Yer mum would be too,' he retorted, his expression showing he was losing confidence in his theory.

Callan kept silent, knowing the silence would gnaw at the boy.

A full two minutes later it did. 'Answer me!'

He didn't give any indication of his presence. As if in support, the grey light around them darkened as clouds gathered overhead.

'Detective?' a whimper came from up the tree.

Callan still waited.

Thud!

Victory! Callan grinned.

A minute later, he heard two feet scampering in his direction.

Just as the boy rounded the tree, Callan stepped into his path and clutched the boy's arms. He barely reached Callan's waist. The gun, as tall as he was, dragged behind him.

Scared eyes met Callan's.

Callan pointed at his badge. 'Want to go in a cell with the bad guys?'

He whimpered, pouting.

Bending lower to the boy's eye level, Callan hid his smile. 'You shot at a police officer. That's against the law. You won't see the light of day for—'

He stopped. A crying child was not what he needed. He hadn't meant to terrify him.

Callan laughed. 'I won't tell anyone, though. Who are ye?'

That restored the lad's cheekiness. He smirked at Callan, using the butt of his gun to lean on. 'I'm Matt.'

'Where do ye stay?'

Matt shuffled his feet, studying the ground. Then, unsure eyes met Callan's. 'Mum said I mustn't talk to strangers.'

If his mum was like the rest, she would've told him not to shoot at strangers, too.

'Are ye from hereabouts?'

No answer.

'I wanted to meet someone who lives in this property.' Callan pointed to the chimney. And then, unsure why, he added, 'I'm looking for a woman named Leana Murry.'

Narrowed eyes met his. 'How do you know about her?'

'I'm the police, remember?'

The gun clattered to the ground as the boy crossed his arms. 'Why aren't you in uniform?'

Callan knew if he got into a question-answer round with a six-year-old he wouldn't ever leave. He needed to walk and talk.

'Why don't I drop ye home and tell ye?'

Before he could respond, thick droplets fell to the ground.

Blast!

'I'll be drenched before I get home. I told Mum I'm at my friends, but they're boring.'

Pleading eyes landed on Callan's. And Callan remembered the reprimanding glare his mother had sent his way when he came home covered in mud.

He surely wouldn't let the boy get wet in this rain. 'Where can we go then?'

A glint shone in Matt's eyes. He grabbed Callan by the hand, gun forgotten, and dashed further into the woods.

Callan didn't know this place, but it felt as if Matt did, trampling the ground like he played here every day.

They raced through the woods, jumping over fallen branches and dry leaves, avoiding the splatters of rain with equal lithe and stamina.

By the time they reached a clearing, both panted, drenched.

Still, Matt continued, pulling Callan behind him.

The area must once have had a fence, but it had fallen into rubble. Mist clung around the trees like a smothering blanket, and the grey light brought along with it an overpowering stench of moss.

Hugging the treeline, they made their way to the other side.

A structure stood there, classical with Corinthian columns. Were they in some English garden from the nineteenth century?

Then Callan saw it. The structure wasn't just an ornamental showpiece; it was a chapel. And they stood behind it. Here, stones – tombstones – covered in moss and grime jutted out from the ground.

Matt pointed to the chapel's porch, and they ducked out of the rain. 'The chapel's closed.'

Callan, too intrigued to let the rain get in his way, commanded, 'Stay here.'

He tried the chapel door. The lock hung in place, still unyielding.

He followed along the white walls, their paint flaky and ivy clinging to them.

The once beautiful stained-glass windows had shattered, leaving behind sharp shards. Inside, amidst the gloom, Callan caught sight of an empty altar and wooden benches and pews, all shoved together on one side. It was a dump. Twigs and bird droppings littered every nook, and the place stank of pungent, putrid fumes.

Feet shuffled to his right. Callan glared at Matt. 'Didn't I ask ye to stay out of the rain?'

Matt shot a shuddering glance behind him. Ah, he was scared to stay alone. Lightning struck, and Matt caught Callan's hand.

'I-I-I know who she is.'

Callan frowned. 'Who?'

Matt dragged him away to the clearing, and they wound their way between the graves until he stopped at a grey stone with a smattering of moss. He pointed to the letters carved on it. 'That's Alfred Murray. At least I think it is.'

Callan crouched beside the boy, studying the tombstone. Alfred *Murray*?

He cleared away the ivy growing over the stone, some stray brambles scratching his exposed skin. A few wilted flower petals peeked out from between the leaves. Had someone left them there or were they from the ivy?

Through the green moss that covered the stone, he made out the embossing. *In Loving Memory*...

Matt pulled Callan out of his thoughts. 'Gramps told me.' He shuffled to the other stone. 'Alfred had two daughters – Isobel and Leana. And Gramps thinks they're gone too.'

Callan stared at Matt slack jawed. Blimey!

Of all the people who'd know about these missing people, Callan had never expected a six-year-old to lead him here.

'Where can I find yer gramps?'

Matt smiled, showing his gums and tiny teeth. 'Gramps says every healthy lad should romp in the mud. Come on – he'll love to meet my new friend.'

New friend?

Callan let Matt pull him towards the woods again. His *new friend* was, apparently, well versed in them as well as romping in the mud.

Hands over the steering wheel, Aileen pulled at her fingers.

She felt drowsy not from sleep but from the emotionally stressful day. She had barely slept these past few nights, and the day had been a challenging one.

Now here she sat, opposite a glass structure that looked like a Rubik's cube mangled by a child.

The glass glittered all shades of red, blue, and green.

Creating computer games surely had to be a blooming industry.

Aileen squared her shoulders. After her meeting with the professor, she had pulled out her phone and done what she should've this morning.

Searching information on Anvit Nair, especially his social media, had paid off. The lad loved to boast about his academic performance and his work as an intern. And he worked at the most coveted gaming company in the north of Scotland, Gammit Inc. Even though it employed a lot of staff from all over the country and abroad, its roots were in Loch Fuar. Douglas Reid, its founder, worked with the crème de la crème of his company here in Loch Fuar.

The man had served as headmaster at the college, then started the company after retiring.

Aileen figured she could wedge her way in, perhaps speak to Anvit's boss. Based on the bragging, that was the top dog himself.

But how did you get an attendance with gaming royalty?

SITTING IN FRONT OF ANVIT'S PLACE OF EMPLOYMENT — though technically it wasn't employment but an unpaid internship — she was still figuring that part out.

Aileen wanted to know if the role was completely unpaid. Working with the boss surely had its benefits.

Get your arse out of the car.

A good starting point.

Aileen pulled her coat closer as she shut her car door using frosty fingers. Every breath puffed out like she'd drawn on a cigarette.

Bouncing on her heels, Aileen contemplated where she should go. The inside, warm and toasty, would be better than the outdoors.

Aileen strode towards the series of stairs leading to the glass doors, hoping her attire fit in at a tech company. The rain soaked her trousers below the knees. She imagined the typical sweatshirt and trainers look most tech people wore and reconsidered the dress shirt underneath her coat. The accountancy and tech worlds didn't define office apparel the same way.

A lavish reception area glowed under stark yellow light. The prism of glasses inside reflected the luminance, making the entire area bloom like a flower in spring – almost as if it was broad daylight.

Aileen reached for the cold metal handle and pulled. The door didn't budge.

She looked around to see if she required an employee ID to get in. But why would someone need an ID to get to the reception area of an office?

Aileen peered through the glass and figured out what the problem was. There was no one sitting behind the desk. They'd shut shop for the day.

So why keep the lights on?

She rolled her eyes at the display of money and power, swishing on her heels.

'Must bear the consequences.'

Stalking towards her car, Aileen almost missed the hushed voices.

She halted mid-step. If someone was loitering around, she could ask them about Anvit. The party boy she knew, but the educational wizard? Aileen wanted to know that lad.

She tiptoed back up the stairs and stuck to the glass then crept towards the end of the wall, praying her visible breath didn't give her away.

The smell of masculine cologne hung in the air.

Aileen took another step and her feet kicked a pebble. The whispers stopped. Crap!

Aileen ducked back, hoping they'd continue. Instead, footsteps sounded, walking towards her.

'What is it?'

A long pause had Aileen's heart palpitating. What would happen if they caught her?

Was this playing things safe?

Stupid woman! Why was she hiding?

'Get back here, ye moron!' A voice hissed.

Aileen clenched her fists, hoping and praying. She couldn't move, could barely breathe, and her heart raced away like a bloody train.

Footsteps again, but this time they receded. A couple of gasps from Aileen and the dialogue resumed.

Somewhere in the few dark trees that survived in the large car park, a bird chirped its final song for the day.

Using it as a cover, Aileen bent lower and inched a couple of feet ahead.

With no lights and, Aileen realised, the path shadowed by a large tree, darkness drenched this side of the building.

A fancy car sat still in the small space between the building and the fence. Could this be a private entrance?

You should come back tomorrow.

That was the safe thing to do. Trespassing would land her in trouble.

'Just issue it. I don't want sniffing noses. Nip the bloody thing.'

'Aye, sir.'

'This is important. Got it?'

Startled, Aileen threw another glance at the alley. This had to be a rendezvous. Who were these men?

'That boy was a thorn, an intelligent thorn, but a thorn. It's a blessing he's gone.' The gruff voice took a pause before muttering, 'But let's be diplomatic.'

Staring into that alley, her eyes adjusted to make out the silhouette of shoes from under the car. Two pairs belonging to two men standing in front.

Crouching lower, Aileen duck-walked her way to the rear of the car, hoping to catch every word.

Which other 'boy' could they be talking about? It had to be Anvit Nair.

'I'll arrange for someone to place a large bouquet at the crime scene tomorrow – make sure it's branded with our logo too.' Then the voice whispered in a gossipy tone. 'Do you know who did it?'

The only answer was a snort followed by chuckles. 'You amuse me.'

Footsteps sounded again, making Aileen want to disappear into the shadows. What was she thinking, hiding behind the car?

Her heart thundered, and her eyes shut. The treads grew louder until they were hammers of doom smacking against her eardrums.

Blood rushed and pounded, encouraged by her palpitating heart.

This was it – they'd caught her.

A click echoed in the night – the click of a gun?

Whrum!

Aileen squealed, hands slapping over her mouth to dwarf the sound.

Hot air blasted against her neck. Someone had started

up the car! And would no doubt reverse it out of its parking space.

Blast! Quite literally, blast.

Just as the car inched backward, Aileen dove into the fence, squeezing against the concrete. She'd rather plaster herself against wet concrete than be tomato puree on the tarmac.

Stupid! Stupid! Stupid!

The angle of the blackness was just enough to hide her from the headlights as the car turned and disappeared around the building.

But she wasn't alone in that alley, not yet.

A suited man hung behind, watching as the car's headlights receded into the distance. Only when it was gone did he move. 'Convenient indeed, Mr Reid. Very convenient.'

With that he strode off, disappearing into a gap in the wall. A white door shut behind him.

CHAPTER SEVEN

Callan followed Matt, drenched and panting, up a long driveway. The mansion emerged from between the trees like something out of a Jane Austen novel. Only the darkening sky gave it an aura of ruthless might, biding time for battle.

They could've been in Bath with the symmetrical Georgian architecture and elaborate friezes. Gargoyles stared at them with dead eyes, mouths green with moss.

Matt led him around the building, leaving the ostentatious entrance with two symmetrical flights of stairs behind.

Callan deduced they used the servant's entrance, especially since it had no gargoyles or friezes, only cold walls and floors.

They hurried up a staircase, emerging into a corridor with pastel-green walls and gold-framed paintings.

'Are ye sure we should drip rainwater on the carpet?'

Matt shrugged. 'It dries.'

The pristine red carpet turned a spotty maroon as they

shuffled up another stairwell and finally pushed through a wooden door.

Leather-bound books lined the walls, their rich scent mingled with the wood polish hanging in the air. A heavy chandelier was suspended from the ceiling. Right beneath it sat a grand mahogany desk.

The man commanding the desk matched its burly girth and age. His dark blue orbs cut through to Callan's. Pink lips peeked from his untamed white beard. He caressed it like a favoured pet – all the way down to his pot belly. 'Made a new friend, eh, lad? What did yer maw tell ye about talking to strangers?'

Matt scampered to the man, climbing up to sit on his lap. 'He's a detective with a real gun, Gramps!'

The man's forehead creased as he lifted his right eyebrow.

Callan pulled out his badge. 'Detective Inspector Callan Cameron.'

Matt butted in. 'He's asking about the Murrays, Leana and Isobel.'

'Why?' The growl reverberated through the study, almost making the dust on the books shudder.

Callan listened to the new gust of rain thrashing against the windowpanes, grateful he wasn't out in those woods.

'I'm investigating a—' Callan cast a glance at Matt, who stared at him with wide eyes, waiting on his words. 'A case regarding Lucas Fraser. I'm told he was romantically linked with Isobel Murray.'

Matt blew a raspberry. 'Why do guys hang out with girls? They like *pink*.'

Callan narrowed his eyes at Matt. He wished it could be that simple with *girls*.

'Matt, why don't ye go find Lucy?'

'But, Gramps—'

'The detective will come meet ye later.' He sent a pointed look Callan's way as he set the boy down.

Callan nodded. 'Aye.'

As Matt scuttled away, the man steepled his fingers. 'And stay inside the house!' His voice softened. 'The wee lad needs a lesson on talking to strangers. If ma daughter found out he'd been frolicking about, she'd have ma hide!'

Callan cleared his throat. 'I'm sorry. Er, Matt didn't give me his last name.'

'He's an only child and gets lonely here, all by himself in a large house.' The man stood up, extending a hand. 'I'm Gregory Winters.'

'Mr Winters.' Callan shuffled his feet, still standing. He didn't want to be crude and soak the upholstered chair in rainwater. Best he got on with it. 'About Lucas—'

'Whisky?'

Callan shook his head. 'I'm on duty, sir. I came here wanting to find out who owned Violet's Rose.'

Glasses clinked, and the amber liquid sloshed into a tumbler. Winters took a gulp that must've burned his throat.

'That's a loaded question, Detective. I've been around for a good seventy years, yet I've never been able to peg it down: is it a story of tragedy or love?'

He sank into his chair again.

'Did ye ken Lucas Fraser?'

Winters chuckled and took a sip. 'That lad knew if he set foot in that house, the old man would have his head.'

What did that even mean?

Callan stared at the pool of water he'd made at his frigid feet. At least the room was warm enough. He eyed the large fireplace where logs crackled behind a glass pane.

Winters followed his gaze and explained, 'Matt's a wee

curious one. He tried crawling in there to search for Santa once.'

Welcoming a bairn meant a huge change – he'd witnessed that with Daniel.

Callan reached into his jacket and felt the soggy paper of his notepad. Damn it!

He hoped his phone hadn't died.

Folding his arms, he kept his mind sharp. 'Who'd have Lucas Fraser's head?'

The whisky vanished, and Winters pointed at the bottle. 'Get me the whole thing.'

If the older man wanted Dutch courage, Callan wouldn't deny him. What was he hiding?

Satisfied at the amount Callan had poured, Winters leaned back. 'Mr Alfred "Stiff" Murray was an arsehole. There's no other way to put it. He wanted a son, had two daughters instead. Well, two legitimate daughters anyway. His wife died ten months after the second one was born, taking with her the chance of a male heir.'

Callan tried to work it out in his head, but couldn't find an answer. 'Why would he need an heir?'

Winters sipped. 'He had more money than entire countries. That house, "Violet's Rose", was one of his many properties. Loch Fuar's a decent place to maintain a household, he'd always say.' He pointed his tumbler at Callan. 'And it's well connected to the city where he ran his businesses from.'

'And what about his daughters?'

Hand on his belly, Winters sat back with a sly smile on his face. 'Isobel and Leana Murray. Isobel, the eldest, worshipped him. He hardly paid her any attention since he'd leave them with a governess when he went away to the city. I reckon she went to a finishing school after being home-schooled.'

Winters snapped his fingers. 'But the younger one, Leana, was a spitfire, she was. Told me off and liked to play with the servant's children. Needless to say, she never saw eye to eye with her father. Caused him plenty of troubles.'

'Do ye ken about the vandalism?'

'Aye, it was all over, but unfortunately I wasn't here to enjoy the ruckus then. Dad had sent me abroad to manage a branch of his business there.'

Wealth – this was the life of the wealthy. Callan dug his hands into his pockets. 'And what about the sisters now?'

The laughter that erupted from beneath the white beard boomed through the room and carried down the corridor. 'That, my lad, is the biggest mystery of all. Talk was, they both vanished the same night, like ghosts. Lucas Fraser, the sisters and their servant, Millie Baines, were never seen after that spring of 1981.'

AILEEN PARKED HER CAR RIGHT NEXT TO ISLA'S. DANIEL had taken little Carly to see his parents. Like most toddlers, she'd picked up on the tense mood, fussing and crying the whole day, and Daniel had thought his wife could use a break.

Now, Aileen rounded the car to greet her best friend outside the pub.

Hanging out with friends was new for Aileen, and she cherished every moment. In the past months, they'd hung out at the beauty salon, chatting as they got their nails done, at Barbara's Tea Room, as well as shopping together until they could barely walk.

Aileen drew Isla into a hug. Her wild hair squashed

against Aileen's, both friends drawing strength from the other.

'How are you?'

Isla clutched Aileen by the arms. 'Not tonight. We talk about anything but our lives tonight. No husbands, no boyfriends, no business, no crimes, just something else.'

Arm in arm, they headed for the bustling pub. Aileen had been here only a handful of times.

The noise pulsed in her ears, slamming her heart against her chest.

Ethan's Pub served all sorts of patrons from pink-faced, bearded old men to starry-eyed, barely legal teens.

Someone hooted with laughter, and another person cursed like a pirate. The wooden stools stamped against the floor and glasses full of alcohol thudded against the counter, staining the brown polish with history.

A musky scent lingered in the air, calming Aileen's aching muscles. For the first time in what felt like forever, a jubilant grin bloomed on her face.

She tugged Isla to the counter and hollered, 'Two pints of draft beer, please!'

'Comin' right up, lassie!'

A short while later, they were settled into a quieter nook with a clear view of the main bar, two dishes of steak and kidney pie between them.

Isla chewed. 'Yum, this is *delish*.'

Aileen grunted her approval, shoving a large piece into her mouth. She hadn't realised how hungry she was. After all, she'd forgotten all about lunch. A piece of toast could only go so far.

They ate in silence, drowning in the cheery atmosphere around them. A fight briefly broke out on the other side of the bar and others broke it apart just as quickly.

Aileen swallowed the crusty pie with a sip of her malty beer.

A twinkle sparkled in Isla's eyes. 'A cutie just walked in.' She pointed at the bar.

Aileen swivelled to see a man wearing plaid and jeans. She gave an approving nod. 'I like his hat, although hats give me the creeps sometimes. Walsh wears them.'

Isla shushed her. 'Fun, remember?'

'Look at the other one, next to him.'

They giggled, heads pressed together, whispering like teenagers.

Isla called up another pint for herself and Aileen.

Twenty minutes later, they were cracking up with laughter, though Aileen couldn't remember what they were laughing at.

They matched the decibel level of the rest of the pub, no longer silent. She threw a cheeky comment at a man passing by. He stopped and furrowed his eyebrows. 'Excuse me, miss?'

Aileen blew a strand of hair from her eyes. 'Ah, don't ya worry, lad. I don't bite!' She hollered the last bit. 'Not unless you ask!'

Isla smacked the table, guffawing. 'Oh, Aileen. At this pace you'll get in a fight and land behind bars.'

She'd never been that wild, but at almost twenty-nine the time had come.

'I've got a candidate I'd like to bash up.' She fisted her hands, shaking them. Then, as loud as she could, she shouted, 'Callan Cameron! I'd like to sock that sod!'

Cheers went up around her, making her grin like an idiot. She'd never felt so good.

Isla poked her side. 'Hey, why don't we call him?'

'Not a chance. I'm not calling that bastard. He'll call if he wants. I'm letting loooose tonight.'

She held up her thumb. 'Ethan! Another round please!'

And so they continued, gossiping about a few men, smacking their hands on the table as they spoke.

'Gah!' Isla wiped the tears leaking out of her eyes from all the laughing. 'Hey, I know.' She pulled out her phone and dialled Daniel. 'I'm prank calling my husband.'

Aileen whipped her phone away. 'If you call him from your phone, he'll know it's you, you idiot.'

'Oh, that's fine!' She snatched the phone back when Daniel answered. 'Hey boo! Guess who is calling who!'

There was a long pause on the line. Then she said, 'No way, we've just had a pint. And you know I can stomach a tr-trunk of alcohol.' She giggled.

Aileen blinked at the glasses on the table. Were there two or four? Three? Six?

'Oh, you're no fun!' Isla pouted. 'Come here and we'll have fun.' She wiggled her eyebrows even though Daniel couldn't see her.

Phone still clutched to her ears, she told Aileen, 'He's coming here to break up the party.'

True to his word, the trusty burly figure of Daniel McIntyre pushed into the crowded pub a short while later. He dwarfed most of the men, eyes hard as they scanned the pub.

'Aww.' Isla gave him a doe-eyed look. 'I love that man. He's my man.'

Aileen smiled at the goofy grin on Isla's face. Married five years and she was still a goner for her husband.

His beige plaid shirt and dark pair of jeans highlighted his muscular physique. Then his gaze landed on the two of them in the corner.

Before she could blink, he was right in front of them. 'Isla! I asked ye to stay home.'

Isla pouted. 'But I was lonely. And you told me to unwind,' she countered.

'Not like this!' Daniel's growl cut through the fuzz in Aileen's brain and for the first time she saw the anger in his eyes. 'Damn it, Isla! I thought you'd be more responsible.'

Isla pushed against the table. 'Don't speak to me like that!'

'I will if you continue to act like a child!'

Aileen blinked, taken aback. Isla and Daniel never fought, ever. And Daniel just didn't have an angry bone in his body. What was wrong?

'Let's go home.'

'No!'

Daniel firmed his lips, finally turning to Aileen. 'How are you getting home?'

A little frightened, she waved her hands. 'I'm fine.'

'Does Callan ken ye're here?'

'Why should he?'

The fight in his shoulders deflated, and he visibly sagged. 'Look, Aileen, it's been a long day. Let's just all get a good night's rest, okay? Drinking yer emotions is never good and, well, I don't want either of ye to wake up hungover. Will you be able to get home alright?'

'I'm fine, Daniel. I am. I'll get a taxi.' The fight had splashed cold water on her face. 'Just take Isla home. She's hurting.'

'I'm fine too,' Isla added, but it was a mumble.

Daniel wrapped his wife in his arms like she was a precious diamond. 'Come on, darling. Let's get ye to bed.'

He nodded a goodnight to Aileen, and she watched the pair walking away, her heart breaking a little.

She checked her phone to reread Callan's message.

'I'm really sorry for not calling. How are you?'

Aileen tugged at her hair. She was sorry too, but she

didn't know what to say. Was Callan so married to his job that she'd always be the mistress?

Holding up her finger, she called out, 'Another pint, Ethan. I don't have anyone to drive me home tonight.'

HE MADE IT BACK TO TOWN AFTER SUNDOWN. THE MIST and clouds hung low, drawing the humidity in the air. Shops had shut for the day, so Callan hurried past Barbara's Tea Room and slammed the brakes outside the florist shop, hoping Mrs Halliday would still be in.

The florist gave him a sly smile after she let him in. 'For someone special?'

Not very subtle, was she?

Callan smiled, showing his teeth. He caught his reflection in the glass case behind her. His smile looked like a grimace.

'Aye, for my mother.'

Mrs Halliday chuckled. 'I just told someone this morning. Lads at eighteen don't buy flowers for their mother on random days. And men don't barge into a florist shop after it's closed to buy their mothers flowers either.'

She pointed at a bouquet. 'Roses to lure a lover?'

Callan crossed his arms and stared at his choice, butterflies fluttering in his stomach.

HE'D DONE WHAT HIS FATHER HAD ALWAYS DONE FOR HIS mother after they had an argument. Sometimes his mother would forgive easily and sometimes his paw grovelled harder, even wearing the cologne she liked.

His gaze flickered to his silent phone. What the hell should he do?

He stuffed the flowers in the back seat of his car, nerves getting the better of him. He couldn't face her. And she hadn't replied to his message, so he likely wasn't welcome at Dachaigh either.

Like a coward, Callan turned and hurried to the police station. At least there he had some semblance of control.

After brewing himself a cup of coffee, he updated the murder board, set Robert to work on searching for information on Millie Baines as well as Gregory Winters. Then he checked for any crimes registered in the last week of May 1981.

He found one missing person report – Lucas Fraser's – but nothing else. It was as Winters had described it – the other sisters had disappeared like ghosts in the night.

And Millie Baines, the servant. They simply had no records of her. She was as lost as the Neolithic people.

What had occurred at Violet's Rose in 1981?

A yawn wrenched open Callan's lips, and he rubbed his stinging eyes. He needed to head home and get some sleep. But he'd just dumped coffee down his throat. Unsure what to do, Callan paced.

Gregory Winters owned an oil rig among many other successful business enterprises. He'd inherited the business from his father and had taken it to the next level. Callan had found photographs of a young Winters, his beard long and a sparkle in his eye. And he'd confirmed that the man had spent the entire spring and summer abroad just like he'd said.

Callan eliminated Winters as a potential murderer. He turned to the other man whom no one cared for.

Sir Alfred 'Stiff' Murray was a typical aristocrat. And what was it Siobhan had said? A patriarch. Would he have killed the man who sought to marry his daughter? Why then would the daughters and servant run?

Did he murder them all? Four murders? Golly!

All the same, the man hadn't cared for his daughters. Would he care whom they married? Unless he wanted to marry them off as pawns to strengthen business connections.

Callan didn't like the idea of mixing family and business, but in the twentieth century, such contracts still occurred. And from what he'd gathered, Murray was a traditionalist.

Facing the board, Callan regarded Lucas Fraser. Was it love or a business opportunity for Lucas? He wasn't sure.

He plopped into his chair and ran a search for Sir Alfred Murray.

A black-and-grey image of a man who looked like he'd be very much at home with royalty popped onto the screen. He wore a moustache, had small sharp eyes and didn't smile, wrinkles drawing sad marks on his face.

He hadn't had much time for his daughters or his first wife, not even attending her funeral. A few months before his daughters disappeared, he had fallen sick and died. With a guilty conscious after abandoning his daughters?

Callan sat back, running a hand over his face. He knew a thing or two about a guilty conscience and ignorance.

He watched the clock ring in the late hour. Tomorrow – he'd get back to this first thing in the morning.

The bouquet glared at him from the back seat of his SUV, making him sigh. He had bought it, handpicking the flowers. Why let them go to waste?

He reached for the car door when the shrill ringing of his phone startled him.

Seeing the caller ID made the blood rush to his ears. Something was wrong.

'Daniel, what is it? Are you and Isla okay?'

Daniel sighed. 'That's a loaded question. I found Isla at the pub, drunk with Aileen. Aileen insists she's okay, but I think she's had one too many. I'm in no mood to argue with a woman, let alone a drunk one, so I thought I'd give ye a call.'

Callan ran a hand through his hair. Aileen drinking? *Shit*, she must really be struggling.

'Ethan's?'

'Aye.'

'Thank ye, Daniel. I'll go get her.' And he could apologise while he was at it.

CHAPTER EIGHT

'I need a minute,' Aileen said to no one in particular. She'd drunk her two pints in complete silence, her happiness dissipating with Isla's absence.

She grabbed the tables as she went, hips bumping into stools.

She needed to take a walk and see straight. Right now, though, she felt joy bubbling inside her like the fizzy beer she'd downed all night.

When she almost lost her footing, Aileen chuckled. 'Silly floor.'

It wobbled under her like jelly again.

Giggling, she clutched another stool and inched towards the door. She mistook a step and almost tumbled, but the stools were her dear friends. They didn't let her fall.

She patted one of them, not sure why the person at the next table eyed her. 'Thank you. Only you care.'

When she almost kissed the floor, the walls came in handy and then the front door.

The cool air slapped her face, and she erupted into giggles as it tickled her nose and fingers.

She thought about getting a taxi. 'No, I'll walk. I'll walk to Callan and show him. Show him, I'm QUEEEEN.' She shrieked and guffawed at herself. 'Ah, ye're rat-arsed.' Aileen mimicked Callan's gruff voice, imagining his face. It sent her cackling again.

She hadn't ever drunk so much, been so happy, or wanted to screech with joy.

Aileen leaned on her car, scratching the back of her neck. Goosebumps popped up on her exposed arms, the breeze setting her tingling skin alight.

What was that?

Her fuzzy mind registered the prickle. She swivelled, gripping the car before she lost her footing.

The pub brimmed with people, some still hopping out of their cars and greeting friends. The car park was crammed with cars.

Aileen narrowed her eyes, still holding on to her car for support. Her eyes scanned every vehicle – as many as she could see at least.

Nothing stuck out as unusual. Perhaps the day's trials had crept up on her.

Aileen leaned her head against the car's frigid metal. 'Urgh.'

She pushed away. 'Walk. Callan. Right.'

Stumbling onto the road, Aileen drew in her lip. Where was the police station? What time was it? Would he still be working?

Of course he would be.

One determined step in front of the other, and Aileen tripped. 'Oops! Silly road.'

Hobbling down the path, she left her car way behind.

'I'm not holding anything back. Not when I'm so YIPEEE.' She did a dance, throwing her hands in the air. 'Hey! Oh!'

A sensible Aileen would've been embarrassed and wondered if anyone had seen her. This emancipated woman, this Amazonian, didn't care.

She picked up the song playing in her head, mumbling it without a care for all the vulgarities spewing from her mouth.

She never noticed when she left the thick of civilisation and took the road she'd driven along earlier. The isolated one that led out of Loch Fuar through the private farms.

It wasn't like she strutted through a forest – besides, an Amazonian could handle herself.

But darkness crept in and so did the cold. A light breeze sent her teeth chattering.

Rubbing her smarting palms against her arms, Aileen hoped to restore some warmth back into her.

Quaint Highland roads like these didn't have street lights. They didn't need them because no one travelled these roads at night. No one, except an inebriated Aileen Mackinnon.

'I'm not stupid – he is!'

Aileen stopped her weird dance and watched her breaths fly away from her.

Walking kerbside, she leaned against the low wall. It might've been low, but for a petite woman, erm, *Amazon* like her, it was waist height.

She ran a palm along the rough stones. 'So cold.' She rested her cheek against one, caressing the stone.

The action caused cold to seep into her skin.

She continued speaking to the wall. The air? To no one in particular. 'Sleep now…'

Five minutes later, she patted the wall. 'I should get back and show Cal-Ca-Callan.' She hiccupped. 'Show him what I can do. I don't need no— Urgh!'

Aileen slipped onto the ground, staining her shirt and trousers. Letting go of the wall had been a bad idea.

Oops.

She straightened, tugging her shirt and patting her trousers. Her arms came up covered in dark brown sludge.

'Eww! I need to – to… Where am I?'

Real horror set in. Aileen looked this way and that until her head spun. Oh no!

She hopped over the smattering of grass. A tiny channel raced by the kerbside, letting excess rainwater run down the hill.

She needed to get back to the pub and reorient herself from there. Yes, the pub! Wasn't she brilliant?

With renewed vigour, Aileen found her way back onto the road, careful not to slip into the small channel with its gurgling water.

On the tar road again, she sang loudly, baseless yet happy.

'Oh! Ah! Hands up in the AIR! I—'

Suddenly, Aileen blinked, blinded. Bright light, the sort to stun someone and rob them of eyesight, pierced her vision.

Aileen raised her arm over her eyes, squinting. They stung from the sudden blast. Who'd opened the curtains? Surely morning didn't just blast in like that – it dawned gently. And since when were there two suns?

The light bulb in her brain switched on a second later. It wasn't *sunlight* but *headlights*. Two headlights in the darkness hurtling towards her at breakneck speed.

A car? Had a car come to take her home?

The air around the lights steamed like fumes, the dust particles glowing in the golden light. She could almost see the veins of the two eyes as the globes increased in size.

She blinked at them, like an enamoured child.

Somewhere, her mind urged her to move. At that speed, that monstrosity would crash into her, crush her!

The headlights grew large, larger and—

Jump! her mind commanded, but it took her feet a while to understand the command.

Jump without tangling your legs!

She leaped, breath hitching, and her entire drunken mass hurtled towards the low wall.

The rumble of the engine filled the air, her eardrums buzzing.

Her legs protested, twirling together and sent her tumbling. Only when her arse crashed onto the ground and her breath had left her lungs in a loud whoosh did she realise the car hadn't even honked to warn her away.

Oh golly! Were they trying to hit her?

She lifted her head from the sludge, not enjoying her mud bath. Blinking the grime from her eyes, she saw the headlights again. But they weren't racing away from her. No, the car had turned, and they were heading *towards* her.

Aileen pushed to get up, but her thoughts swam, eyes blinking, unfocused, and her limbs turned to mush.

Oh hell!

CALLAN WRAPPED HIS CLAMMY HANDS AROUND THE steering wheel.

He could hardly keep up with a sane Aileen. How could he deal with an inebriated one?

She'd never drunk herself into oblivion before. Aileen would never like that loss of control.

But the day must've taken a toll on her. He knew about the nightmares she suffered from, had woken her up from a couple in the past, and he also knew seeing Anvit Nair's body with all its gory details had to have left an unwanted stain.

He hit the accelerator and was at the pub in no time.

Just as he turned into the car park, another vehicle left. Grateful to the stars, Callan parked in its spot and raced inside.

'Callan!'

He headed towards Ethan, who for a man with two hands worked like he had ten. 'Funny seeing ye here. Aileen was talking about socking ye in the face. What did ye do, man?'

Callan took a deep breath, tasting the whisky fumes in the air. Ah, so she was angry not cold.

'Where is she?'

Ethan pointed to the front door. 'She walked out, but I've got her car keys here. Nicked them when she ordered her fourth pint – just in case.'

'Thank ye.'

'Hold on!' Ethan called out. 'She left her coat behind. It's right over that chair.'

Callan nodded his thanks, grabbed the woollen coat and raced out.

Where could his *banlaoch* have gone?

He scanned the car park. Not many people were hanging around and most were just talking between themselves.

Could someone have taken her? Dread filled him. No, she knew how to defend herself.

Even if she'd drunk a pint too many?

Callan tempered his fear and got into the car. It was the fastest way to search.

Since he'd driven in from the main square, Callan took the road that led away from it.

Usually it lay deserted at this time of night, but now Callan's lights caught something metallic in the distance.

A car.

It drove languorously, too slowly and without any lights on. Every hair on his body stood to alert and his eyes sharpened.

Callan cut his own lights, blinking to see in the dark. He couldn't make out a number plate, but he could see the car was a dark colour.

Something was afoot.

He waited for the car to turn its headlights on. What was the driver playing at? Could they be intoxicated? And Aileen? Where the hell was she? Eejit woman! He'd lock her up for sure.

He heard it before he saw her through the darkness, someone screaming like a drunkard. When his eyes adjusted, he made out a petite silhouette, dancing and wiggling her torso.

She was sloshed.

Suddenly, the perp in the car hit the lights – two sharp headlights – aimed directly at his pissed *banlaoch*.

A moment was all it took for Callan's heart to leap into his mouth. *Aileen!*

Before he could react, the car made for her, and she didn't move.

He fumbled with the gears, but his legs lost all their strength when Aileen gaped, frozen to the spot. 'Move, ye bampot!' he roared in his car, but no one heard a word.

Aileen, mouth open, stared at the car and then leaped. Her body crashed to the ground just as the car reached the spot where she'd stood. The eejit behind the wheel jumped into action, swivelling the car and making for her again.

And Aileen sprawled kerbside, a sitting duck, too drunk to move.

Callan found the gear and floored the accelerator.

His car almost unbalanced as he raced down the road, headlights glaring at the other car.

It had no number plate. Damn it!

His hand pressed against the horn, blasting it like his life depended on it. Aye, his life did depend on it!

He shocked the other car into a screeching halt. The driver didn't waste time, turning around like a race-car driver on adrenaline and dashing down the road, headlights disappearing at once.

Callan hit the brakes right when his rat-arsed *banlaoch* turned and... '*Bluck*!' She retched all over the ground.

Was there a point in asking why she'd walked down a pitch-black road alone?

Later, he thought before hitting the brakes with the same intensity as he'd floored the accelerator, all but smashing himself against the windshield.

He tumbled out of the car, letting it rumble in the middle of the road, and hurried towards the vomiting form of Ms Aileen Mackinnon.

'There's no point in telling ye to keep out of danger, is there?' he shouted at her as he held her lush brown locks off her face. She bent to empty the remnants of her stomach.

Her hair was soft, although matted with sweat and sludge. Her clothes were a mess and she reeked of alcohol. Not to mention she shivered from the cold.

When she dry-heaved, Callan hissed, 'Done boking all over someone's farm?'

She swiped at her face and tried to swing a fist at him, but it missed its destination, landing on his knee.

Callan didn't waste much time. She would all but fall asleep in the mud at this rate.

Wrapping his muscled arms around her, he cradled her into his chest.

'That car—' Hiccup. 'Callan, the car—' Hiccup. 'What was it doing?'

He stalked over to his SUV and opened the front passenger door. Careful not to hit her head, he sat her down and buckled her in. She grumbled incoherent words but had no strength to shove at him.

He reached into his glovebox and pulled out a packet of tissues.

Gently, minding any scratches, he wiped her face. Her glassy eyes locked on his turned to chocolate lava. 'What're y-you doing here?'

He shot her a glare. 'I could ask ye the same.'

After cleaning three tissues' worth of grime from her face, he turned to her hand. Jerking his head to the bottle of water between the two seats, he ordered, 'Drink up.'

Aileen giggled. 'Already did.'

Satisfied that her hands were as clean as he could get them without water, he narrowed his eyes. 'I can see that. When did ye start drinking yerself silly?'

But she'd moved on from their conversation. 'I like it when you're gentle like this, cleaning my face.'

Aye, she was a goner. He tried to withdraw his hand from hers, wanting to wrap her in a coat, but she clutched it tight, interlocking their fingers. 'I missed you.'

He had missed her, too. He caressed her face, pulling her to his chest. 'Darling, why must ye get yerself in harm's way?'

Her eyes fluttered with sleep. 'Not— I didn't know the car would... I...'

Something rustled in the hedges, bringing him back from the trance she held him in. He had all but blocked the road, and Aileen's injuries needed to be tended to.

She snored like a beast all the way to Dachaigh, the woollen coat tucked around her. He carried her upstairs and ran a warm bath.

'You can't step in here!'

'I need to check ye for injuries.'

She swatted his chest. 'In your dreams!'

'Aileen.'

'Callan.'

A face-off ensued.

She was too drunk to keep from blinking. 'Fine!'

He sighed and then proceeded to inspect her torso, where a black and blue bruise had already formed on the left side.

Using the antiseptic, he dabbed the cuts on her elbow and forearms. 'Why didn't ye wear your coat?'

'Dunno. That hurts, you moron!' she grumbled.

After cleaning all her wounds, he instructed her to step into the bath. 'Stay here. I'll make some tea.'

'You'll burn down my kitchen.'

But she stayed put while he carefully brewed some tea. Aye, he burned his forefinger, but at least he made a cup.

He dumped her soiled clothes in the bin. They'd been torn in a few places, muddied beyond repair and they stank, soaked in mud and manure. Not to mention the vomit and alcohol.

Now wrapped in her towel, Aileen blew a raspberry at him. 'You ever been this drunk?'

'Maybe.'

She chuckled, caressing his chin as he tried to stop a wound from bleeding – it had opened up again after she'd picked up her cup. 'It hurts!' A hysterical laugh escaped through her lips. 'Hey! Did you have snobby-bobby teachers?'

Her hands pushed at him. Annoyed, Callan straightened. 'Ye're hurting yerself!'

Aileen nodded. 'Can I sleep?' She blinked her large eyes at him, still unfocused.

'In a min—'

Before he finished his sentence, her arms came around him and the next minute, she was snoring against his neck.

Callan sighed, revelling in this new experience of caring for someone. He bent and pressed a kiss to her head.

Someone had tried to kill her. He'd almost lost her – again.

He settled her into the bed and looked at his badge. Would he let it rule his decisions like it had this past couple of days? Could he stand losing Aileen because of it?

Aileen snored, petite under the soft duvet.

He leaned down and whispered in her ear. 'I'm sorry, I'm so sorry for the hurt I've caused. But ye always come first.'

CHAPTER NINE

Aileen rolled to her side. 'Ouch! My head.'

A beam of early morning sunlight escaped from the drawn curtains, straining Aileen's throbbing eyes.

'Urgh! Fine, I'll wake up.'

She struggled to sit up and peered at the clock on the bedside table. It was nine – she'd slept in again.

Scrubbing her eyes, she yawned wide and saw it.

A cluster of wildflowers sat behind the clock.

Tiny petals in all the colours she could imagine twinkled in the dark bedroom. The green ferns cradling them – surely some incredibly aromatic herbs – lifted her lips in a smile.

A tiny card rested against the vase he'd put them in. The illegible chicken scrawl on it, Aileen recognised from afar, but she needed a moment to comprehend the words.

Their colours remind me of you.

Her smile bloomed into a full-on grin. He might annoy her, but he still made her heart sing.

What was she to do with him?

After swallowing the pills he'd left for her with a glass of water, Aileen hurriedly showered and dressed.

She'd decided to take him breakfast as a 'thank you' for saving her life again, but when she descended the stairs, she stopped short.

Fire! Something was burning!

She hurried into the kitchen, where Callan, in his all-black sweats, was struggling with the toaster. 'Aileen!'

She saw two mangled omelettes on two dishes and two slices of crusty brown toast. The other two – burned beyond recognition – Callan plucked from the toaster and dropped onto the other dish.

'Er, I, er might have smashed two eggs on the floor. But I cleaned it up, I swear!' He blushed a deep red.

Aileen's heart performed an elaborate somersault. 'You made breakfast? And you burned yourself?'

For the first time, she stared at someone's bruises doe-eyed. A man who'd rather watch a post-mortem than wear an apron had cooked for her?

'It's nothing, just a little er— Why don't ye sit? I'll bring the coffee.'

A minute of clatter and curses followed. They settled with their mangled omelettes and black coffees.

Aileen took a refreshing sip, steeling herself as she cut into the omelette.

Callan grimaced when he bit into his. He set his cutlery down and stared at her with serious eyes. 'Aileen, I'm really sorry for my behaviour this past week. I didn't mean to hurt ye or cause ye stress. Especially after Blaine, I should know better than to take relationships for granted.'

She'd been apologised to before and hurt again. Aileen swallowed the salty omelette and took his words the same way, with a grain of salt.

'I felt lonely, Callan, not just hurt. I thought you simply couldn't be bothered. And you didn't even call Daniel.'

His shoulders dropped. 'I cannae call them, Aileen. It could jeopardise Andrew's case. Being a police officer, I can't let them in on the details or be too chummy with them while the investigation's underway.'

'But you could lend Daniel an ear. He looked stressed yesterday.'

Callan's blue eyes darkened into sad pools. 'I will.'

Aileen leaned forward, broaching the topic she knew Callan didn't like to talk about. 'And what about Blaine? Have they found anything?'

Callan pushed his plate away. He couldn't cook to save his life, but at least he'd tried. 'Dr Brown's working on it.'

They fell silent, thinking about Callan's deceased best friend. Aileen knew if or when they found him, Callan would need her by his side. That's what friends were for.

His loud sigh echoed through the silent room. 'Now, about what happened last night. We need to head to the police station and register a complaint.'

Aileen opened her mouth to protest when Callan cut her off. 'For the record. It's vital. I'm a witness, and the skid marks should be visible on the road. I'll get Robert to check them out. I thought about it last night and I think ye angered someone, darling. Ye got close to someone's secret when they wanted it hidden. We need to figure out who it was.'

We?

Aileen nodded. 'Thank you for being there last night.'

Callan waved a hand. 'Don't thank me—'

'But I'll do this on my own,' she finished.

He shot her a glare. 'And land yerself in more trouble? Let me help ye—'

Aileen shook her head. 'No, Callan, you can't help me. I need to do this alone. I'm not a fool—'

'Never said ye were,' he cut her off, not wanting to let her be.

She reached out, enveloping his calloused hands in her soft ones. 'Look, Walsh is your colleague. And after what happened with Candace Willoughby last time, I don't want you to bend the law. I know you've got my back, but I need to do this.'

Their eyes locked for a long moment. He finally nodded. 'Alright, but be safe and—' He sighed. 'We're okay, aren't we?'

She smiled, leaning in for a kiss. 'We are, but do that again, Callan, and you'll wish you'd never met me.'

AILEEN SAT BACK AND STARED AT THE ROOM AROUND HER. She'd never been in an actual interview room at the police station. She had observed, heard Callan talk about it, but never had the experience herself.

With a loud wall clock, no windows and dull walls, she understood why perpetrators often broke down and confessed. The white light made the pale-yellow walls sterile, and the desk and chair in the centre under the light bulb felt cold. She sat in a hot seat, heart palpitating for no other reason than the gnawing ticking of the clock.

She fidgeted with her shirt sleeve, hands clammy, nerves wrought.

Robert sat opposite, unperturbed as he penned down all she'd said. The plastic beneath her arse burned like a furnace.

Robert did a good job of maintaining a straight face

and she gathered Callan had already given him the gist of what had transpired.

'Callan, er, Detective Inspector Callan Cameron jumped out of his car and helped me,' she finished.

Robert nodded as his pen clicked shut. 'Thank ye for coming in here. This is the only place we won't be disturbed.'

Aileen smiled but it didn't meet her eyes. She cast a glance at the tinted glass that stood between this room and the observation chamber.

Eighteen-year-old Andrew had been here.

'Have you made any progress with Andrew's case?'

Robert bit his lip. 'Ye ken I cannae tell ye about it.'

Aileen huffed. 'Is Andrew DI Walsh's only suspect?'

The police constable hung his head. 'We're done here.'

Knowing he meant well, Aileen let it go. She couldn't take out her frustrations on him; he'd done nothing wrong.

Once out of the interview room, she waved at Rory, who gestured as he hissed words down the phone.

Beside her, Robert cleared his throat. 'Fancy a walk? He's been on the phone like that all week, what with all the cases and media calls. Then there's this new member of the council who wants to discuss the Christmas tree lighting.'

Aileen cast him a sideway glance. 'It's October.'

'Tell her that! Apparently, it's only a month away and it would take that long to find the perfect fir tree.'

Chuckling, they walked out of the police station, the door swinging shut behind them.

Instead of heading towards the market square, they took the road away from it.

'How's your wee one?'

'Growing up. Lizzy wants another one.' He sighed with

exasperation before chuckling. 'Can't say I don't want another. Just that this one's a handful.'

Aileen grinned at him. She hadn't ever thought about the whole marriage and family scenario when she'd been in her corporate job.

She gulped when memories of those horrendous hours spent in a cubical threatened to resurface. With the current business Dachaigh brought in, she'd be headed back there sooner than later.

Aileen had never imagined herself as a wife or mother. Ever. But now she'd seen Isla, Rory and Robert speak fondly about families and her chest fluttered, as if in longing.

In the city, she'd seen more fragmented families than happy ones, and as for herself, she only had the stories her gran had told her about her short – albeit happy, passionate – marriage.

When the breeze picked up, Aileen got her head back to business. 'Why are we taking a walk?'

Robert shoved his hands into his pockets. 'Look, I can't imagine Andrew hurting anyone, let alone killing a friend, but he won't say what he was doing in the library that night or in those woods. He's stubborn. The blood on his clothes doesn't help his case. But' – his voice dropped to a whisper, and he leaned in – 'Anvit Nair had secrets.'

Aileen waited for more, but Robert didn't elaborate.

An elderly couple with a trolley full of groceries strolled by, paying them no heed, lost in their own world, holding hands like teenagers in love.

Before her eyes turned into longing pools, Aileen asked, 'What sort of secrets?'

'Dinnae ken. His friends just say he worked hard and partied hard. Andrew won't talk, but I keep wondering: where do teenagers store their information?'

Her forehead wrinkled, and she shook her head. 'Diary?'

'He's not a thirteen-year-old girl from the noughties.'

Aileen pouted, but her cheeks deflated at once. 'You mean on his devices? Can't you unlock them.'

Robert bobbed his head, a twinkle in his eyes. 'Only if Walsh and his team can find them.'

Was he saying what she thought he was? They hadn't found Anvit's devices? No phone, laptop or tablet?

'I'm sure he had a phone – all teens do.'

'And a computer – top-of-the-range laptop that his boss gave him as a gift apparently – and a tablet,' Robert added.

Mr Douglas Reid had given a boy who was a pain in his arse a top-of-the-range laptop? That seemed unlikely. Unless it was a bribe. Or they'd had a falling out at some point after he'd received it?

She shuffled her feet. 'And they searched his room, the rest of the house?'

Robert hummed, looking around. 'His locker at the college swimming pool and at the gym. Nothing – no sign of them or of any calendar to shed light on what he was doing in the woods.'

Aileen blushed and told Robert, 'Andrew said that place was known for nefarious activities. Maybe he was meeting someone?'

'As yet we don't know,' Robert whispered and pointed backward. 'I need to head back, and if anyone asks—'

'You bored me to death with images of your wean.'

She waved him off as she continued to walk, her mind churning a hundred miles an hour. But an hour later, she was nowhere close to having any concrete answers.

What was Anvit doing in those woods? And why had his boss gifted him a top-of-the-range laptop? To buy him off? To keep him quiet?

'Are ye certain?' Callan's voice held awe.

'Aye. The smear of blood we found on Fraser's handkerchief doesn't match his DNA.'

Callan sat back. 'And do we have a match in our system?'

A long pause met his question. 'Unfortunately, no. Although we can't say for certain that blood is the murderer's either.'

But they'd found some DNA, potentially that of Lucas Fraser's killer. If they could find a match, it would be the best evidence they could get for court.

'I'll get ye a swab to run the test against.'

At the moment, he had only one person connected to Lucas. Perhaps it was time to pay Logan Fraser another visit.

Charlotte Fraser appeared flustered as she gestured him inside and called for Logan. 'Oh, we've been dusting up the entire house today. And… and…' She sneezed loudly.

Their home smelled of detergent and soap rather than warm cookies to Callan's disappointment.

Logan Fraser appeared from behind a table, his face pink, tears of sweat rushing down his forehead, a duster in his hand.

'Detective! It's madness I tell ye. Madness!' He managed to stand up, wobbling so much he had to clutch the table. 'Marry a woman, buy a house and the next thing ye ken, there's a bloody duster in your hands and ye're on yer knees, sweating like a pig!'

Charlotte set her hands on her hips and glared. 'At least the house is clean!'

'All we wanted were Lucas's belongings, not to ready the house for some TV decorating show!' Logan shouted back, apparently not bothering to avoid the decibel levels that hurt his 'babies'.

Callan regretted his decision. He'd stepped into a marital fight and had no chances of getting more of Charlotte's home-made cookies.

He shuffled his feet, unsure what to say or whether to say anything at all. 'Er, I had some questions regarding Lucas.'

That got the couple out of fighting mode – they were instantly back to being a team.

As one, they gestured for Callan to take a chair in the kitchen. Charlotte tied her apron. 'Tea or coffee?'

'Coffee would be great, thank ye.'

As she stirred and asked him his preferences, Callan admired the yellow walls and pastel-green cabinets. Herbs bobbed on the windowsill, bright green and wafting a refreshing smell through the room.

He plucked a biscuit from the offered plate, barely containing a groan of appreciation. His satisfaction showed on his face since Charlotte flushed. 'It's nice to cook for a young man.'

'I'm the one on hands and knees, woman!' Logan grumbled, sipping his tea.

Callan took a sip of hot coffee and almost burned his tongue. He reached for another biscuit.

Charlotte dusted her hands off and slid in next to her husband. 'Ye aren't here to only eat my biscuits, are ye, Detective?'

Her not-so-subtle probe burned his ears. 'Er, I, er…'

He cleared his throat. 'Mr Fraser, Mrs Fraser, we have come to the conclusion that Lucas was murdered.'

This was the worst part of his job, telling the kin of the deceased that someone had killed their loved one.

The cup clattered, china clinking like it would crack. Logan Fraser turned white as a sheet while his wife gaped, tears pooling faster than water out of a dam.

'I'm sorry,' was all he could say. He'd lost his appetite for those biscuits baked with so much love.

Finally, Logan whispered, 'So ye're looking for Lucas's murderer. That's why ye wanted his belongings.'

Callan nodded. 'We hope to find something in there.'

Logan covered his face with his hands, his shoulders shaking as he silently wept.

To tell someone their missing loved one had been murdered after having only recently found them was gut-wrenching. Callan knew just how it felt. Though in Blaine's case, he still didn't have a body.

Charlotte pushed her cup and saucer away, too. 'Are ye sure? Perhaps he hit his head and—'

'I wondered,' Logan cut her off. 'I wondered if... What the hell would he do at that peatland? Lucas would go to the beach, on a hike, the woods or any place other than that bloody secluded peatland. Just not there, not alone. He hated being alone.'

Callan's heart reached out in shared grief. 'Do ye recall any fights or disagreements? Did he upset someone?'

'I wasn't here. But no one hated him enough to...'

Charlotte refilled Logan's cup and pushed it towards him. 'Drink some. Ye'll feel better.'

Unlike most men, he listened to his wife and seemed to feel better for it.

Callan hated to push on, but he needed the info. 'Mr Fraser, it's come to my attention since the last time we spoke that Lucas had plans to propose to his girlfriend, Isobel Murray.'

Logan snorted, a stray tear leaking down his wrinkled cheek. 'I told ye, he didn't have a girlfriend. I never met any Isobel Murray. As far as I know, he'd never even got her here to meet the parents.'

Charlotte tucked a strand of hair behind her ears. 'I never met Logan's parents. They were gone before we met. But we went through the family albums and Lucas never had his arms around any one woman. He had many friends though.'

But Callan already knew that Lucas had had acquaintances not friends truly close to his heart. And not many knew anything about the man.

Forty years played with human memory, though. Logan might know Isobel, and perhaps had just blocked her out. 'Do ye remember any woman who hung around a lot? Someone he perhaps spoke to or about? Or someone who helped yer family look for Lucas when yer parents organised search parties?'

Logan sat back, thinking. 'I recall coming home and seeing people searching, the posters all over the neighbourhood. We gave up after two months. This was a grown man. Where would a man of thirty go?' He shook his head. 'No one comes to mind at all.'

Callan sighed. 'And what about Violet's Rose? Does that ring any bells?'

Charlotte blinked. 'That vandalised house? What's that got to do with Lucas?'

Logan sat back, narrowing his eyes at Callan. 'That belonged to a Murray, didn't it? A friend of mine worked in the newspaper at the time and he grumbled about how everything about that case was kept hush-hush.'

Callan explained that one of the daughters who'd lived

there went by the name of Isobel. But Logan insisted he hadn't heard of her before.

Thanking the Frasers, Callan pushed away from the table.

They followed him into the hall. 'So I dusted the loft after you called,' Charlotte told him. 'It took me ages really, but I found some boxes. They must belong to Lucas. And I thought you'd like to look through them?'

'Aye, I'd like to take them with me, if that's okay?'

Logan waved his hands. 'Whatever helps. They're under that table.'

When Logan bent to extract them, Callan touched his arm. 'Let me.'

He studied the brown cardboard boxes. Charlotte had dusted them, yet some granules stuck to the paper like old friends. They weren't labelled but − Callan sighed with satisfaction − paper's old enemy, moisture, hadn't gripped its claws into the cardboard.

'I'll give ye a receipt for these and return them to ye as soon as we're done.'

Carefully, he hefted each box into the car, grateful for the extra space in his SUV. When he handed over the receipt, Callan respectfully asked if they'd be willing to hand him their DNA swabs.

If he'd expected resistance, he'd have been disappointed. He wished other people he interviewed would be so polite. Callan thanked them, then headed back to his car.

To his surprise, Logan followed him out, hands in his pockets. 'Detective, um, I asked around after ye dropped by before and Mrs Douglas says you're the best detective there is hereabouts.'

Mrs Douglas had praised him? Callan felt his cheeks warm.

Logan chuckled. 'Perhaps it was the first time she and Lt General Warren agreed on anything.'

It would be the first time Callan had heard of them agreeing, too. How many times had he visited them because they couldn't bury the hatchet?

'To be honest, Callan – if I may call ye Callan – when I saw him, my big brother, he looked the same as I remember him. I spoke to Lottie after. She'd come with me to the viewing. I'm very lucky to have her. I know what ye're going through, looking for yer mate.

'I broke down when I saw Lucas, but, I think, I'd sort of already said my goodbyes to him. Lottie helped me through it when we met. That's why she kens about everything and has seen all our pictures. She helped me say goodbye. Seeing him now and finding his killer might help, but the work to find peace comes from within. The pain will never leave my heart, I ken that, but it will ease and open yer heart for more love. I just thought... Well, I thought it might help with what ye're going through.'

Emotion crowded Callan's throat until it almost choked him. Blaine hadn't left his mind the entire time they'd been looking for him. And he hadn't really entertained the possibility that they mightn't find him.

But Logan might be onto something. The act of finding peace had to come from within. Did he have the ability to find it and say goodbye?

CHAPTER TEN

Aileen played the previous evening's interaction between those two men at Gammit Inc over again her mind.

Boy, thorn, blessing he's gone.

The man who'd called Anvit's death convenient sent an unwelcome shiver through her.

Anvit had worked for Reid, and it seemed like one of those two men had been the top man. Now she'd head over to discover for sure whom she'd eavesdropped on.

Since the property wasn't exactly in the town centre, Aileen took a good thirty minutes to get there. And when she did, rain pounded on her windshield.

The glass doors welcomed her into the warmth, unlike yesterday.

Dripping water on the floor, Aileen hurried to the neatly dressed woman behind the counter. She curled her lips at Aileen in contempt, clearly upset at the water pooling on the pristine floors.

Aileen kept her smile on even though it pained her cheeks. 'I'm here to see Mr Douglas Reid.'

The receptionist sneered. 'And do you have an appointment, Ms...?'

'Aileen Mackinnon. And no, I don't have an appointment, but I'm a friend of Mr Anvit Nair.'

Sceptical eyes scanned Aileen's wet hair and coat. Maybe she should've used the umbrella in her car, but her stupid brain had believed she could dash into the headquarters before the rain had a chance to do much damage.

Aileen reached into her pocket to pull out a card when she realised she didn't have one anymore.

You're not a forensic accountant now.

She'd reached for her business card so often in formal environments, it was second nature.

'Ms Mackinnon, is it?' A pleasant voice made the hair on the back of her neck perk up.

Aileen swivelled to look into smiling eyes, then took in the tall gentleman before her. His dark hair was ruffled and his expensive-looking suit fitted his frame as if he'd been born in it. Then her gaze settled on his gleaming shoes – shoes she recognised.

With a voice laced with poisoned honey, he asked, 'Would you like some coffee?'

Aileen twiddled her thumbs, waiting for Langdon to return to their table in the cafeteria with coffees.

Mr Allister Langdon had introduced himself as a lawyer and Douglas Reid's right-hand man. Judging by the look on the receptionist's face, he was second in command, too.

Aileen imagined him as a Groom of the Stool, whispering gossip into King Reid's ears as he wiped his bottom.

She stared at his back as he stood by the counter, desperately trying to hold in her giggles as she reached into her pocket.

The cafeteria might be a hive of activity, but she had to learn from her mistakes. If nothing else, she'd ensure her phone had battery and reception.

That way she could ask for help if she needed.

'Ms Mackinnon.' Langdon placed a tray on the circular table overlooking the car park. Unbuttoning his blazer, he took a seat. 'Please, take one.'

She'd asked for a basic cappuccino with no interest in injecting it into her system. Another precautionary step.

Sipping at his brew, Langdon assessed her over the rim of the go-cup.

He broke the silence. 'You've got quite the reputation, Ms Mackinnon.'

Aileen raised an eyebrow. 'Reputation?'

He grinned, showing pearly whites. 'And you're modest. But they also like to say I've got laser-sharp eyesight, so let's not beat about the bush.'

Contradicting her earlier intentions, Aileen took a sip of the warm brew. It wasn't because her throat resembled sandpaper – she just wanted to buy time before answering his comment, maybe encourage him to say more.

And it worked. 'It's my eyes and also my security cameras. So I know you heard that conversation last night. My only question is why.'

'Why what?'

Langdon chuckled, but the laughter didn't light up his eyes. 'I stand mistaken. Not modest then. Coy.'

'I would appreciate it if you spoke plainly. All these riddles are muddling my brain.'

Langdon smiled. 'Why were you here last night?'

Aileen ran her hand over the rim of the cup. She didn't know this man. Should she trust him?

'Anvit Nair worked for your boss.'

'He did.' At least he didn't deny that fact.

'Anvit Nair is dead. Murdered.'

Langdon nodded, taking another small sip. 'And you think after what you heard last night that Mr Reid is responsible.'

Aileen tilted her head, studying the expensive suit and well-combed hair. He didn't look very techie. 'What do you think?'

He blinked at that question and then laughed, turning a few heads their way. 'I think we should go out for dinner.'

She inhaled a sharp breath, straightening her shoulders. Why did all men think she was stupid enough to be brought around by flattery?

Wildflowers and salty, burned omelettes do the job.

Aileen shook her head. 'I think you aren't sure about your boss's innocence.'

'I never said I thought he was guilty.'

A couple of people took a seat at the table next to theirs. Their laptops clattered on the table as they set up their equipment, chatting at the same time.

Aileen looked Langdon straight in the eye. 'You're speaking in riddles again.'

'Must be the lawyer in me.' He pointed at her ring finger. 'Is there a husband?'

Don't need one – my fist can mangle your face just fine.

Aileen grinned. 'Maybe. Tell me, why was Mr Nair a thorn in your boss's side?'

He waved his hands like he was swatting a fly. 'Smart people have a way of irritating others with their smartness.'

'So he was irritating.'

'A know-it-all.' His phone chimed, drawing his attention away from her eyes and to the screen. Abruptly, he pushed his chair back. 'Sorry, I must get going.'

'Run away you mean?'

She wanted to smack her mouth and find the missing filter.

The smile disappeared from Langdon's face. 'You must know, Ms Mackinnon, Nair was no saint, and that extended to his career. He'd tear anyone and anything down. That's what it takes to reach the pinnacle. And you make several enemies that way.'

Having pulled the nib on that grenade, Langdon walked off.

What did he mean by that?

CALLAN STARED AT THE MESS ON HIS DESK AND THEN AT the additional boxes he'd been given by the Frasers. It made no sense to empty them here – Lucas's belongings would just get lost in this.

A head poked into his office, wearily eying the mess. 'Rory's asked me to take yer printer away,' Robert ventured.

'Sod off!' Callan grumbled, contemplating moving the boxes into the interview room or to that horrendous closet-like room opposite his.

Robert waltzed in instead. 'Come on – boss's orders.'

Callan crossed his arms, glaring at him. 'Sod off, buzz off, bugger off.'

'What's with these boxes?'

Robert was like that annoying sibling who didn't value

your privacy. An idea flashed through his mind. 'Haven't ye got anything to do?'

'I have!'

Callan decided to rile him up. 'Why do we keep ye on the payroll if ye only do calligraphy on that monster called paper?'

'It's *paperwork*, Callan. The sort that ye refuse to work through and create more of with that printer.' Robert bent over to study the boxes. 'They stink of dust.'

'That's 'cause they've been kept in a loft. They're Lucas Fraser's belongings.'

Robert straightened, hands in his pockets and wrinkles on his forehead. 'Wouldn't the brother have hidden any object he doesn't want us finding?'

Callan shoved a pile into the bin he'd categorised as rough paper a few weeks ago. Yet the wooden top of his desk still evaded him. 'I've cross-checked and we know for certain he was in the US between the time Lucas was last seen and when the complaint was lodged with the police. The detective who worked his case did a good job.'

Robert gnawed on the information, head tilted. 'Alright.'

'And the Frasers gave me their swabs. Dr Brown is running them against the DNA she found as we speak.'

Callan flicked his hand over the boxes. 'Since ye have all the time in the world, why don't ye head over to the hill and cross-check what Winters told us about the sisters? Ask the neighbours, note down what the tattle says. Get a feel about the community.'

Robert pointed to the door. 'I have paperwork—'

'Go door-to-door, ask questions. Then ye can practise bloody calligraphy with those stupid leaky pens.'

'They're fountain pens, Callan. They don't leak unless ye break the nib!' With that, he stalked off.

At peace, Callan then pushed open the door to the interview room, confident they wouldn't need it anytime soon – at least not until he cracked these cases.

Moving the boxes again made him regret his decision, but then finally he settled in, the aroma of coffee filling the banal room.

One of the things Aileen had taught him included data searching. He tried to be as organised as she was, sifting through one box at a time.

Callan had got lucky with the Frasers. Whoever had piled up Lucas's things had done so with the utmost care, as if he'd one day come home and unpack it all. His shirts, all neatly ironed, sat in a proper pile on one side. On the other were his jeans and trousers.

His heart shuddered to think of the parents who'd died without ever knowing what had happened to their son.

Callan sipped his smouldering coffee, the burn in his throat wrenching his mind from emotional thoughts. He needed to be objective – to see the logical facts.

He pulled out the shirts and set them on the table where criminals confessed crimes, then went through the pockets, seams and the space in between their collars.

Ten shirts and five T-shirts later, he'd worked through the heap but found nothing apart from clothes that would've fitted a healthy thirty-year-old in 1980.

Next, he approached the jeans. Jeans had many pockets, and he hoped, prayed, he'd find something.

He checked the front pockets, then moved to the back. Running his hands through the seams, his hand caught on something. Callan tugged at it, heart hammering. He turned the jeans around and tried to make out what it was.

But it was just a label.

And so it continued, jeans followed by trousers.

An hour later, his skull throbbed like music through

loudspeakers. He'd hadn't yet worked through one box and he had two more to go. Above all, he wondered if Lucas's killer would leave any trace for his meticulous parents to find.

This was as wild a goose chase as any.

Despite the low possibility of any crucial discovery, Callan tugged the jumpers and gave them a similar inspection.

Half an hour later, he was left with nothing except for the knowledge that Lucas apparently loved olive green.

Courtesy and manners nagging at him, he placed everything neatly inside the box again, feeling his mother's reprimanding stare over his shoulder. Try as she might, she'd never instilled the habit of tidying up in him. She'd even made him fold laundry all summer while his friends were out playing because he'd made the unfortunate mistake of rifling through her kitchen cabinets and not setting the items inside to rights again.

Callan huffed, reaching for the next box.

When he saw the brown hardbound books, nascent rays of hope bloomed. Finally, some place Lucas could hide data.

He picked up the first and saw it was a copy of *David Copperfield*. Reading was another hobby he didn't share with his mother. And classical English literature?

Good heavens!

But with a detective's eye, he perused the thin paper, the brown spots on it tugging at his nostrils. He stifled a sneeze and eventually lost to it.

The door to the interview room creaked open. 'Ah, did the papers in yer office kick ye out?'

Boss or not, Callan glared at him. 'These are Lucas Fraser's belongings.'

Rory strolled in, a sheet of paper in his hand. 'And?'

Callan shrugged. 'He was mental about the classics. He's got Chaucer, Shakespeare, Voltaire in *French* and Dickens. There are more in this pile.'

When Rory picked up Chaucer, Callan reached for what appeared to be a ledger. 'And he geeked out on bookkeeping as much as Aileen does.'

It didn't astonish him to find small bits of paper, coarse with faded ink. Lucas had pencilled in the bill amounts in a neat hand to remember after the ink had faded.

And he liked to make notes too.

He'd noted down recipes Isobel liked, their date nights and what they'd eaten. These receipts were his own personal diary.

Callan deduced the man had been smitten with his fiancée. Where was she, though?

Finally, he found a single receipt dated 12th May 1981. Was that the day he disappeared?

He froze, reading it. Lucas hadn't pencilled in anything except for the amount. Whatever it was for had evaporated with the ink.

Bloody hell!

Callan handed the receipt to Rory, who'd been working through the books.

He frowned. 'Why hasn't he written on it like the rest of them?'

'Look at the total on the receipt. He's traced the numbers using a pencil.' Callan grinned. 'I reckon it's his killer who's done that.'

Rory frowned, holding the receipt up to the light. 'But there's no way to ken who wrote it.'

He'd made a start. They'd found something even if they didn't yet know its significance.

Callan dug in with more vigour. Only when his coffee mug beckoned for more did he surface.

Rory too had his head buried in a book, eyes frantic as they scanned the sheet.

'Anything?' Callan's voice broke at the dryness in his throat.

'He's made notes on the phrases, words but nothing about a potential killer. You?'

Callan shook his head. 'Nothing. Coffee?'

Rory nodded. 'Ah, that reminds me, I had a little call today followed by this email.'

He handed over a piece of paper. 'It's a complaint by Reid and Co about Aileen Mackinnon trespassing on their property. They've requested we ask her to keep off it. Next time they'll file a formal complaint.'

Callan frowned. 'And this isn't formal?'

'Apparently they don't want us to record it but just warn her.'

'Threaten her?' Callan's belly churned with anger. 'As far as I'm aware, Gammit Inc is part of a shared working space that's open to anyone who works there or visits.'

Aileen would never be so stupid as to trespass and show herself.

Rory smirked. 'Bet ye're right. Ask her to tread carefully. If that car attack was Reid's doing, she'd best be cautious. And ye should ken what this shows. Reid's got something to hide.'

Aileen mulled everything over as she jotted points down in her yellow notepad.

Like she'd watched Callan do, she made a list of her suspects and things about the evening she'd found Anvit.

She'd told her inner voice to shut up every time it tried to bring up the debacle outside the pub. No, someone trying to attack her meant she was on the right path.

In her clear, careful handwriting, she made a note of Langdon. Something told her he had a lot to hide, or at least his boss had.

Something about her presence yesterday had scared them. What could he want to hide?

She needed to speak with Andrew, too. Perhaps he could shed some light.

Aileen turned the key in the ignition and pulled out of her parking spot. Ten minutes later, she was at the bakery. With relief, she inhaled the scent of bread and watched the two redheads behind the counter.

Her heart sang to see Isla in her element, Andrew beside her. Wasn't it commendable that the boy was back to work despite all that had happened? His entire life was at stake! Aileen couldn't fathom how she'd have coped with it.

She pushed the door open and comforted herself with the warmth of the bakery. If she'd expected a hug from Isla, she'd have been disappointed.

For the first time, Isla sent her a glare. So she wasn't in her friend's good books. But why?

Aileen let it go and waited in the queue. When she reached the counter, she said, 'A lemon tart and a moment of your time please, Andrew.'

The lad looked at her, green eyes clouding over.

'I just want to talk.'

Throwing a glance at Isla, he nodded. 'Er, can you give me a couple of minutes?'

Aileen smiled. 'Let me sink my teeth into the tart until then.'

Throwing a wistful glance at the chocolate eclairs, she added, 'Can you box those up for later? Four of them.'

Aileen spent a good ten minutes watching the queue move and Andrew work. His years of work had made him quick at his job. He smiled and chatted, greeting the young and old regulars. Not a hint of sorrow or stress.

What had he been doing around the woods that night?

When the queue eased, Andrew could finally break away from his duties.

'I've a ten-minute break. Isla said we can use her office.'

Aileen nodded. 'Come on.'

They settled in and she began. 'Last time we spoke, before…' She didn't need to remind him. 'You never told me what you were doing in those woods, Andrew.'

He had told her what he'd done, about traipsing around the murder scene, but he'd deflected that question like a well-rehearsed politician.

Even now, he sat twiddling his thumbs as the clock ticked by. What was he afraid of?

'Look, Andrew, you have to tell me, so I can help.'

He shook his head. 'I can't. Just, I didn't do it.'

'The police have matched his blood to your clothes, Andrew!'

Slapping his hands on the desk, he shouted, 'Because I touched him! I tried to save him.'

Aileen wasn't taking that excuse. If the lad was interested in forensics, he would have known not to go anywhere near the body, especially as the lad was clearly dead – it had been clear even in the darkness of the night.

She tried again. 'What were you doing that night?'

'What does anyone do at the library?'

Aileen narrowed her eyes at him. She was offering help, yet he wanted to be difficult.

Angry at people underestimating her, Aileen braced her palms on the table and looked Andrew dead in the eyes. 'I spoke with Zay that day I came to find you and she deflected when I asked where you were. Then she gave me the long route, through the bloody woods to get to you. And now you won't tell me about the library. I'm not an eejit. Now, you either tell me or I'll make it my business to find out much more than you want me to.'

Andrew didn't shudder, although his eyes flickered with fear.

Satisfied, she smiled thinly, without a hint of friendliness. 'I hope Isla's told you about my special talents of finding dirt on people, Mr Mackay. And you are no exception. I *will* find it if you don't tell me.'

He gulped just as the clock struck the hour. Unfolding his arms, he spluttered, 'I can't tell ye, ye must understand but… but Anvit was about to expose them. It was supposed to be a big bang that would roll a lot of heads, if you ken what I mean.'

'Elaborate.'

He didn't. Eyes pleading with hers, he hung his head and left the room.

Aileen smacked her palm against the table, not paying heed to the sting. 'Damn it!'

She stepped out of Isla's office while Andrew tied up his apron. She tried to catch Isla's eye, but her friend avoided her. She'd have to resolve this soon.

Later – she'd speak with Isla when she didn't feel like strangling her nephew.

Just when she rounded the counter to the customer's side, a man dressed in a suit and tie waltzed in. He smiled at Aileen and tipped his cap. 'Fine weather, isn't it?'

Aileen hadn't taken the time to think about the weather.

Now she cast the window a glance, watching the grey light mix with the yellow. 'I assume so.'

The man roared a hearty laugh as he turned to Andrew, not reading the tension behind the counter. 'The usual for me, lad.'

He thanked Andrew as he handed him the money and plucked his paper bag from the counter.

The white bag with 'Isla's Bakery' written in pink cursive crackled as he pulled out his scone.

'The best I've ever had, although don't tell ma daughter. She loves to bake those low-sugar diet ones for me.' He shook his head and waltzed out the way he'd come.

Aileen cast a look at Andrew. 'You know where to find me if you want to add anything. You know I'm not the police.'

She stalked out of the bakery and tipped her head towards the cloudy sky. A cool breeze blew over her, making her brown locks flutter and fall over her face.

How freeing would it be to be a bird and fly with the wind.

She smiled and turned to head for her car.

The man who'd bought the scone sat on the bench, enjoying his snack. A jolly sort, she pegged him.

She'd only just passed his bench, smiling her greeting as she went, when he choked, coughed and wheezed.

At first, she thought he'd gulped before chewing.

She swivelled just as he shuddered, hands reaching for her, eyes begging for help.

When a seizure hit him, Aileen screamed. Foam began to gather at his mouth, the jolliness all lost.

'Help!'

'I'm a doctor!' someone shouted over her shoulder.

A man with strawberry-blond hair rushed towards the older man.

'Call an ambulance,' he instructed over his shoulder.

Aileen fumbled for her phone – where was the bloody thing when she needed it – and dialled 999.

'Ambulance,' she spluttered. 'Ambulance at Isla's Bakery.'

CHAPTER ELEVEN

By evening, Callan considered slamming his forehead against the wall. At least it would ease the pounding in his head.

He'd brewed himself a coffee, headed out to sort out another one of Douglas and Warren's fights and cleared up some paperwork.

Now he sat in front of Lucas's belongings, hoping the box and a half he'd yet to go through held answers.

With his aches and pains, he considered calling it quits for the day. The loyalty in him wouldn't let him up and leave, though. Logan might've said it didn't matter to him, but it did matter to Callan. That way, he'd have done his job. Forty years was too long for a killer to roam free.

Callan reached into the second box and brought out shoes. He inspected them in under five minutes.

The knock on the door drew him from his perusal.

Robert stuck his head into the interview room and chuckled. 'We have electricity and ye look like shite.'

He switched the light and took the opposite chair.

Callan raised an eyebrow. 'What did ye find?'

'That not all rich folks are snobs. I spoke with every home owner in the locality around Mr Winters' home as well as Violet's Rose.'

When he sat back and crossed one leg over the other, Callan shot him a glare. 'And?'

'Winters told ye the truth. Alfred Murray never stayed for more than a week at Violet's Rose. And after his wife died, he spent even less time there. The neighbours say the two daughters didn't attend school. They had a governess home-schooling them.'

Robert plucked out his notepad. 'One very old Mrs Hudson said she'd once gone to their home to introduce herself with her mother. She recalls the elder sister sat there haughtily while the younger one spoke of "preposterous things no lady should know of, let alone discuss".

'The sisters kept their distance from everyone – that's the common thread. And one night in the spring of 1981, they vanished. Winters was the only one the younger sibling ever spoke to. The owner of the property opposite *Violet's Rose* says the house had three servants. One went missing with the girls. The butler and the housekeeper, who were married, left after two weeks when they didn't hear from anyone. They didn't file a complaint because they simply thought the daughters had taken off with their lady's maid to another property. The house unnerved the daughters since it was where their mother had passed.'

Robert snapped his notepad shut. 'And that's that.'

'No one remembers how the sisters looked? Where they might've gone?'

'Those houses with large gardens are so disconnected, ye'd think they lived in the middle of the forest. No one kens anything about the neighbours.'

Callan pushed away from the table. 'That gets us

bloody nowhere. Do we ken whether Winters was here that spring?'

Robert nodded. 'He isn't lying, and he's got a lot of friends. They all attest to his claims of being abroad.'

Callan took to pacing, his footsteps echoing in the small space, the smell of sterilised floor cleaner smothering him. 'Bloody hell! Where did the sisters go?'

Robert pointed at the boxes. 'Need help?'

He shook his head. 'It's late. Let's get back to this tomorrow.' And he needed something to eat and a quick shower to clear his head.

Should he head to Dachaigh?

The shrill ringing of the station's telephone snubbed his thoughts. Callan answered. 'Hello?'

'Detective, I would like to report a possible crime...'

HOSPITALS AND CALLAN DIDN'T GET ALONG. HE'D BEEN TO them a lot lately for his trouble-seeking girlfriend. Now he wondered what the nurse had meant.

Nurse Jackie, as she'd introduced herself with a heavy accent, nodded at him sombrely. 'Thank you for getting here so soon. We got Mr West in this afternoon, and he's been unconscious the entire time. We've run a few tests to figure out what happened.'

She angled the computer screen to show Callan records that his brain couldn't comprehend. 'We spoke to the family and his GP. Mr West has no history of seizures or any other issues. We found it unusual he'd choke on a scone, so the doctor had him tested.' She pointed to something on the screen. 'If you see his blood report right here, it shows traces of potassium cyanide.'

Callan frowned. 'Hold on. Could ye tell me when the patient checked in?'

The nurse bobbed her head, her eyes diverting to the other nurse at their station. 'Keep an eye on things.' Then she jerked her head towards the door that read *'Staff Only'*.

Callan took a seat in the break room. Its pistachio-coloured walls were as mundane as the interview room he'd spent the day in. The plastic chair creaked under his weight.

With a loud groan, Jackie sat opposite him, cracking a container open.

The smell of fresh salad wafted through the room. 'Sorry – I missed my dinner,' the nurse said.

Callan had missed his, too, and it was already 8 p.m. 'What about Mr West?'

'We got a call that a man had choked near *Isla's Bakery*. Mr West had sat on the benches outside the bakery to eat a scone. After he came into A & E, we stabilised him, but as I said, the doctor ran checks on his blood and we found potassium cyanide.'

Callan pulled out his notepad and made a quick note of what she'd said. Then he asked his questions.

He jotted down the time the call had come and the time West had been brought in. Jackie answered him precisely.

'Would Mr West regain consciousness anytime soon?'

She chewed on a salad leaf while nodding. 'But the doctor won't allow you to meet him.'

'Would you know how the potassium cyanide got into his system?'

Now her eyes flittered around the room, a guarded expression setting in. 'We're not sure yet, but, well, the gossip is that he'd eaten a scone from Isla's Bakery. Look, if he had that level of poison in him, he would've suffered a seizure at once. So the poison had to be in the scone. If he'd had another bite, he surely would've died.'

Callan's fingers froze, the pen hovering over the paper. 'Mr West was poisoned by a scone Isla McIntyre made?'

Jackie gulped. 'I mean, I heard the doctors say so, so I'm sure that's the case.'

He narrowed his eyes. 'Ye're either sure or ye're not.'

The door to the break room opened and a familiar face wearing scrubs stepped in.

Callan blinked at him. He looked so much like his father. And they had only met that summer at a victim's house.

'We meet again, Dr Eric Macdonald.'

They shook hands.

'Please call me Eric. They said ye're in here.' He eyed Jackie. 'And Jackie always has her gossipmonger's tales ready.'

'Dr Macdonald!' she reprimanded him, snapping the container shut. 'I was merely being an ideal citizen.'

Wiping her mouth, she stood up. 'Now, if ye'll excuse me…'

When it was just the two of them, Eric settled in the chair Jackie had occupied. 'She's right, though. The tests suggest he consumed potassium cyanide and I believe it was that scone. Potassium cyanide tastes bitter and smells like bitter almonds. I reckon he took a small bite, since a bigger one would've killed him on the spot.'

Callan sighed. 'So this was attempted murder?'

Eric shrugged. 'All I can say is that it was a lethal dose. But it's unlikely Isla would do something to sabotage her own business.'

Unlikely didn't make it impossible. Callan stood. 'Thank ye. I'll look into it.'

AILEEN STRAIGHTENED HER SHOULDERS, RUBBING THE SLEEP from her eyes and boosting her morale as she drove into town. Callan had called her last night, saying he couldn't come over. So she'd gone to bed, thoroughly exhausted. But nightmares had still crept in.

Her phone chimed with Daniel's number as she parked. He'd asked her to come over.

She hurried through the market square, ignoring the crowd outside the bakery, and walked a couple of buildings down to Daniel's handyman shop.

No one stood behind the counter. A couple of plaid and thick-boot-wearing customers gave her a once-over. Compared to their hefty frames, she looked like a mouse.

Unsure, she walked towards the shelves and squeaked, 'Daniel?'

His golden-brown hair appeared from behind the shelf. He waved at her as he uncurled. 'Hold on.'

A crash sounded, followed by cursing.

He wound his way behind the counter, rubbing a hand over his neck. 'Sorry. Coffee?'

She refused, but he filled a mug to the brim, dark circles under his eyes. 'This lack of sleep is leaving me a zombie these days.'

Aileen could sympathise. Isla didn't hold back her emotions, positive or negative. And being afraid of tears like Daniel was, having a toddler and an emotional wife would be stressful.

'Are you alright? Maybe you should take some time off?'

'I'm fine,' came the automatic response. Daniel rubbed a hand over his eyes. 'It's just that— There's no point in lying to a friend, is there? Isla and I, we're having issues, and this case, the circumstances, is making it all worse. We had a mental row last night. It was so bad, I had my mum take Carly away for the night.'

Aileen's breath caught. She didn't know anything about this. The last she'd seen them together, Isla had been all over him.

She'd held them to the ideal of the perfect couple.

'Anything I can do to help?'

Daniel slurped his coffee. 'Not now, just don't mention this to her. She'd have my hide. Working here's like a break. But that's not why I called you.'

He took his time ringing up some customers and then waved them off. Swishing the 'Open' sign to 'Closed', he trundled back to the counter.

'The police called. Well, the man who… the man who had that seizure yesterday, outside the bakery… They found poison in his blood. And the doctor's sure it was in that scone. The police want to ken how it got there.'

Aileen gaped. '*In* the scone, or perhaps, I don't know, in the paper bag?'

Slowly, he shook his head. 'I didn't ask. After the shitty night, I just… They've launched an investigation into the bakery, with a warrant too. It's a bloody mess, and Callan can't get involved, since we're best pals. Rory's at the bakery right now.'

Aileen hadn't paid heed to the gathered crowd, thinking it was the usual rush-hour traffic. But a police investigation! 'Why aren't you with her?'

Daniel sighed. 'I'm not sure she wants me anywhere near her right now.'

Aileen's heart shattered at the pain clouding Daniel's eyes. The man adored his family and loved his wife to pieces. She knew this because she'd seen the fake act couples put on, at least in the city, where ambition so often overruled love.

She gave Daniel's drooping shoulders a pat. 'Don't worry. You focus on your daughter, okay? She might be a wee thing, but she needs you.'

'I ken.' The lines on his face darkened, signs of wear. But the battle still lay ahead of them.

Aileen made her way to the bakery and found Isla leaning against a car right outside.

Silently, she mimicked Isla's pose, their shoulders brushing, but she didn't initiate conversation.

When the door opened and some police constables stepped outside with evidence bags, Isla's hand sneaked into Aileen's.

Rory appeared behind them. He gave Aileen a nod and said, 'Morning.' Clearing his throat, he spoke to Isla. 'I request you keep yer bakery closed for the day.'

Aileen gripped Isla's hand. 'What did you find?'

Rory tugged at his hair. 'We only want to make sure the poison they found on the scone isn't—'

'There was no poison!' Isla shouted. 'I clean the place every night and have a cleaning company give it a deep clean every week. I have certificates from the food department and I'm fire compliant and all that. The doctor's got it wrong, just like you've got the wrong murder suspect!'

'Police incompetence!' someone from the gathered crowd shouted in Isla's support.

A chorus of 'ayes' went around.

Rory shook his head. 'We're only trying to keep you safe. A man nearly died yesterday.'

'Lies!' Isla snapped. 'He must have a condition. He's eaten at the bakery every day for years now. And you expect me to believe he got poisoned when he hasn't complained of so much as a cramp after eating our food all this time?'

'Aye, no one's ever had a complaint about the quality of the food at the bakery,' another one of Isla's supporters chimed in.

'Why is he in the hospital then?' someone retorted.

'Andrew Mackay!' another responded. 'He was working there yesterday, wasn't he?'

'Aye, and he's got a new liking for bloodshed.'

Beside her, Isla tensed. Aileen gritted her teeth, fighting the urge to pound the accuser's face.

'That's baseless!' she snapped instead. 'You've got no proof he'd do anything like that!'

'And you've got no proof otherwise!'

Before Aileen could physically harm the other person, strong arms pulled her back. 'Not on the street!' Callan hissed in her ear. 'Take Isla home, darling. I'll deal with this.'

Aileen frowned at Callan. 'Why're ye here?'

He whispered hastily. 'Look, we need to do this by the book, and Rory won't have me work Mr West's case. He's got the warrant to search the place, but it's good that Isla agreed rather than resisting. Just take her home and I'll deal with the crowd.'

She looked into his troubled eyes. At least Callan was here. He hadn't shut them out.

Aileen nodded. Isla didn't deserve this hullabaloo or these accusations.

Clasping her friend's arm in a tight grip, Aileen led Isla to her car. She moved as if in a trance. They drove to Isla's house in abject silence.

Once she'd pushed a glass of wine into her hands, despite the early hour, Aileen asked, 'Where is Andrew?'

Isla stared at the red liquid listlessly.

'Isla?'

She blinked, her green orbs watery pools. Worry lines were etched on her face, deepening the crinkles around her usually smiling eyes.

'He was distraught after what happened to that man. Andrew rung him through, placed that scone in the paper bag, gave him his change and waved him off. And the next thing, he's choking on that very same scone.' Her voice was barely a whisper. 'I told him to take the day off. Lord knows he needs it.'

Aileen took to pacing, mind churning. The situation wasn't only puzzling but very coincidental. The only time Andrew had interacted with Mr West was when he'd handed over his order.

'The scones – who made them?'

Isla lifted her eyes. 'Me, who else? Susan helped out.'

'How many did you make?'

Taking a small sip, Isla whispered, 'Twenty. I wasn't expecting to sell more at that time of day. They're usually lunchtime sellers.'

Aileen processed that information. 'And did you sell all twenty?'

She hadn't noticed the counter when she'd left the other day. Hell, she hadn't even realised that Andrew had helped the man until Isla reminded her.

And she'd been standing right there!

Isla's reply brought her back to the room. 'The scone Andrew sold was the second to last one.'

'And none of the other customers complained?'

Her red hair flopped around her face. 'Not one. They never have.' She choked on a sob. 'Oh, Aileen, my life's a mess.'

Aileen pulled Isla into a tight hug. 'We'll get through this nightmare together. I promise you.'

Pulling out her phone, she typed up all that Isla had said. 'Okay, tell me how you make the scones. Do you add something on top once they're baked?'

'Why are you asking me this?'

Aileen pursed her lips. Isla was in pain, otherwise she'd have pieced it together. 'Isla, think! None of your customers complained. Only Mr West fell ill. So it's something added at the last minute or—'

'My scones aren't poisoned! Are you like those bloody scumbags? Didn't you hear a word I said? Not. My. Scones!' Isla wheezed, coarse breaths reverberating through the silent room.

'I'm not saying you did anything wrong. And if the test results say it was the food he ate, I want to know how the poison got into one scone and not the rest.'

Isla sat back. 'They said another bite would've killed him.'

In one big gulp, she downed the wine, then pointed at the glass. 'More.'

A ray of sunlight glinted off the crystal, reminding Aileen it wasn't even ten in the morning.

Aileen didn't argue. Maybe wine would loosen her friend's tongue and cut the sniping.

Dipping her nose into the glass, Isla inhaled the fruity scent. 'Like blood but way thinner,' she mumbled to herself. 'Andrew would never do this. Not once, let alone twice.'

'I believe you and I hear you.' Aileen reached for her hand, but Isla withdrew hers. It stung, but she let Isla be.

'Icing sugar. All the scones have icing sugar on top.'

Icing sugar. A poison could appear like icing sugar.

'How do you sprinkle it?' Aileen asked.

Isla gesticulated. 'Pick it up from the packet and sprinkle it on the scones.'

'So you don't coat them individually?'

'I don't *coat* them with icing sugar. It's only a light dusting.' Isla lifted her chin. 'I know what I'm doing in the kitchen.'

If Isla had sprinkled the icing sugar on all the scones at once and that's where the poison had been, the others would've been affected, too. So how did the poison get into that particular scone?

She remembered what she'd said to Daniel earlier and thought back to the scene. She saw Mr West walking in, saw Andrew pick up the scone with purple tongs, the second last of twenty, and drop it in a paper bag.

'What about the paper bags? Where do they come from?'

Isla scowled. 'A company – they print the logo on each bag and supply them.'

Now she was getting somewhere. 'How many bags do you have in stock?'

The glass was empty once again, and Aileen refilled it without question.

Isla frowned at the liquid now and muttered to herself. 'It's strange, so strange. I know I ordered three thousand last week and they would last a fortnight at least, but we had a new shipment today and the other bags were gone. No, not gone – Susan said she'd found them dripping wet and that the new shipment had arrived on time. But she's new, so she wouldn't know I don't order until a week before we need more. I didn't ask for them, but maybe Andrew did?'

Aileen had heard enough. 'One paper bag, Isla. One paper bag and a bit of confusion was all it took. Someone added a powdered poison, purposefully or mistakenly, to one of your paper bags and poor Mr West swallowed it.'

Isla nodded, her eyes heavy. Aileen helped her to the couch and speed-dialled Callan.

If only the eejit would pick up his bloody phone!

CHAPTER TWELVE

He'd somehow managed to dissipate the crowd outside the bakery and make space for the officers to load the collected samples into the vehicle.

Now, he'd drowned his worries in two cups of coffee and it wasn't even 11 a.m.!

Callan massaged the back of his neck, where pain throbbed steadily. Stretching out his spasming muscles, he headed for the interview room, determined to find something, anything to connect Lucas with his killer.

Unless they had a crazed serial killer on the loose – the possibility of which sounded as preposterous as him cooking a meal – Lucas had most likely known his murderer.

He eyed the leftover items in the second box.

Hefting dusty books, he rifled through their pages.

The second book could've been used as a doorstopper. A brick would fall to shame next to its thick width. And it weighed a ton, too.

He split open the sandwiched pages and leafed through them. Finding nothing, he reached for the back cover.

It had gone damp with age. He went back through the pages once more and stopped.

Ah, that felt weird. The book had page 467 but no 468 or 469. Lucas or possibly his killer had stuck the pages together.

Excitement bloomed in his gut, the dull room no longer threatening to swallow him in its boredom.

He rubbed his fingers against the paper, but it didn't budge. Callan turned the book over to examine the pages from the top. There, he saw the thin fracture between the two sheets.

Pursing his lips, he blew into the paper and it crackled, splitting apart to let the air through.

He tried it again, sticking a finger in when the two ends blew apart. Someone had stuck the other edges together. Using the torch on his phone, Callan inspected the small pocket.

Golly! Was it empty?

He felt around with his forefinger. 'Ah, bastard!' Something smooth touched his skin and he, as carefully as he could, used a knife to extract it.

There, from the pages, emerged a photograph, sticky to the touch. It wasn't just any image, but one of Lucas Fraser and – Callan gawked at the other name on the back – Douglas Reid. The date scrawled below the names read '8th May 1981'.

Just before Lucas Fraser had disappeared.

Reid and Lucas knew each other? The same Douglas Reid who ran Gammit Inc? Who'd threatened Aileen?

Sitting back in his chair, Callan recalled what Dr Brown had said. The two murders, she'd mused, were very similar in the way the killer had dispatched their victims.

She'd been quick to dismiss them as the work of the same killer though. Forty years between murders just seemed too long.

Callan stared at the picture. The two men had their arms around each other's shoulders, grinning at the camera in complete camaraderie.

Had their friendship soured after that photo was taken?

What connection did Reid have to Isobel, Leana Murray, and Millie Baines?

He dialled Dr Brown, hands trembling with excitement. 'Doctor, could you please cross-check the DNA found on Lucas Fraser's handkerchief with that found at Anvit Nair's crime scene? I think we might have the same killer.'

A stunned silence echoed down the line. 'Detective? That's highly unlikely. The murders are decades apart.'

'Please just run the tests because I'm staring at an image of Lucas Fraser and Douglas Reid taken on the 8th of May, not long before he was last seen.'

She spluttered. 'Goodness! That's unexpected. I'll run the tests now.'

Callan wanted to punch the air, but he knew the dangers of counting his chickens before they hatched. Everyone in Loch Fuar's meagre populace knew each other, and this picture could've just been one of many Fraser took with his hoard of acquaintances.

Why keep it hidden then?

He picked up the book and checked the title. It had various plays by the Bard – *Hamlet* and *The Merchant of Venice* to name a few.

He knew those two stories. Callan frowned. What an odd place to store pictures, though.

He checked the index, tracing the page numbers and

found page 466 covering *Hamlet*, right where he'd found this photograph.

Did the theme of the plays mean anything to Lucas? In that case, what would be a befitting story for Lucas and Isobel?

Again, he perused the index.

'That lad knew if he set foot in that house, the old man would have his head,' Winters had said about Lucas.

Callan found *Romeo and Juliet* on page 201.

And then he struck gold. Pages 212 and 213 were missing, stuck to each other.

Did Lucas have a photograph of his fiancée? Callan's fingers shook in such excitement that he had to take calming breaths. Finally, he'd add a face to the name.

Carefully, he found the thin gap and blew into it. The edge split in two. Again, using his torch, he caught something inside – something that looked like paper. Multiple pictures?

Callan set the book down, reaching for his multi-purpose knife again. So as not to damage anything, he inserted the knife carefully, using it like a letter opener to unstick the pages. Then he tilted the book.

To his utter astonishment, out slid a folded piece of paper!

'Bloody hell!' He unfolded it gently. The fragile paper had browned with age. It would likely crumble to dust if he didn't handle it with care.

He'd worn blue surgical gloves, but he had to be careful not to rub his finger against the paper.

Callan opened the whole sheet and gasped.

Dear Lucas,
 Words are not enough to express the sorrow I feel in my heart for

what I did. I shouldn't have had blind faith in the whispers. You have asked me to trust, and I do have faith in you, in us. Although sometimes, like last time, I... I deeply apologise for my hurtful accusations.

You might grin as you read these words, but I was in the wrong. I can't ever get a sense of where I stand with my sister. The way she barged into my bedroom, going on about how we don't deserve to be together, my dearest Lucas, the spiteful girl made sure I thought you'd chosen her over me.

What we have, Lucas, is strong. I won't let my sister take you away from me as she did our mother.

Sometimes, my heart cries out for me to leave it all behind. Leave it and run away to sunny Côte d'Azur with you.

Ever since Mother left this earth, I've felt so lost. Oh, dear Lucas, I miss you so much. Would you please come over for lunch at Violet's Rose?

I have so much to tell you. So much to share.

Violet's Rose is as peaceful as always, and I find myself in the gardens, staring at the leaves shivering in the breeze, wondering what I should do with myself. I am, for all purposes, an orphan, given how little Father cares for us. Despite staying with Leana, I do not have a family or friends close to my heart.

Leana, with all her rude friends, ensures the house is a circus. Her ghastly friends ridiculing Mother's taste is like a knife to my heart. She had the most exquisite sense of decor and elegance, qualities Leana will never possess.

Oh, Lucas, you must come over as soon as you can. I need to speak with you, see your handsome face and hold your hand.

And I want to say yes to the question you asked me last time. When I so rudely suggested that you'd been unfaithful.

Oh, dearest, I'd be honoured to call you my husband and carry your last name.

I must end this letter here for I hear my sister and her friends screaming down the hallway, playing the music they say is all the rage in London.

Help me, Lucas. Take me away to bliss.
Yours lovingly,
Isobel M.

CALLAN BLEW OUT A LOUD BREATH. NOT A PHOTOGRAPH, but he'd found Isobel's voice in a letter she'd written to her lover. A letter Lucas had preserved because it had meant so much to him.

He stared at the picture of Lucas and Reid. What meaning did that photograph have?

Callan slid the letter back into its spot.

He'd head to Gammit Inc and figure it out for himself.

AILEEN LEFT ISLA'S AND HEADED OVER TO THE POLICE station to find out more about the complaint against the bakery.

A notification popped up on her phone screen. It was a text from Zay.

'*Need you.*'

Aileen frowned at the odd message. Had Zay found something in the house? She texted back saying she'd be there in half an hour and raced to Loch Heaven.

The rain came on, hindering her visibility, and Aileen cursed as she drove along the winding roads. Just when things couldn't get more stressful!

When Aileen arrived at the house, her shoulders ached and her head throbbed. But a promise was a promise.

She made a dash for the door.

Zay, with her hair all over the place and still wearing her pyjamas, answered, gaping at her. 'Aileen! Ms Mackinnon!'

Gripping Aileen by the arm, Zay pulled her inside. 'Oh, thank God you're here! Oh, Ms Mackinnon, I searched, and I searched, and he's nowhere. He's not answering his phone, and he didn't come home last night.'

Aileen held Zay by the shoulders and shook her until she stopped rambling and gasping. 'Who, Zay? Who are you searching for?'

'Andrew! Andrew's missing!'

AILEEN CLICKED PHOTOGRAPHS OF ANDREW'S ROOM AFTER asking Zay if she had gloves.

Zay handed her a pair of stinky blue surgical gloves. 'I like to set up science experiments at home sometimes,' she muttered through rapidly gathering tears.

Aileen gingerly stepped into the neat room, Zay looking over her shoulders from the threshold.

'Where have you looked for him?'

Zay ticked off the places on her fingers. 'The gym, pool, library, classrooms, lab, park. I know he didn't head off into the woods. He hasn't worn his boots or the warm scarf his mum gave him for Christmas. They're right there.' She pointed at the rack behind her in the hall which held jackets, coats, scarves and hats. A pair of shoes sat below it.

The room was spotless. All of Andrew's clothes sat in two piles, one lot in a cotton bag and the other folded into wicker baskets. His narrow desk overlooked the neighbour's garden, and his books sat stacked in one corner, the pen stand glittering like a rainbow with highlighters, pens and pencils.

'He's very organised,' Zay wheezed. 'Nothing's ever out of place.'

'Could he have stayed over at a friend's?' Aileen asked.

Zay shook her head. 'He never does that. He hasn't got friends like that. We're his friends.'

Aileen pursed her lips. 'When did you last see him?'

'We met at the cafeteria for dinner last night at six. He said he'd be right back but never came home. And… and he had a class today with Professor Robertson.'

Aileen checked her watch. It was ten. Andrew had been missing for several hours. She'd give it another one before reporting him missing.

'Where are Finlay and Leith?'

Zay waved her hands. 'Out?' She was on the verge of a breakdown and not much help.

'Why don't you call them? Let's spread the word through social media channels – see who last saw him where, okay?'

Zay only nodded, fumbling for her phone. When her hands trembled and she couldn't get a good grip, Aileen led her to the kitchen and made her some tea.

Leith and Finlay arrived a short while after they'd put out the first message.

Leith rubbed circles on Zay's back. 'Why didn't you tell us?' But his eyes gave away his distress.

Aileen stared at her silent phone, fidgeting with the string of the teabag.

Leith and Finlay had last seen Andrew at dinner, too. 'He headed to the library to study for an hour,' Finlay had explained while furiously tapping on the phone.

Finally, a message chimed – then another and another.

Leith pulled it up on Zay's phone. Heads pressed together, they read the missives.

'Someone saw him at the library.'

'The woods – have you checked there? Maybe he went there without his scarf,' Aileen whispered.

Zay shrieked, unable to bear it any longer. 'He'd never go there again!' She tugged at her colourful hair. 'Do something! Where could he be? He wouldn't go *there*, not now!'

'Not in the gym,' Leith updated them.

'Staff room!' he shouted with his next breath. 'Someone caught him heading to the staff rooms yesterday.' The glee on Leith's face vanished. 'And someone saw him leave at about half seven.'

'Does he have a bike?' Aileen gestured. 'How does he get to the bakery?'

Zay blinked at her.

Aileen wanted to kick herself. Why hadn't she thought of this before?

'He's got a bike,' Zay mumbled. 'He bought a brand new one. Loved to show it off.'

Finlay nodded. 'He said it helped him get some cardio in on his way to the bakery and back.'

Aileen went to the window and peered out. 'Where is it then?'

'He must've taken it with him.'

Shit! Aileen was tempted to kick something, but she didn't want to put Zay off.

'Okay, any more news, Leith?'

'He hasn't been at the cafeteria all morning and no one's seen him at any of the bus stops.'

Aileen crossed her arms and leaned against the windowsill. 'What does his bike look like?'

'Like any bike?' Finlay looked up, lips set in a line. 'I've got the word out, but it looks like no one knows anything concrete. We haven't got time for this!'

Aileen checked her watch. Forty-five minutes.

'Does he have any other friends on campus or in town? Would he go to the cinema? The theatre?' She'd known it was a long shot before she suggested it. 'The museum? A hike to clear his head?'

Zay pushed away from the table. 'Not without telling us!' A sob left her lips. 'Oh, where are you, Andy?'

Finlay reached over to comfort her, but Zay shrugged his hand away.

'What a bastard! Someone murders one roommate and now another's missing.' Zay paused in her rant. 'Do you think someone took him?' Now the real horror set in.

Aileen's watch signalled that her time was up. She pulled out her phone and dialled the station.

She'd penned down all that they knew about Andrew before Walsh got there. He must've raced like the hounds were nipping at his heels.

'Let me go check his room.'

Aileen and Zay shared a look, each sure what he'd find: nothing. Leith pointed at the door. 'Let me go ask around if any of the neighbours saw him return last night.'

Ten minutes later, Walsh had asked for forensics to come dust Andrew's room. Leith hadn't yet returned, so Walsh assembled the rest of them in the kitchen.

He sat at the counter, hands around a coffee mug Finlay had placed in front of him, his sharp eyes sweeping over their faces. 'If you know where he's hiding, you'd better fess up.'

Zay shook her head, displacing the tear bobbing on her eyelashes. 'We don't know. Why would Ms Mackinnon have called you?'

Walsh sighed. 'Let me arrange a team to canvas the area. He might have decided he needed a break, but he's a prime suspect in a murder. And if I discover you've been hiding his whereabouts from me, I will charge you with obstruction of justice.' His dark eyes settled on Aileen's. 'I heard you upset Reid.'

Aileen pursed her lips, but before she could ask what he meant, a knock sounded at the door, breaking the tension. Hope bloomed in Zay's eyes as she dashed towards it.

The door creaked, and Aileen caught the bulky silhouette of Callan. He strode into the kitchen behind Zay and nodded at Walsh. 'Thank ye for the head's up.'

Crossing his arms, Callan met Aileen's eyes. 'Where did ye look for him?'

She showed him the timeline they had of Andrew's whereabouts. Callan scrunched his nose as he read. 'The last time anyone's seen him is last night. He wasn't at Moira Robertson's class then?'

Zay shook her head. 'Nope. He never misses class unless he has to.'

Finlay leaned on the countertop. 'Aye, but she never took the class either. Robertson's off on a conference.'

The group fell silent, unsure what to say. Zay smacked the countertop. 'None of his things are missing. He hasn't even taken his scarf.'

Finlay draped a hand over her shoulders. 'He's got nothing except for his backpack and the clothes on his back.'

Walsh picked up his phone. 'Let me call the bank and see if he's withdrawn any cash.' He walked out of the room, busy dialling.

Zay's shoulders dropped. 'Why would he run away? He's got nowhere to go.'

Aileen turned to Callan, who jerked his head to the front door. 'A word?'

They headed out in silence, both lost in their own thoughts. Callan shut the door and leaned against the front wall. 'I was going through Lucas Fraser's things, and I think I've got a connection between him and Reid. And' –

he pulled out a rumpled paper – 'he's made an unofficial complaint against ye.'

Aileen plucked the paper from his hands. It crackled, fluttering in the breeze. 'An unofficial complaint to the police?'

Callan placed a hand over her shoulder. 'Someone tried to murder ye, and would've if… and now this sort of warning.'

'And you think Reid's got something to hide?' Aileen finished his thought.

They faced the quaint street, watching the sun and clouds play peekaboo. The shadows of the trees on the pavement drew patterns like an ever-changing kaleidoscope.

'How did I scare him? All I did that day was head over to that shared working space and accidentally overhear their conversation.' Aileen sighed.

Callan pulled her into his chest, stroking her back. 'Darling, they've got surveillance cameras. His security team might've spotted ye.'

Aileen looked deep into his eyes. 'What if it wasn't him that night? What if someone else tried to hurt me?'

'And who'd that be?'

She didn't know. They stood there in an embrace for a while, drawing strength from each other.

When the door opened, Callan released her. Walsh popped his head out. 'Detective, Ms Mackinnon.' His eyes flitted between them. 'Erm, sorry for the interruption.'

He shut the door behind him, tugging at his trench. 'The bank, after a lot of cajoling, told us he hadn't withdrawn any large sums. We're working on keeping tabs on any card transactions he might do. And we've also asked the bank to inform us if he withdraws cash. So he's nowhere to go if he's running.'

Callan pushed off the wall. 'Ye also need to canvas public transport or any surveillance cams.'

'I've set a team on that and contacted the traffic police. So far they've got nothing.'

Aileen rubbed her forehead, anxiety squeezing her heart. 'Isla! I have to call her.'

'Ye do that, and let's see if she kens where he might go if he's stressed. Perhaps she lent him money.'

But Aileen knew that wasn't the case. If Andrew had gone to Isla, she would've sent him back to class. She dialled her friend anyway to shove more bad news onto her.

Oh, Andrew, where are you?

CHAPTER THIRTEEN

Isla didn't know where Andrew was. Between her contacts and the police's resources, they'd set up a search party by the afternoon.

The Loch Fuar grapevine worked double time, trying to search for the red-headed lad who served them their coffee and bread with a smile every day.

Callan had made his way to the swimming pool and checked the gym. He'd headed over to the security team of the university and gone through their surveillance. As Zay had claimed, the camera showed Andrew wave his friends off after dinner and head in the direction of the library.

At two, Callan's stomach growled, reminding him he'd missed lunch. Aileen was at Andrew's house with Finlay, the tech wizard, trying to locate Andrew's devices.

Callan thumped the sergeant's chair. 'Call me if ye find anything. I'll head over to the house and see if the search party's found anything.'

He'd just reversed out of the car park when his phone rang.

Aileen spluttered, 'Isla called. She says the search party's found nothing. She's barely holding on, Callan.'

He frowned, thoughts whirling. 'I'm heading back to Loch Fuar. Perhaps Andrew went there to catch a bus or train?'

A long silence made him wonder if she'd hung up. Then a murmur drifted down the line. 'Are you sure he ran off?'

No, he wasn't sure. The more they searched and drew up blanks, the more his gut told him something had happened. Something wrong.

'Why don't you come here? I'd like to have a word with you,' Aileen murmured.

When he got there, she scrambled into the car. Dark circles beneath her eyes made them look pensive.

They sat in silence until Callan hit the road, just driving.

When she gazed out of the window without speaking, he found a lay-by on the road and parked there. 'Okay, what is it?'

'Isla.' She spoke in a small voice. 'Callan, she's doing poorly.' Tears in her brown eyes caught him unawares. He placed a hand on her thigh that Aileen gripped like her life depended on it.

'Someone broke into her bakery, poisoned a customer, and Andrew's vanished after being accused of murdering his friend. Andrew's mum is worried but can't come here since her youngest isn't in school yet and there's no one to take care of her. To add to the stress, Isla and Daniel are having marital trouble.'

Callan blinked at the last bit. Daniel had told him the same, though not in so many words, but Callan had put it down to stress. Only a few weeks ago, Callan had been giving Daniel hell for going soft because of Isla.

'How long have they been having trouble?'

Aileen looked at her lap and shook her head. 'Dunno. We need to find Andrew, Callan, and the killer – the real killer.'

Callan sat back in his seat. 'Aye, as long as something lets up. Hell, it's like we're coming to one dead end after another. Whoever this person is wants something to do with—'

Thump! Both of them jolted.

A rustle followed, making Aileen unbuckle her seat belt and Callan reached for his gun.

A familiar memory from that summer popped into Callan's head. They shared a look as he reached into the back and pulled up a messy blond head.

'Ye ken this eejit?'

Aileen gasped. 'Leith! Honestly! I thought you were a criminal.' She waved at Callan. 'He stays with Andrew and, well, lived with Anvit as well. That's Leith.'

Uncurling from his spot in the gap between the front and back seats, Leith sat up, hands up in surrender.

'Next time, I will check my car!' Callan growled. 'How the bloody hell did ye get in?'

Leith had the gall to blush. 'When ye unlocked the door for Ms Mackinnon.'

Aileen gasped. 'You were following me? I thought you were off asking your neighbours if they'd seen Andrew!'

Leith nodded. 'I did but found nothing. I wasn't following you! I planned on speaking with you, not to the police though. It's— I've some confidential information to give. I wanted to visit you at Dachaigh alone, but if you trust this detective—'

Aileen tilted her head. 'What have you done, Leith?'

He cleared his throat, flitting his gaze between them. 'So, I may have nicked Anvit's phone, tablet and laptop—'

An hour later, Aileen scrolled through the laptop, rummaging through Anvit's data. They sat at Dachaigh's kitchen counter, the light from the picture windows shining on the marble countertops.

Callan glared at Leith, who tried to look sheepish but failed miserably.

He pointed at the laptop. 'I can charge you for withholding evidence and obstruction of justice. Not to mention ye just broke into a detective's car.'

Leith raised a shoulder. 'Sorry?'

He glowered. 'Ye've got to be more convincing than that.'

Aileen pushed the laptop aside. 'How is this related to Andrew's disappearance? You think Reid took him?'

Leith chewed on his bottom lip, perhaps mulling over his thoughts. 'I don't know exactly. I just wanted to hand over the laptop, phone and tablet in case… in case…'

'In case ye ended up potentially harming yer pal? Ye've already caused Andrew harm, ye bampot.' Callan jerked his head to the doorway. 'Got a minute, Aileen?'

Once Leith was out of earshot, Callan glared his way. 'Why do ye think he hid the info all this time?'

Aileen dropped her chin until her hair curtained her face. She'd left it loose. Callan's fingers itched to twirl a soft strand.

'I can't believe I trusted him. He had access to Anvit and Andrew's schedules and, like he just showed us, to their personal items. Why would he murder Anvit though?'

Callan waved his hands, speaking in whispers. 'Let's not jump to conclusions. What do ye think is on Anvit's devices? What did ye find?'

She gave the laptop on the table a once-over. 'He's got

copies of Douglas Reid's company accounts. But I checked the data on his phone and there's no calendar entry regarding what he was up to that night.'

'Why don't ye go through the financials and I'll put out feelers for Reid's company? Like I said, we've got a potential connection between him and Lucas, not to mention that warning he sent ye. If ye do find any dodgy data, it should help us secure a warrant. Until then, I'll haul this bastard's arse to the station and detain him for a bit. Next time he thinks it's funny to remove evidence – important evidence – he'll think twice.'

Aileen placed a hand on Callan's heaving chest. 'He's spooked, Callan.'

'What?'

Giving a shake of her head, she looked into his frowning eyes. 'Leith's spooked because he's not alone in this.'

She strutted over to the counter with determined steps and slid onto a stool. 'Okay, I might not have truth serum with me, but I can sense a lie. Now tell me, who're involved in this plan? And what's the plan?'

Leith frowned. 'Plan?'

He had a lot of work to do, and babysitting this teenager only added to his to-dos, but Callan would support Aileen, even if what she'd just said made no sense to him. Her hunches were usually spot on.

Holding up her fingers, she counted. 'One, the night I got to your house looking for Andrew, Zay sent me through the woods so I wouldn't be near the library. I chanced upon Anvit and Andrew, but they weren't supposed to be there, were they? Now, if Zay wasn't involved, she wouldn't have sent me the wrong way. Second, when I asked Andrew what he'd been up to that night, he wouldn't tell me.

'Now you tell us. You've got Anvit's laptop and other devices, so I'm sure you've gone through them and know what he'd been up to. And I know it's something to do with Douglas Reid. Why have you been investigating him? Why not contact the police?'

Leith's skin matched the marble countertops. His eyes splayed wide. She saw the remnants of childish innocence on his face.

Callan cursed. 'Stop lying to us. That includes not telling us things. I've got to find Andrew. If ye hide information and something happens to him—'

Leith blinked. 'Something happens as in he dies?' Now his eyes held fear. 'I don't know where he is, I swear! Please believe me.'

Pushing the stool beside Leith to one side, Callan loomed over him. 'Tell us everything!' he hissed.

The lad's terrified eyes danced between Aileen and Callan. He wetted his lips. 'Water?' he squeaked.

Aileen pushed a glass at him while Callan scratched his jaw, considering strapping the lad in handcuffs. 'Go on!'

Wetting his lips, Leith began. 'Anvit worked under Douglas Reid. It was a dream internship, and he slogged for it. Once he'd been working late and got into the company files on an older machine, he was using. The machine had more access than an intern would normally have, and he found sensitive data. Just weird details like log-in times and random names. He thought it was someone messing around and he let it go. But a few months later, after he'd got a handle on things, he was working on a new game and there too he found anomalies. You know, in the database. The app would store people's data, watch them as they played – spooky stuff. And there wasn't even a warning of any kind or permission asked.'

Leith's hands wrapped around the empty glass. He held it up, watching it sparkle as it caught the light.

'Anvit spoke to Reid about it. The man brushed him off. A week later, he's gifted a new laptop and tablet and asked to work on another project. Then the company announced they were launching the thing. Curious, he looked through that game's files when he wasn't supposed to, hacked into them. The problem still persisted, and the company didn't mention that they were gathering data. He didn't know what to do. He approached the lawyer man, Langdon?' Leith shrugged.

Aileen intertwined her fingers. 'And he was asked to look at it from a different perspective.'

'Something like that. Anvit was sure they wanted to sell the data, make some bucks from it. After all, data's currency.'

Callan leaned on his elbows. 'Why not come to us? What was he doing in those woods?'

Leith shook his head. 'Reid is an influential man – he's got connections. Who'd take an intern seriously? And Langdon kept saying Anvit had made a mistake. The sod could rival Einstein, but even he was wrong sometimes.

'As for those woods, he was supposed to go through Reid's data with Andrew that night.' He waved a hand. 'Not in the woods, though. And Zay didn't want you to know. Most people worship Reid.'

Aileen tapped a finger against the cold marble. 'Only Andrew and Anvit knew what they were doing there then?'

Leith hummed. 'That's the whole truth.'

Callan pointed to the computer. 'And what did you find on here?'

'Financials,' Aileen answered. 'And they look funny.'

After Callan hauled Leith to the police station, taking Anvit's laptop with him, Aileen settled in with the data she'd copied from it. Callan could get the police IT team to search the data, but time was of the essence, and if anyone could find the anomaly in the numbers, it was her.

An afternoon of data searching and number crunching – Aileen rubbed her palms and smacked her lips. She might have left her job as a forensic accountant, but she always enjoyed digging into numbers and figuring out what they said.

It didn't take her long to find out that the accounts Reid shared publicly were different from the books Anvit had uncovered. The lad was no financial genius, so he hadn't figured out the discrepancies beyond a few obvious issues.

An hour later, Aileen emerged from behind the screen, bleary-eyed yet grinning.

She'd caught the bastard alright. Not for murder, but for material misstatements in his financials. They had been glaringly obvious to her trained eye.

The bills didn't match the sales book and the suppliers didn't really exist. He'd used shell companies that he owned, which Aileen thought was the stupidest thing she'd ever seen. No wonder he had an accountant cook a different set of accounts to share with Companies House.

Reid had also perhaps paid off the statutory auditors to hand in a favourable audit report.

Aileen huffed. She had caught him, but she had a thing or two to clarify first. Should she head there? It could be dangerous.

William Black, of William Black and Co., was one of Gammit Inc's customers and had registered his business using his home address. They had sold bicycles until a few years ago.

Aileen tapped the steering wheel as she eyed the house. Fresh, verdant plants sprouted from between the picket fence. A name plate on the front door, designed in coral shells read 'Black'.

The curtains in the house were pulled wide open to reveal a library, a dining table set up for a meal, a few trinkets on the windowsill that Aileen deduced were gifts from the beloved grandchild who even now squealed in the front yard as Grandpa Black wheeled her around on a bicycle.

The man, a little stout, with a white beard enveloping a pink face, didn't look like a fraudster.

Aileen huffed. Was she wrong? Maybe, but she still had to check him out given that Reid had charged invoices to his company.

She pulled the car away from the kerb and made her way to another address – this time to the ex-owner of a beauty salon.

Bettie Ray had sold her salon to PC Robert Davis's wife a couple of years ago. She'd left the town last year only to return when her daughter fell pregnant.

Oldies and their affection for grandbabies. Aileen rolled her eyes as she turned onto the road and saw a house similar to the one she'd just left. Bettie was hunched over a shrub, whistling to herself as she pruned it.

When Aileen pulled up in front of her house, her whistling broke off.

'Just cutting these to make tea. Want to join me?'

Well, she hadn't expected an invitation. Aileen nodded. Tea would be divine in this frigid weather.

Soon her palms wrapped around a steaming cuppa that tasted of flowers and honey.

Bettie, her wrinkled hands showing off a huge sapphire ring, tapped a cookbook. 'I'm learning about teas and their benefits. So I'm growing herbs and flowers in my garden – as many as I can at least.'

Aileen smiled. 'You have a lovely garden and a lovely home.'

If fraudsters had pictures of their family plastered on every surface possible, Bettie would be one.

Her bright cabinets showed off her cat mug collection and a few more pictures of a balding man, a young woman and a bairn wrapped in another young man's arm.

Bettie grinned. 'Now that we're staying here for good…' She followed Aileen's gaze. 'I got my husband a Polaroid camera on our twentieth wedding anniversary. Then I got him a DSLR a decade later. Now he moonlights as a photographer. Living the wild life.'

Aileen sipped her tea. 'I'm sorry to—' What? She hadn't visited unannounced; Bettie had invited her in. Aileen tried again. 'Well, I wanted to speak to you about your salon.'

'Oh, I sold it.' Bettie's neat eyebrows formed a line on her forehead. 'Are you here about a case?'

Aileen pursed her lips. 'I found your salon mentioned as one who purchases games by Gammit Inc. Some kind of beauty/ fashion game with lots of add-ons. According to them, you've been a customer for years.'

Bettie gasped, manicured nails shining as she covered her mouth. 'Me? I can barely start and shut off a computer. Who is Game It?'

'Gammit like damn it.' Aileen pushed her cup away. 'I thought so, Bettie. Thanks for confirming. The tea was lovely.'

'Am I in trouble with the police?'

With that fluffy white hair and kind eyes? Aileen didn't think so.

BACK IN HER CAR, AILEEN GNAWED ON HER LIP. Her search for Reid's 'customers' had fallen through. She'd driven around to three more modest houses, all belonging to retired business people.

Why would Reid use their names? He had detailed information about these former business owners, especially their addresses.

Aileen tapped a rhythm, thinking. If Reid wanted to target business owners, he could've picked ones currently trading. But he'd picked retired ones. Why?

Maybe he'd got access to their data?

Aileen eased her car onto the road again, this time returning to a place that had helped them break open the previous case.

THE YOUNG WOMAN BEHIND THE COUNTER EYED AILEEN. Her baby face had slimmed, and the easy trust in her twinkling eyes had dulled. All because of Aileen.

She sniffed, patting the fragrant lilies on the counter. 'You're Aileen Mackinnon, aren't you? Your grandmother is just *fine*.'

A blush reeking of humiliation stamped Aileen's cheeks. 'I'm sorry, Charmaine. I was only looking for justice.'

A deep chuckle sounded from behind her. The fact that the man wore a white lab coat and his laugh lit up his eyes like his father's told Aileen he was the new consulting doctor at the Senior Citizen Care Centre.

Eric Macdonald looked like his father, DCI Rory Macdonald, right down to those expressive eyes. 'Does Callan ken ye're here nosing about?'

Another blush. 'I'm helping!'

He sashayed over to them and leaned a hip on the red counter. His gaze fell on Charmaine. 'Why don't you head out? I'll be here for a while so I'll lock up when I'm done.'

Charmaine shot him a kind smile, tucked her brown curls behind her ears, and fired a glare at Aileen. 'Gladly.'

She pulled out her purse and shut the door on the wall behind her as she walked away. Rambunctious oldies didn't populate the hall behind the reception this time. But the pinboards still overflowed with activities. And, Aileen noticed, Zumba had taken over the timings for doctor's appointments.

'What are ye here about?'

Aileen gave Eric her attention. 'I've been looking into a few people in association with a suspect.' She ticked off names with her fingers. 'William Black, Bettie Ray, Thomas Moore, Julie Saunders and Seamus Wayne.'

He frowned. 'Those are patients here at the centre. They like to come here instead of the GP since we started our drop-in clinic.'

'Are you sure?'

Eric rounded the desk and tapped a few keys to start up the desktop. 'We have a database here with all of their medical data. It's very basic – the password is written on this sticky note here.' He tapped a yellow note stuck to the desktop's frame.

Aileen tutted. 'Even a child could steal that info.'

'Essentially.' He clicked the mouse and pointed at the

spreadsheet. 'Here you go. A list of all the patients I've done a check-up for.'

Aileen read the long list. 'Goodness! So many of them? They sure keep you busy.'

Eric chuckled, his eyes lighting up again. 'This is Loch Fuar. Most of them have seen me as a wee bairn. So they like a blether as well as a check-up.'

Of course they did.

Aileen gave the room another look. 'No surveillance cameras.'

'Not in Loch Fuar.'

Aileen straightened. 'But this helps. Thank you.'

'Sure thing.' He waved. 'For the record, Mr West, the man who was poisoned? He shows signs of a full recovery.'

Aileen smiled at Eric. 'I'll tell Isla for sure. It'll make her feel better.'

But Aileen knew that finding Andrew safe was the only way to make her best friend feel like herself again.

CHAPTER FOURTEEN

Callan clutched the steering wheel in a death grip. Beside him, Robert tried unsuccessfully to slow them down.

'Ye ken they could fine ye.'

Not now. Not when no one had seen Andrew for almost a day now. Every second ticking away would cost them.

Callan had to track him down, starting with speaking to Reid.

Aileen – thank God for her financial brains – had found just enough. They'd then had their team search for the data legitimately, helping them get a warrant. Reid's company had misstated the financials, indicating money-laundering schemes and a false list of debtors.

Slimy pig!

Callan strode towards the weirdly shaped office with 'Gammit Inc' flashing in all sorts of colours at the summit. They cut through to the reception desk.

The receptionist gave them a warm yet poisonous smile from behind the desk. 'How can I help you?'

Callan took a deep breath and pierced the woman with a glare. 'Douglas Reid. Where is he?'

A laugh burbled through her tight lips. 'Do you have an appointment?'

He smacked the warrant on the white countertop. 'No, but I do have a warrant.'

She scrambled towards the phone, stabbing the buttons with her manicured nails.

When she snapped the phone down, her lips in a tense line, she spat, 'If you could just follow that corridor and take the lift to the fifth floor.'

Callan snatched up the warrant sheet and strode towards the corridor on the left.

In a modern building such as this, the glass lift added to its stark aesthetics. Callan wondered if people realised how fickle and transparent glass was, unlike the company's financials.

Soon they were on a quieter fifth floor. He'd read about open-plan offices and sweatshirt-wearing employees. But this floor resembled an accounting firm: greys, whites and silver in slick lines.

The place felt cold and banal. And the suit-wearing eejit standing underneath a geometric chandelier had to be Langdon.

His sleazy smile boiled Callan's blood. He stifled the urge to deck him.

Langdon stretched soft, manicured hands to Callan. Perhaps it was company policy to look after nails.

'Langdon,' he introduced himself. 'To what do we owe this pleasure?'

Pleasure indeed.

Callan smirked. 'DI Callan Cameron and PC Robert Davis. We're here to speak with Douglas Reid.'

The argument formed on his face before he opened his mouth. 'Sorry, he's a bit busy. Would you—'

He wasn't bloody here for tea and a blether! Callan dangled the warrant. 'Where is he?'

'I'm not sure on what basis you've got this, but if you'll wait here please, I need to speak with my client before—'

Robert had walked a bit away to the glass walls overlooking the woods around the college. A blanket of darkness sat over the entire landscape, muffling any signs of life beneath it.

Now he ambled back to Callan's side, smirking. 'Douglas Reid's offices are that way. He seems to be on a call.'

Callan didn't waste more time, stalking towards his office. One knock was all Reid got.

When Callan saw his red constipated face, he didn't hide his smug smile. The man had aged considerably. His mop of hair had fallen away, leaving a shiny ball that reflected the light from the bulb above him. His pale lips parted to show corroded yellow teeth.

Ruby cufflinks clinked at his wrists. His cologne made Callan's stomach turn. His ludicrous tie had to cost Callan's entire monthly salary.

Pompous and ridiculous were the words that came to mind.

With his spluttering lawyer behind him, Douglas Reid gave Callan one look and snapped at Langdon, 'Get a proper lawyer on the line, ye useless twit! I'll come with ye.'

Callan and Robert flanked him as they walked to the lifts. If Reid wanted to run, he didn't try. Instead, he muttered, 'Why I pay that numpty I can't say. Useless bampot.'

He continued muttering all the way to the police station. Callan let him be, exchanging amused glances with Robert.

However he'd imagined the owner of a gaming company to look, it wasn't like this. And he couldn't wait to hear what he had to say.

CALLAN PLACED THE FALSIFIED FINANCIAL RECORDS, THE list of shell companies, complaints Anvit had placed about the lack of data privacy, and names of his 'customers' on the table between him and Douglas Reid.

Reid didn't balk at the sight of them.

His numpty lawyer, Langdon, had managed to send another twit since he didn't deal with criminal law and they'd been in consultation for a good half hour. Callan, tired of them, had considered barging in when the Rolex-wearing Mr Killick strutted towards him and announced they were ready for the interview.

Now with Rory beside him and Robert in observation, they got to work.

Callan placed a palm on one paper. 'Who is Balehoff Inc?'

Killick's head bobbed slightly.

Reid sat back, crossing his legs. 'A software company.'

'Setze Software?'

'Another software company.'

Callan looked Reid in the eye. 'And how are they connected to you?'

The lawyer butted in. 'How's this relevant to why you've dragged my client in here?'

Sitting back, Callan crossed his arms and let the silence build up. He wanted Reid to sweat. The man looked too smug, hiding behind his lawyer.

Another minute later, Callan smirked. 'As you might know, Anvit Nair, one of his interns, has been murdered and we've found misstated financial statements belonging to Gammit Inc marred with fraudulent transactions. So, Mr Reid, how are Balehoff Inc and Setze Software related to you?'

Reid got an all-clear from his lawyer. 'I don't know them personally. They are vendors of Gammit Inc.'

Rory had sat silently the entire time. Now he took to tapping a staccato on the floor. The steady beat made Reid gulp.

Pausing for dramatic effect, Callan went for the jugular. 'Professional connection? But I found Setze Software lists you as one of their shareholders. Companies House says you own a whopping thirty per cent and have done since their inception seven years ago.'

A muscle on Reid's forehead twitched. He leaned in to spit words at Callan, but his lawyer held him back. 'My client has no comment on the matter.'

Callan grinned. 'Okay. Why don't ye tell me about Balehoff Inc?' He studied the papers to add more drama. 'It says here the owner is Lucas Fraser?'

'No—' the lawyer began.

'I don't know anyone by that name,' Reid butted in. He turned to his lawyer, shaking his head. 'This is harassment. Oh God. Get me out of here!'

Killick turned to Callan. 'Please, Detective, get to the point. My client's clearly been duped.'

Rory smirked, speaking for the first time. 'By whom?'

Spreading his hands wide, the golden Rolex glinted under the single light bulb. 'Mr Langdon's played my client. He made him sign papers and create these companies.'

'Mr Reid is the CEO of a world-famous gaming company and yet he signed papers without reading them?'

'I trusted my lawyer. I pay him big bucks,' Reid replied.

Callan sat back in his chair and, tilting his head, asked, 'And where does the money for that come from?'

Killick snorted. 'As you pointed out, Detective, Mr Reid is the owner of Gammit Inc, a globally successful company. Money isn't in short supply.'

'No? But it hardly comes from legitimate gaming sources, does it? Word on the forums is ye've leeched games from amateur indie developers.'

'No comment.'

He swivelled to another topic. 'Tell me, Mr Reid, ye said ye didn't know anyone by the name of Mr Lucas Fraser, yet there are photographs of ye with the man and claims from yer old friends that ye were close pals forty years ago.'

Reid shrugged. 'That was a long time ago.'

Callan slapped down a picture of Lucas's body, followed by a picture of the two men together. 'This picture was taken not long before he was murdered. Care to elaborate how he went from enjoying drinks with his pals to being dead?'

Reid's face turned ashen. 'Ye should ask that bloodsucking witch of a fiancée. Jealous of him she was. Wasn't satisfied with that big rock he'd bought for her.'

Callan leaned his forearms on the desk. 'Are ye referring to Isobel Murray?'

'Aye. More likely, it was her old man. Detested my Lucas, he did.'

My Lucas?

Callan stopped short and really studied Douglas Reid. His wrinkles had deepened, and his cheekbones protruded.

He hung his head and Callan watched, horrified, as a tear slid down his cheeks. Douglas Reid had been in *love* with Lucas Fraser?

'Ye called Isobel Murray his fiancée. Did you know her? Where did she go?'

Reid chuckled. 'To hell! Luc bought the biggest diamond he could. He showed the ring to me, asked if it looked good. Damn it! She never really cared!'

Callan felt a headache come on. 'Why did ye use his name to create those companies, then?'

Douglas Reid shook his head. 'No comment.'

AILEEN'S MUSCLES CRAMPED. SHE'D HEADED TO THE grocery store after her visit to the Senior Citizen Care Centre, begged the grocer to stay open ten minutes longer and purchased ingredients for pasta with a red wine sauce.

Restless sleep, the stress of solving a murder to save her friend's nephew and now searching for said nephew had played with her nerves like Mozart had the piano.

She made her way back to Dachaigh, clutching the steering wheel as her mind threw questions at her.

Where were Andrew's devices? What information had Anvit found? What were the two of them doing in those woods? Were Andrew's devices synced to the cloud? Or did he make manual backups?

Seeing the inn emerge up ahead soothed the intensity of her thoughts. She knew once the cutting board came out, she'd lose herself in her cooking. Then her mind would ease up.

When she turned her car into the parking area, Aileen stepped on the brake, hands turning clammy with sweat.

An unknown black car sat in one of the spots. Thick dried sludge coated every part, but its number plates gleamed under the grey light. Who cleaned number plates but not the rest of the car?

There were all kinds of weird folk living in Loch Fuar though – solving murders had taught her that.

Perhaps it was a tourist. And she was always glad to welcome those, especially if they dropped in as a surprise and paid money.

Aileen pulled out the bag of groceries and hurried inside to welcome her unexpected guest.

The pastel-blue door shut behind her and silence spread its arms in welcome. Puzzled, her heart thudding in her chest, mind flashing images of her recurring nightmares, Aileen tiptoed her way to the kitchen.

Her shopping bag clattered onto the marble countertop, and Aileen groped for a knife from the stand.

With a steady mind and agile feet, she made her way to the living area. Nothing sat skewed, broken, or amiss.

She did as Callan had taught her: ears perked up to hear any noise, eyes searching for the slightest of movement.

Finding nothing in the reception or living areas, Aileen tiptoed towards the library.

Someone had meant to murder her the other night. With her other hand, she drew up the station's number and was ready to click on it if need be. No more mistakes!

Pressing her back against the wall, she angled her gleaming knife to use as a mirror. She saw nothing except for the reflection of the picture window; the moonbeam sparkling onto the polished floor.

Eyeing the room she was leaving behind, she stealthily inched into the library and saw *him*.

'Hands where I can see them!' She shouted. 'Don't move! I've got a knife.'

She thought she sounded a little pathetic, so she added, 'And I won't hesitate to use it.'

The chuckle rang ripe with familiarity. 'Do you welcome all your guests this way, Aileen?'

Aileen reached for the switch and blinked when light poured into the room. What kind of creepy idiot stood in a room in the dark?

She eyed the expensive-looking suit and leather shoes: all shiny black and sophisticated. No wonder he skulked about. *Slimeball.*

What did I ever like in those shoes?

She cleared her throat to focus on the situation at hand. 'Sorry, I thought it was an intruder.'

Langdon swivelled, hands still raised beside his ears.

Aileen gestured with her knife, then realised what she was doing and used the other hand. 'You can— I'm sorry. To what do I owe the pleasure of this visit?'

He smiled, a pleasant mega-watt smile that would sway judges and hard-to-please women. But Aileen didn't sway – her intuition rendered her immune, blaring an alarm in her ears.

Langdon spread his hands, undeterred by Aileen's guarded stance. 'You said you can't have dinner, so I was wondering if you'd like to have lunch tomorrow?'

She was ready to use her knife then. Since moving to Loch Fuar, she'd gained an animosity to this kind of suited man. Pompous shallow bastards, the lot of them, who never heard a woman. Especially when she said 'no'.

'Thank you for the offer but if I wasn't clear last time, I'm not interested.'

But the eejit continued to smile smugly. 'That's where our differences lie. What interests you, I find odious and vice versa.'

Aileen crossed her arms. 'Then I don't see the point of asking me for a date.'

'I always thought I could persuade you.'

Oh yes, chauvinistic pig, a woman's mind is fickle. Now she imagined biting his head off.

Tucking his hands in his trouser pockets, he stood as if he was royalty. 'Tell me, Ms Mackinnon.' Aileen noted he'd moved back to her last name. 'How much profit does an old inn like this make?'

What an odd question. And how did it matter to him?

'You're a man of business – I'm sure you can guess.'

He shrugged. 'Not enough to live the lifestyle you'd be used to.'

'And how would you know my lifestyle?' Fear muffled her sternness. How did he know *anything* about her?

The arrogant smirk was back on his face. He waved towards the car park. 'I've seen your car. It's a high-end model, isn't it? And I heard you were the auditor who unveiled the scandal at—'

So he'd done research on her, perhaps stalked her. Aileen narrowed her eyes, wanting to cut to the chase. 'Get to the point, Mr Langdon.'

He nodded with a simper. 'I like a woman who doesn't beat around the bush.'

Oh really? He did an awful lot of circling around, not nailing any point on the head.

Pausing for dramatic effect, he smoothed his crisp blazer. 'I can help you.' He plucked out a thick envelope from his pocket. 'I can help you very handsomely, but I need your assistance too.'

It was on the tip of her tongue to order him to get out when she reined it in. All in good time.

'And what help is that?'

He tilted his head and made Aileen want to find a duster and mop up that arrogance.

'How should I say it?'

'Plainly,' Aileen whipped out.

He waved her off. 'I believe we should use the words we learn well, Ms Mackinnon.'

Staring at the envelope, he said, 'Let's just say this is just the first of many. A little incentive. Twenty-five grand to divert your attention to the upkeep of this inn.'

Ah, he was finally on point. What a typical lawyer!

'I wasn't aware my attention was anywhere but on the inn.'

He sighed. 'You and I both know that isn't true. An inn such as this one is a legacy to cherish. It would be a shame to see it reduced to shambles.'

Was the bastard threatening her gran's inn?

Aileen hissed, but he continued without missing a beat. 'You need to be here to greet guests, market it on social media, etc.'

'And on what superfluous activities do I spend time on now, Mr Langdon?'

He chuckled; it sounded like air leaving a balloon. 'Gossiping, let's just say, comes to mind.' He offered her the envelope. 'Twenty-five grand as an incentive and the rest will follow every week as a reward for your concentrated efforts on the inn.'

Aileen didn't heed the envelope another glance. She stood aside and gestured to the door. 'The door's that way.'

'Ms Mackinnon.' He adopted a patronising tone. 'You must listen well.'

'Or?'

'It's really a benefit I'm offering you.'

She chuckled now, and guffaws of laughter pealed out of her.

He smirked. 'The idea appeals to you, then?'

Aileen shook her head. 'Your need to grovel does. Let me inform you, Mr Langdon, I'm not one of those items your money can buy. Let me show you the way out.'

'Ms Mackinnon—'

'Get out or I'll boot your nether regions so hard you won't ever feel them again.'

Holding up his hands, he backed away, as if scared. Yet he didn't leave.

Aileen flashed her teeth. 'In all the research you've done on me, you'll know I'm excellent at that shot. So if you care about your safety, please leave.'

He looked into her eyes, leaning down to place the envelope on the side table.

'With that envelope, Mr Langdon,' she spat.

As soon as he was out the door, Aileen shut it and turned the locks. Then she hurried to the kitchen and peered out her window. Her angry tantrum would have to wait.

She snapped pictures of his car until it all but disappeared down the road.

Her next action was to go through the surveillance footage of the car park. She might've been sloshed the night she'd been attacked outside the pub and blinded by the headlights, but Callan was not. And perhaps between them, they'd catch the bastard who'd tried to run her over.

She paused the voice recorder app on her phone – it had recorded her entire conversation with Langdon.

Langdon had indeed offered her a boon coming here like he had. It told her he had something to hide and that her investigation had spooked him. But what could be his motive for murder? Or was this his employer's tactic to scare her away now that the 'unofficial warning' hadn't worked?

CHAPTER FIFTEEN

Aileen scrubbed the counter with all her might, thinking about Andrew. Where did teenagers go when they wanted to get away from it all?

A yawn slipped past her lips, driving home the fact that she'd spent last night entrenched in another nightmare. This one had been worse because of all her worries about Andrew.

Stressed, her muscles ached and her body sagged, ready to give out. No sleep for the wicked – or for those who had to find a missing person.

Andrew couldn't have run away. So where could he have gone?

Aileen straightened after winning her fight with the stubborn stain. If she truly believed he'd not absconded of his own free will, that meant somebody had kidnapped him.

She draped the duster onto the hook and reached for the pans in the dishwasher.

Kidnapped.

Aileen clutched the handle of the machine. He was the

one who'd found Anvit's body. So he might have seen the killer.

Bloody hell! What had Andrew and Anvit being doing in those woods?

She reached for the phone, dialling Callan. As usual, he didn't answer. But he'd spent the night questioning Reid and then headed over to Loch Heaven to pour over CCTV footage. His early morning message had revealed they still didn't know where Andrew was, though.

More than twenty-four hours and no ransom note.

Fear clawed its way under her skin. No, she'd find him, for sure.

When she'd placed the fresh-smelling pots in their places, Aileen folded the laundry. She liked to clean when nerves got the better of her.

Callan had warned her to stay put either at Dachaigh or with someone she trusted. He wasn't sure what Reid was capable of and worried she'd get herself killed.

Aileen had rolled her eyes at his choice of words, but then he'd recounted every incident her life had been in jeopardy since he'd met her. She was 'too civilian' to encounter so many threats. *Arsehole*, she thought, chuckling to herself.

A groan from the back door startled her.

Aileen dashed into the kitchen, a shirt dangling from her shoulder, ready to strike the intruder – then stilled. 'Oh, darling!'

Isla, her frenzied red hair resembling a forest fire, her green eyes droopy pools, shut the door behind her.

Spots on her face matched her hair colour, as did her eyes. The rest of her skin was dull, a patch peeling at the nose. Wordlessly, she slid onto a stool.

Mimicking her, Aileen pulled up the stool next to hers and sat. Intertwining her hands on the white marble top,

Aileen studied her nails, waiting but not pushing Isla to speak.

The clock in the living room cuckooed, but the two remained still. After a minute, Aileen's lemon-scented diffuser puffed out aromatic smoke, yet the silence continued.

Isla pressed her forehead against the cool marble. The rust-coloured sweater she wore rounded over her hunched shoulders.

Running out of patience, Aileen filled a glass of water and slid it to Isla. Next, she ventured to the cabinets and pulled out the teabags.

'I'm sorry. It was stupid of me to pull away from you.' Isla's muffled voice finally filled the empty air.

Taking that as her cue, Aileen dropped what she'd been doing and sat across from Isla. 'They've been a difficult couple of days. You don't need to apologise.'

Placing her palms flat against the countertop, Isla pushed up and took another moment to swallow the tears crowding her eyes. 'If only it were that easy. I've been a disaster and angry at myself for it. And I took it all out on you.'

Aileen reached for Isla's hand. Her fingers were cold to the touch. Aileen gave them a slight squeeze. 'We'll find him, Isla.'

Isla's eyes met Aileen's and held. 'I don't need to be coddled. It's been more than twenty-four hours. He's not taken anything: no money, no food, no keys; nor has he used his phone – that's what the police officer outside our house said. I know the chances.'

'Police officer outside your house?' Aileen gaped.

Isla bobbed her head. 'Aye, in case Andrew comes there or reaches out to us. They've been working through the night to locate him. I'm not sure if it's because he's a suspect or they worry he's been hurt or... or worse.'

Aileen didn't want to think about worse. 'Is there a cabin in the forest? Perhaps he went to camp out there? It could explain why we can't reach him.'

Isla slurped the water. 'None of his clothes are gone, though. And he wouldn't leave unless the police cleared him.'

'He's organised, but if he took a day bag or a weekend's worth of clothes, say two T-shirts and a pair of jeans, it's unlikely we'd realise. And he won't need money if he's staying in the forest.'

'His bike, Aileen! It's gone too. It's a road bike – it would be no use in the forest. And don't forget the fact that he went missing at night.'

Aileen rubbed her tired eyes. She had spent a lot of hours in front of her laptop screen, going through the financials and the names again last night. Anvit's data held a lot of other information, but she'd stuck to what she knew.

She'd done nothing but unearthed a few more shell companies and frauds.

The data wouldn't lead them to Andrew, so despite her findings, she considered her night's sleuthing a failure.

That morning, before rolling out of bed, Aileen had reached for the laptop to dig into Andrew's online presence. He didn't appreciate social media and didn't own any accounts.

Then she'd checked in with Zay and Finlay, who spoke in subdued tones – whether from the chastisement Callan had given them all after his encounter with Leith or from missing Andrew. Finlay hadn't made any progress with locating Andrew's devices. He'd set up the locator app on

Andrew's phone after Anvit died, but it couldn't find a signal.

According to Finlay, Andrew's devices had either broken, or he'd switched them off.

Isla pushed at her hair, but the frizz popped back up. 'I couldn't sit still. I can't, not anymore. I'm not a stupid damsel who falls apart at everything. I've decided to do some of my own digging. I'll help you find Andrew.'

Seeing the gleam in Isla's eyes swept Aileen up in a wave of relief. It wasn't her usual unbridled twinkle, but it was a start.

'I won't sit about moping when I can be of use,' she said in a firm voice. 'I called up Edith at the company who supplies those paper bags. She said she herself took the call. And she told me she was surprised to hear a lad ask for those bags, given that they'd just dispatched a delivery to us. But she assumed we were running short and, in her haste, didn't question.'

Reaching into her purse, Isla pulled out her phone. 'She said the call came at half past four.'

'Half past four,' Aileen repeated to make sure she had the chronology right.

Isla bobbed her head, all business now. 'That's the odd bit. We have a new batch that rolls out at five every evening on the dot, but we're out of supplies at that time – which is common knowledge. Most customers don't come in until five minutes to five.'

Aileen scribbled it all down. 'So there was no one in the storefront. But surely anyone could've placed that call?'

Isla shook her head. 'Edith says it was the bakery's number. She remembers it well and also has a call history. It matches.'

'So someone got into the bakery and placed a call? But wouldn't you be there?'

'Nope. I can't hear anything in the back. I usually have music on at that point. After twelve hours on my feet, I'm knackered.'

'What about your assistants?'

Isla's lips curled. 'Andrew wasn't in. I'd asked Susan to clean the counters. I questioned her about it, and she confessed she stepped out back to take a phone call she thought was from her boyfriend.'

Leaving the bakery unattended. The perfect time to place a call.

Isla held up a finger. 'But it wasn't her boyfriend, Susan said. It was someone else enquiring about her course at uni and such. A bunch of shite since that call lasted just long enough for someone to put the call through to the paper bag company and get out.'

Aileen's eyes sparkled. 'CCTV footage?'

Isla smirked. 'I haven't checked it yet. Want to join me?'

CALLAN STARTLED AWAKE, GASPING AS THE WORLD careened and snapped.

'Bloody—'

The air left his lungs. He landed on his side, knocking his elbows against the pile of papers on the floor. Who needed a coffee to wake up when you could fall and hurt your arse?

Callan grunted. After spending the night going through the surveillance footage with the traffic police and then heading to the train station to question the staff working there, he'd crashed at his office. None of his legwork had paid off, and neither had Walsh's questioning of Isla's neighbours. Not one of Loch Fuar's sharp eyes had seen

Andrew. It led Callan to deduce he simply hadn't come to Loch Fuar.

Callan pushed off the floor, letting the dislodged papers crumple under his palms. They might be a pain, but they'd just protected his elbow from the floor at least.

His phone blared in his ears, subduing any embers of sleep left in his foggy brain. No wonder he'd crashed awake. Someone had rung him.

He hadn't meant to fall asleep in his office chair, but early that morning his eyes had closed of their own accord.

'Hello?' Callan rasped.

'Ah, Detective, I'm so glad I caught you. I've been trying to call you for a while now.'

He squinted at his watch, cursing when he noticed it was almost noon. Where were Robert and Rory?

'Dr Brown,' Callan acknowledged. 'I'm sorry. Did you find a match?'

Scrapes and tinkering came down the line until something thudded and Dr Brown spoke. 'You, DI Cameron, are a genius. Why don't you come over? I'd like to explain it all in person.'

He heard the inappropriate glee in her voice. But in their profession, success meant finding clues about dead bodies.

He raced to Dr Brown's. The glass screen on her office door had white blinds on the back. It reflected the dark circles around his eyes, making the blue of his irises appear more radiant. A sleep line marred his left cheek.

Dr Brown was bent over an open drawer, rummaging into it. She turned when the door clicked behind Callan.

Her cropped hair frizzed in a haphazard fashion, as if she too had slept in her office. But the stains on her coat and the circles around her gleaming eyes told him another story.

She gestured to a visitor chair. 'Just a minute please.'

A minute later, the door to her office opened again and in walked a trench-coat-and-hat-wearing detective.

Detective Inspector Declan Walsh raised his eyebrows at Callan. 'Afternoon.' His drawl echoed off the four walls in the tiny room.

The two burly detectives filled out the space, but Dr Brown didn't seem bothered. She slapped a couple of files on her littered desk and plopped into her seat.

It creaked, then bobbed a bit, giving her enough time to slip on her spectacles. 'Perfect. I called the two of you here because I simply do not have time to explain the same thing over and over.'

Reaching for two files, she sprawled them open. None of them flinched at the gruesome images of the crime scenes.

'This is Lucas Fraser and this is Anvit Nair. They were both killed after being bludgeoned by an object. A shinty stick in Mr Nair's case because we found it. The murder instrument for Fraser, as I mentioned, is different and we've yet to find it at the crime scene. However, as I told DI Cameron, I found a handkerchief in the deceased's pockets with a swab of blood on it. I thought it was a bit unusual given that the blood doesn't match Mr Fraser's.'

She held up a hand. 'So, as the detective suggested, I tested it against Mr Fraser's brother's DNA. Logan Fraser's DNA doesn't match the blood at all.'

Callan leaned in. 'He was never a primary suspect.'

Walsh, who'd been silent this entire time, interrupted. 'That blood swab couldn't have been the killer's either, surely? If they were injured, why would they wipe their blood on a handkerchief then push it in the victim's pocket?'

Dr Brown grinned. 'DNA profiling was still in the early

phases in the 1980s. Our killer was careful not to leave fingerprints, but they might have seen no issue with leaving their blood behind. However, what DI Walsh says is also a possibility. Fraser could have just lent his handkerchief to someone who'd cut themselves – someone completely unconnected to the case.'

'Or' – Callan's eyes glittered – 'he did loan the handkerchief to his killer when they were out in the peatland on an "excursion" and the killer just forgot about it.'

Dr Brown shrugged. 'That's your area to figure out. But I ran another test, since you'd said you'd found a picture of Douglas Reid and Lucas Fraser together.'

'There was some DNA on the stick, a hair that belonged to neither Andrew Mackay nor Anvit Nair.' She dropped her voice to a whisper, so the detectives had to bend to hear her. 'And the DNA on that hair and the DNA on Fraser's handkerchief are a *perfect match*.'

Stunned silence, astonishment and excitement popped up in the form of goosebumps on Callan's skin. He sat mum though, shocked.

'Holy hell!' Walsh gaped. 'Connected? So the killer must be in their fifties at least. And strong if they were able to take a young lad like Anvit down.'

Dr Brown scrambled over to the end of the table and dug out another file. 'Maybe. But it's possible the killer just caught him unawares. One smack on the right spot would've done the trick.' She held up a finger. 'Imagine you and I are speaking, then you turn your back on me. Perhaps we quarrel, and you ask me to leave. I turn around and so do you. But then I change my mind and strike you down. You're hurt and have nothing to protect yourself with bar your own body.'

Walsh hummed. 'Anvit had bruises on his arms which we deduced were from him trying to protect himself.'

'From the marks in the soil and the stains on his shirt, we know he turned over onto his stomach and scrambled a short distance into the woods. He was killed after that, so the killer followed him.' Dr Brown's eyes were wide as she explained. 'The entire thing would've taken five to ten minutes.'

She opened up another file and rifled through the pages before turning it to face them. 'If the killer was thinking straight, they'd have chosen a better spot to attack him and wouldn't have left the murder weapon behind. I think they would've buried him like they did Fraser if they hadn't been interrupted.'

Holding up a finger, she wagged it. 'What I'm getting at is this is a crime of passion. Both these murders are. The killer was angry at the victims, and that sort of anger can result in unusual strength. The mind knows no boundaries when the red mist descends.'

CHAPTER SIXTEEN

The drive to the bakery was a silent one – a formal kind of silence, Aileen would call it. Isla still sat withdrawn into her own thoughts, and Aileen didn't know whether to try to bring her out of her shell.

She wanted to figure out who'd tried poisoning Mr West, though there was no guarantee solving that mystery would get Andrew back if he had indeed been kidnapped.

At the bakery, she pulled up the CCTV footage. Dachaigh used the same software, so she knew how to sift through the data. 'When did Edith say the call came?'

Isla gave her the precise day and time, and Aileen skipped through the footage until she and Isla were watching the afternoon crowd come and go.

'This person had to have dropped by before to assess where the phone was and how you ordered the bags.'

Isla stared wide-eyed at the screen. 'Maybe I'll recognise them.'

Aileen nodded, and they continued to watch. As they did, the warm aroma of bread tickled Aileen's nostrils and tugged at her stomach, followed by an irresistible molten chocolate scent. How did Isla manage to be around this and not eat it all?

'There!' Isla snapped her fingers, drawing Aileen's attention back to their task.

She hurriedly paused the video. 'Damn it! I missed it.'

So they rewound the footage and this time, Aileen stared at the screen.

The timer in the bottom right-hand corner showed 4.25 p.m. The shop lay empty apart from Isla's assistant Susan, diligently cleaning the empty counter.

At 4.27 p.m. she stepped out of view, phone clutched to her ear.

Beside Aileen, Isla rolled her eyes. 'The amount of times I've asked her to keep her phone in her locker.' She sighed loudly. 'This'll teach her.'

As soon as Susan disappeared, the front door opened. The person had obviously been waiting for her to leave.

The hooded figure was most likely a lad, given his height. That was Aileen's first thought. He stood tall and wore a cap to hide his hair and face.

He hid himself from the camera lens but moved deftly behind the counter. Hesitating for a second, he picked up the telephone, then punched the buttons.

Aileen's breath caught, hoping to see some skin. But he'd pulled up the hood of his sweatshirt and wore gloves.

'He's memorised the phone number,' Isla muttered with some emotion. 'How could someone be so vile?'

Aileen reached over and placed an arm round Isla's shoulders. Isla leaned in, her red curls squashed against Aileen's brown ones. 'We'll find him.'

They watched the screen together. The entire while, the lad showed no skin, covered from head to toe in black.

He replaced the handset on the receiver and, without a backward glance, strolled out the way he'd come.

Susan returned a couple of seconds later, frowning.

Aileen whispered as they watched her resume her cleaning, 'Is it a long shot to ask if you've seen a person that looks like that?'

Isla shook her head. 'In all black? Do you know how many people own black trousers and hoodies?'

They sat in silence for a few minutes. 'Why don't we go through it again?' Aileen suggested.

They watched it again twice before Isla slapped her palms on the table. 'This is useless!'

Aileen rubbed circles on Isla's back. 'Let's slow it down and watch it again. How about some coffee?'

They settled down with steaming cups, the aroma soothing Aileen's cravings.

Aileen jostled in her seat before settling down, a thought forming in her mind. 'What happened when the bags were delivered?'

Isla rubbed her eyes. 'That day was a frenzy. I had to prepare cupcakes for a school trip and a couple of birthday cakes. I got in early, made the cupcakes and pastries the teacher had ordered and got Andrew to deliver them.'

Aileen took a sip. 'How did he seem then – Andrew? Was he stressed?'

Isla shook her head. 'He was himself.' A tear trickled from her eye, then she sobbed before wrapping her fingers around her mouth and steadying herself. 'Aye, he was himself. Cracked some stupid joke about those raspberry cheesecakes looking like blood. The eejit. I smacked him on the head and sent him away.'

A small smile graced Aileen's lips. 'Tell me, how are the bags delivered?'

'Andrew or someone collects them from one of Edith's people. They come here in a van.'

'Wrapped in plastic?' Aileen enquired.

Isla bobbed her head. 'Usually, but actually, now I think on it, these had been opened. I thought Andrew or Susan had done it. I didn't even realise it was a new batch until—' She cleared her throat. 'So you think someone picked up the parcel, tampered with it, and then put it in the stacks?'

Aileen mulled over what Isla had said. 'Why not just dump the poison in one of the paper bags behind the counter and leave?'

'He'd have to face the camera to do that. I keep them under the till and the camera looks directly at it.'

The lad knew about this arrangement then.

'Isla, did anyone looking like that work for you recently? Think about the height, the walking style.'

Isla huffed. 'I had some people in for work experience over the summer. But anyone could've told them how we work. Hell, Andrew could have; I could have. It's not really a secret where we keep our bags. Customers would see it too.'

Suddenly, Isla clicked her fingers. 'I have a camera facing the storefront. Edith drops the bags at the door early in the mornings. Why don't we go through that?'

Early for Isla meant four in the morning. Aileen couldn't fathom waking up at that hour. But then again, in her previous career, she'd often worked till that sort of hour, returning for a full working day at eight thirty the next morning.

No wonder she'd burned out and left it all behind on a whim in pursuit of this amazing life. A life that she was struggling to maintain.

Aileen navigated to the time slot they were looking for and rewound the footage.

'There – you've got it!' Isla pointed.

They slowed the video, leaning in as it played. A white van parked right in front of the store. The printing company's logo pasted on the side.

Despite the dark grainy images, they could see the burly van driver's face. He wore a dark cap that matched his uniform.

As soon as he fetched the bags from the back, a familiar hooded figure, hair still hidden beneath a cap, stepped into view of the camera.

Once again, he'd hidden all his skin, wearing a shapeless jacket. The van driver wouldn't question the lad's fashion choice, given the freezing temperatures.

The driver handed the parcel over, not asking for identification, just asking him to sign. These were paper bags, hardly gold. Then he climbed into his van and set off.

Watching the truck leave, the lad turned his back to the camera. He bent lower, taking out a small something from his pocket.

Isla smacked her fingers on her lips. 'Oh gosh, that's the poison!'

They couldn't see what he did, but when he was done, he stood up and crossed his arms.

Something about the lad's posture tickled Aileen's memory. However, she focused on the scene.

He'd brought the poison in a vial and planted it in a paper bag.

Hefting the bags up, he walked to the entrance of the bakery, closer to the camera. They could still only see his back.

The door though swung to the outside. So he had to turn to get the bags in and therein lay his mistake.

Aileen and Isla both gasped when the lad turned sideways, showing his side profile before ducking his head.

'I know him!' Aileen whispered. She'd never forget him. 'That's no *lad*.'

※

CALLAN BEGAN TO PACE, HIS MIND WHIRLING IN ALL directions as he processed Dr Brown's revelations.

What were they missing?

Walsh sat in the visitor's chair, fiddling with his hat. 'What do you reckon we do? My officers say there's no sign of Andrew at the McIntyres' place. He hasn't turned up for work. He hasn't gone back to his house. His housemates don't know anything about him. And we are nowhere close to finding him.'

Callan stopped pacing. 'So chances are he's been kidnapped. But there's no ransom note. Unless…' He let his sentence trail off.

Unless the murderer had struck again, his mind finished.

'We have to be missing something, a common link.' He gestured, frustration making his movements desperate.

Would it be Reid? At this point, that possibility seemed impossible. For one, the team hadn't found anyone at his mansion. They had searched it after his arrest the previous night.

Who were they missing? What were they missing?

'Look, here's what I think.' Walsh stood. 'Let's go speak with Reid – he might know something, and you haven't really questioned him about Anvit Nair.'

With no other lead to follow, the two detectives headed off in Callan's car.

The afternoon dragged on as people went about their daily duties.

All members of their respective teams had tried so hard to find Andrew. Forty-eight hours later, the chances of finding him lessened like sand through an hourglass.

Callan gripped the steering wheel tight. He would find Andrew – he had to.

The sunlight danced through the trees as their leaves fluttered in the breeze, drawing patterns on the car's bonnet. The road wound around a river, twisting and bending to its curves.

Half an hour later, they plopped their arses on hard chairs in front of a prison-garb-wearing Reid.

The man scowled at the detectives. 'Have you realised your mistake?'

Walsh placed his hands on the table. 'Stop playing around. Tell us what you know, what you've done.'

'I've done nothing,' he hissed, spittle flying from his mouth.

Jail was clearly a struggle for him. He hadn't shaved that morning, and his white stubble had grown like little spurts of grass on his pampered cheeks. His fingernails looked as if he'd been biting them all night. Dark circles made his eyes look heavy and worn.

Reid glared at them. 'Get me out of here!'

But his orders held no sway in jail.

Callan crossed his arms across his chest, knowing that his bulging biceps would be intimidating.

His ploy worked. Reid sat back, but still didn't drop his upturned nose. Walsh took off his hat and tucked it under his arm, perhaps not wanting to spoil it on the sticky table.

'Mr Reid,' he began, 'where were you the night Anvit Nair died?'

Reid glared at him. 'I know what you're trying to do. You're trying to intimidate me into confessing to a crime I didn't commit. You have no evidence, I know.'

Callan stared at the blank walls and steel furniture around them. It was a sad place to be, jail. He didn't pretend to know what it was like being behind bars, but he'd suffered in the prison of his mind.

He focused back on Reid. 'Where were you when Mr Nair was found dead in the woods near the college?'

'I was at a meeting, as I have told this detective countless times.' Reid pointed at Walsh. 'And' – he faced Callan to glare into his eyes; anger made the muscles in his forehead twitch – 'I also instructed my lawyer to contact your office and keep that innkeeper away. I have done nothing wrong.'

Callan smirked, lifting the left side of his lips. 'It was yer idea then to intimidate her. What did she do to scare ye so much?'

Reid tried to push away from the table, but one smouldering glare from Callan had him sitting right back down. The seat groaned under his weight.

'Look, the more you talk, the better things will go.' Walsh leaned in, placing his hands on the table. 'Tell us what you know, and we'll help you.'

But Reid wouldn't listen. His gaze travelled up and down, never settling on either of them. He was acting like a petulant child, throwing a temper tantrum because he couldn't have a cookie before dinner.

Callan and Walsh dealt with this often; it didn't faze them.

Callan turned to Walsh. 'His silence tells us a lot, doesn't it? It's a guilty conscience.'

Walsh chuckled. 'Aye, a guilty conscience. What was it he said about Anvit to his lawyer? Ah, *blessing he's gone*, a *thorn* in his side.'

Reid might have turned his eyes away, but his ears perked up.

He faced them again, thumped a fist on the table and said in a loud voice, 'I didn't kill him.'

But Callan knew he had more to say than that. 'Tell us where ye were the night Anvit Nair died.'

'As I told your colleague, I was in a meeting. I gave you contacts to cross-check my alibi.' He spoke like he was schooling a child.

'They were your employees, Mr Reid.' Walsh shook his head. 'Of course they would corroborate your statement if they want to keep their job.'

'I didn't threaten anyone – I didn't.'

Callan tutted at the lies. 'Why then did ye insist ye didn't know Lucas Fraser when first asked? You were clearly friends.'

'Because it was private. But I told you he was an important person in my life,' Reid said adamantly.

'Why did ye use his name to start those companies?' Callan persisted.

'It was his idea, okay? It was his idea to start Gammit Inc. Bloody hell! I did what he wanted to do,' Reid spluttered.

'And what was it he wanted to do with the money?'

'It was for that stupid wench! Isobel Murray. He would do anything for her, even steal. And that's precisely what he wanted to do with Gammit Inc.'

Callan took it all with a pinch of salt. 'You expect me to believe that Lucas Fraser wanted to start a tech company in a time when smartphones weren't even around?'

Callan might be an amateur at technology, but he knew smartphones hadn't been a thing in the 1980s. He wasn't an eejit, even if Aileen might contest that statement.

Reid placed his palms flat against the table, looking at the two detectives with sorrowful eyes. 'No, it wasn't about smartphones or apps or anything of that sort. He just wanted to steal money from people by threatening them, bribing them, blackmailing them. That was his plan. How much do you think scientists make?'

Walsh butted in. 'You mean to say that it was Lucas Fraser's dream to start a company to make money for his fiancée. A dream you picked up. Why would you do that? You hated his fiancée. And as a good friend, shouldn't you have urged him to take the legal path?'

Reid stared at his fingers, plucking at a piece of loose skin. He fell silent for a good two minutes. 'I was young, and I was heartbroken. I told you. I loved Lucas. After losing him, I lost sight of what was right and wrong.

'I wandered from one job to another, one city to another. And then when I became headmaster at the college. It was so… I saw… I wanted a change and left the place. I couldn't stand it. I couldn't stand the sniggers from my colleagues and I couldn't stand… couldn't stand…'

'What couldn't you stand?' Callan asked.

'Look, I had to leave that place. And then I remembered what Lucas had said about starting that company. And then I did it.' He swallowed, his wrinkled neck jiggling. 'You've got to believe me. Why would I lie? I have no one. All this money goes to no one. I never married, never had any children, don't have any family left.'

'What were Lucas Fraser's plans for Gammit Inc?' Walsh had pulled out his notepad, eyebrows set in a line as he wrote.

Reid hunched his shoulders. 'He was a scientist and dabbled in anthropology as an amateur. What he was good at was making friends and keeping them at a distance. Lucas knew every single thing about them. He maintained detailed accounts. Isobel Murray broke through his walls.

That's what I think. But she was rich. And I always wondered if that played a part in his feelings for her.'

Callan tilted his head. 'Did you ask him about it?'

'Not to his face. I wasn't sure he'd appreciate my nosiness, as he liked to say when I got too close. But out of all his friends, I was the closest, and he would go on and on about her. Lucas never mentioned if he really loved her or was with her because of her father. Then the Murray sisters went missing too, and I just let it all go. Let it stay in the past because I couldn't… I knew something – it was something she'd done. She's vile, I tell you, vile.'

Callan heard it, the present tense. 'Is?' he questioned.

'Nothing's going to happen to her. Nothing! Wealth, arrogance and unbridled anger – no one's touching her.'

Walsh stared Reid in the eye. 'Is. Do you know where she is?'

'No.' Reid pushed away from the table. 'I don't.' His eyes had curtained, hiding secrets once more.

Callan tried one last time. 'Look, she might be responsible for another murder – Anvit Nair's murder. We need to speak to her. Who is she? Isobel?'

Reid, head bowed, turned his back on the astonished detectives, heading to the guards who'd escort him back to his quarters.

Did what he'd said make sense, or was he pushing the blame onto someone who didn't have a voice to defend themselves? Perhaps, in his fit of rage, he had murdered the two sisters and Lucas. Maybe Millie was a casualty of what happened at Violet's Rose that night. And now he'd murdered his intern.

Maybe he was the one with anger issues.

Reid was certainly on the large side, broad and tall, hefty even. He would certainly be capable of smacking an eighteen-year-old over the head and killing him – and overpowering Lucas Fraser.

But at this point, they didn't have any evidence pointing towards Reid. Callan really hoped the DNA was a match.

But then a thought struck him and he pulled his mobile phone out and typed a message to Dr Brown. *'Does the DNA you found belong to a man or a woman?'*

CHAPTER SEVENTEEN

When Callan messaged to say her he'd call her back later, Aileen considered chewing his head off.

'He never picks up my calls – never!' She gestured frantically to a stunned Isla.

'Why don't we go to the police station ourselves?' Isla asked.

The two of them bundled into Aileen's car and sped down the road, heading for the market square.

Stepping inside the coffee-scented office, they found only Robert behind the reception desk.

Aileen hissed. 'Crap!'

Robert's eyes widened. 'Aileen! Isla! What's the matter?'

Aileen narrowed her eyes. 'Where is he?'

The police constable scratched the back of his head. 'Callan? He's at—'

Robert was saved from answering when a car engine rumbled into the silent street outside the police station.

Aileen watched as the two burly detectives got out of the car, mentally spewing curses at them.

The sun hung precariously close to the horizon. Another day, another sunset, and no sign of Andrew.

Aileen clutched her hands into fists. At least now they knew who had tried to poison Mr West at Isla's Bakery.

Callan walked towards the front door and saw her leaning on the doorframe. He frowned. 'What are ye doing here?'

'We've managed to do something you haven't,' she snapped back.

Walsh chuckled. 'It's good to know you're still as persistent.'

Isla sniggered next to a scowling Aileen. 'He's right, you know – you are tenacious.'

Aileen shook her head, and gestured for Callan to enter. 'We found out who tried to poison Isla's customer.'

Callan touched his fingers to Aileen's exposed hand. She jumped.

'It's freezing,' he said. 'First, coffee, and then ye tell us.'

THE TWO DETECTIVES AND ISLA SAT IN SILENCE, HANDS wrapped around steaming mugs as they watched Aileen pace the floor of Callan's small office, wary of the papers scattered around.

She would do what she had promised Isla. She would save Andrew, even if it was the most difficult task she'd ever undertaken. This was the new adventurous and courageous Aileen, the one who would fight to give a teenager the right to live a full life. Even if her own dreams of running the inn and staying in Loch Fuar were inching to an end.

Aileen swallowed the negative emotions roiling in her heart and turned to Callan. 'Isla and I were thinking of ways someone could have poisoned Mr West. And the only way is to have placed the poison inside the paper bags.'

Walsh set his mug on the table, the muffled thud ringing out like a drumbeat. 'We considered that option, but there was no opportunity for someone to poison one of the bags.'

Isla turned in her chair to face Walsh. 'That's not true. We saw it happen. It's in the CCTV footage.'

'CCTV footage?' Walsh frowned. 'I never saw anyone in that. I've been through it myself.'

Aileen opened her mouth to reprimand him for his sloppy job, but Isla cut her off. 'It took him a fraction of a second. That's all.' She held up a pen drive. 'I have a copy of the footage right here.' She dropped it into Callan's palm.

Aileen crossed her arms across her chest and studied the two detectives from under her nose. 'It's Langdon, in case you're wondering. *Langdon* tried to hurt Mr West.'

Callan plugged the pen drive into his computer and tapped on the keyboard with vigour.

Aileen didn't interfere to tell him what to do. Her mind replayed the previous night instead, when she'd returned to Dachaigh to find Langdon in the library.

'He was at Dachaigh too, the creep!' she mumbled. 'Standing there in the dark, looking at God knows what. That's how I recognised him in the video.'

Callan cursed from across the room. She ignored him again, assuming he was berating the computer as he usually did.

'Repeat that!' he roared from behind her, popping goosebumps on her skin.

Aileen whirled around. 'Excuse me?'

'Repeat what ye just said.'

'I said it's Langdon.' Aileen's head started to throb. She didn't fancy arguing with him.

'No, no.' He waved his hands. 'Ye just said Langdon came to Dachaigh in the middle of the night.'

Bloody hell!

Aileen sighed dramatically. 'It wasn't that late.'

'Late enough that it was dark,' Callan retorted. 'What did he want?'

Deer caught in headlights, Aileen gaped, unsure what to say. In the end, she went with the truth, shrugging it off like Langdon's presence hadn't scared her witless. 'Nothing. He just snuck in to Dachaigh before I returned – to bribe me. He wants me to focus my attention on the inn and not on him or his boss.'

Walsh stood up now. 'What exactly did he mean by that? Bribe you for what exactly?'

Not wanting to relay the conversation herself, she pulled out her phone and shoved it into Callan's hands. 'I've got the entire recording.'

'Good,' he snapped at her, deftly pressing keys to play the recording for everyone to hear. Was he finally learning tech?

A loud silence blanketed the room as three inquisitive pairs of ears focused on her and Langdon's voices.

Aileen continued her pacing, trying to slow down her nerves.

The door finally clicked shut behind Langdon and the recording ended.

Isla turned wide eyes to Aileen. 'Why didn't you tell me? This man's dangerous. He could've hurt you!'

Aileen switched to the Photos app and showed them the pictures she'd clicked of Langdon's car.

Walsh pointed at the number plates. 'That's weird. Why are they so clean when the rest of the car's a state?'

'Exactly.' She smiled, happy that he understood what she was trying to get at.

Callan didn't look amused. He gripped her arms so tight it would leave marks. 'Ye should've called us right away! Don't ye see? Anything could have happened to ye last night, anything! Ye're out there all alone with no neighbours. He could have done anything. The car I saw that night outside the pub looks just like this one. Bloody hell!'

He slammed his hands on the table. 'How many times do I have to ask ye, plead with ye to stay safe?'

Aileen hadn't come to Loch Fuar in search of safety or stability. She had come seeking adventure, seeking a new Aileen. And this new Aileen didn't back down. 'Look, there's something I've done. It's riled him up. We need to figure out what it is. Maybe it's the link to finding Andrew.'

Isla's eyes shone. She pulled her chair nearer to the table and looked at each of them in turn. 'What if Douglas Reid hasn't actually committed a crime? What if Langdon did it on his behalf?'

Walsh nodded, his hat bobbing up and down. 'That's a possibility we haven't yet explored.'

Callan sat back in his chair, hands caressing his prickly jaw. 'We'll do that. Let's get Langdon in for questioning. After all, we've questioned his boss but not him, and he is in all but name Reid's right-hand man.'

When Aileen strutted towards the door, keen to resume her search for Andrew, Callan's voice halted her mid-step.

'No, ye're staying right here out of harm's way.'

Hands on her hips, she wagged her finger at him. 'You can't keep me here!'

'I am a detective, and I swear, Aileen, the next time ye

find yerself in danger, or even close to it, I will lock ye up for obstruction of justice!'

His voice brokered no arguments. It floated into her ears loud and clear, a command. Aileen loved pushing her own limits but knew better than to press Callan's buttons when he was wound up like this. It would only end in disaster.

Isla and Aileen watched Walsh and Callan get into Callan's SUV and tumble down the road, eager to get Langdon in for questioning.

Isla draped an arm over Aileen's shoulders. 'They will find Langdon and the answers.'

Aileen wasn't sure, though. Ducking underneath Isla's arm, she stepped away. Then she gripped her friend's forearm and pulled her towards her own car.

'Come on! Callan warned me against getting into danger, but he didn't say anything about me doing some harmless sleuthing.'

He would lose the plot when he found out – she knew it. But Andrew had taken precedence over everything else.

So Isla got in the driver's seat, Aileen next to her, and they made for Langdon's house.

Isla, of course, being the queen of gossipmongers, knew who lived where. She maintained a safe distance from Callan's car, ensuring that he couldn't make them out in his mirrors.

Soon, they entered a plush neighbourhood which Aileen had visited during a previous case.

Houses stood a little apart, with wide gardens and long driveways packed with high-end cars. Some even had garages. Isla parked a few houses away from Langdon's.

From here, they could see Callan's car outside Langdon's massive property. No one occupied the vehicle. Aileen assumed they'd already found their target.

Curious, the two women got out and crouched low as they steadily made their way to the hedges opposite Langdon's house, Aileen leading the way, Isla following closely behind. Once or twice, Aileen slipped when her foot landed on green moss, but luckily, she didn't hurt herself.

Finally, they came to a car parked opposite the house. Aileen crouched behind it, then rose slightly to peer through its windows, her breath misting on the glass as Isla squashed in beside her, jostling her. They had done the same thing only a few weeks ago.

Aileen's heart began to hammer at the memory, pushing against her ribs. Her breath came in fast puffs as if she'd run all the way here. The sweet smell of wildflowers wafted through the air, but couldn't calm her down.

Isla's green eyes rounded and then narrowed to scan Langdon's property.

The front yard lay resplendent, beautifully manicured, just like the other properties. Aileen knew little about gardening, but from the look of it, most of the planted shrubs came from exotic places.

Her gaze travelled up the driveway where expensive, customised cars faced a grand house in the centre. Sleek lines and geometric patterns gave the house an air of efficiency.

Isla grasped Aileen's shoulder. 'Look!' she exclaimed in a whisper. 'The house seems empty.'

Empty? Aileen squinted through the glass. Whoever the owner of this car was, they hadn't bothered to clean it. Her view wasn't exactly high definition. She shifted a little and peered over the bonnet instead. Nothing hindered her eyesight now, helping her really see the place.

Dark windows, no light on the porch, just a silhouette against the sky. The chimney sat silent too, the cars quiet.

The house looked like an empty husk with all its open blackened windows.

Where were the detectives?

Bolder now and slightly worried, especially about her boyfriend, Aileen dashed across the street towards Langdon's place. Isla whispered, motioning Aileen to return to their hiding place, but Aileen paid her no heed. Isla followed them, muttering under her breath about the repercussions if Callan found them.

Aileen halted outside Langdon's gate studied the property again, her limbs turning heavy as the reality of where she was settled in. This was just how her nightmares began, right there, standing in that nothingness, knocking on a wooden door and stepping into a museum-like house.

When something rustled, she flicked on her torch, and flashed it into the hedges.

Two eyes – two *familiar* eyes – stared at her from the darkness. Aileen shrieked, images from her nightmares flashing through her mind.

Ice-cold veins slithered up her limbs, taking hold of all the warm blood in her, and her heart squeezed, every thud painful. She froze up entirely, unable to do anything but watch as Langdon leaped from the hedge like Superman on steroids. Before Isla could react and pull Aileen aside, he was on top of her, shoving her to the pavement.

Aileen's back crashed into the tarmac, yet still her limbs wouldn't move. Langdon reached for her arms, pulling her up to use her body as a shield.

A loud crash sounded from somewhere above them and Isla screamed the place down.

Aileen's ears buzzed, and then another sound came from Langdon and her eyes watched as if they weren't a part of her, like an omniscient observer.

Langdon fell to the ground beside her, clutching his

head. Poised with a backpack swinging from her arms, Isla loomed over them. Her terrified yet sure eyes met Aileen's.

Another pair of footsteps neared, the boots smacking against hard stones.

'Isla! Aileen!' a husky voice shouted. Walsh.

Where was Callan?

Like an angel manifested from heaven, a pair of hands encircled her, pulling her off the ground and into a familiar warm chest.

Aileen sagged, gasping for breath as if someone had choked all the oxygen from her lungs.

Callan ran his hands through her hair, then cupped her head and massaged it gently. 'Are ye alright?'

She didn't answer because her voice had left her along with the strength in her legs.

The crackle of a radio met her ears, followed by the clicking of handcuffs as Walsh led Langdon towards Callan's car.

Isla drew Aileen from Callan's chest and said, 'You take care of Langdon. I'll take her back.'

Callan's dark eyes ran over Aileen. 'Get her to Dr Macdonald please.'

Instead of reprimanding Aileen for what she'd done, Callan bent until his forehead pressed against hers. He looked Aileen in the eye, his worried gaze caressing her, so warm. Then he leaned in and pressed a tender kiss to her lips.

'Ye'll send me to an early grave, Ms Mackinnon.' Then he turned and walked away, eyes focused on the man who had just tried to hurt her for perhaps the second time in less than a week.

She hoped all this trouble paid off.

❋

'No comment.'

Callan wanted to yank his hair out. This is what he'd been doing for the last thirty minutes. He'd expected Langdon to talk, but so far he'd been disappointed.

Here they sat in the eventless interview room, he and Walsh, banging their heads against the brick wall that was Langdon.

Walsh leaned in and placed his hands over the files spread between them.

'Where were you between four and seven thirty Wednesday evening?'

Langdon glanced at his lawyer who gave a slight nod. 'In my office.'

'Can anyone confirm that?'

Langdon sighed. 'The CCTV can.'

Callan smiled caustically at the man. 'Oh, but there isn't any CCTV in your office, is there? Nor is there any at the back entrance that has a staircase leading directly up to the fifth floor where you and your boss work?'

Langdon laughed. 'It's a fire exit!'

'And ye could still use it. Have yer car waiting for you on the road and drive to the woods, do the deed and then leave. After all, Anvit's death, as yer boss described it, was a *blessing*.'

Langdon's smirk vanished. He scowled. 'He said it, I didn't.'

Callan changed course. 'Where is Andrew?'

'Who?'

He'd had it with this man. Callan imagined wrapping his hands around Langdon's neck and smacking it against the desk till he talked. Aye, he'd become that frustrated.

Hoping to try another approach, he reached for a closed file containing images of Langdon at Isla's Bakery in his all-black outfit, avoiding the camera lens.

He sprawled those out above images of Anvit's and Lucas's bodies and their respective crime scenes.

'What's this?'

Langdon tilted his head to study the pictures. Another silent communication with his lawyer later, he said, 'A good bakery.'

Callan stubbed at the black silhouette. 'Who is this?'

As if seeing the figure for the first time, Langdon narrowed his eyes. 'Er, can't say. The picture's *hazy*.'

Walsh smirked. 'Just like your memory, I think.'

Langdon spread his fingers wide, in mock confusion. 'I don't know what you're getting at.'

Done with this shite, Callan shuffled through the pictures and found the one with Langdon's side profile. 'Recognise this eejit?'

Langdon opened his mouth to snap a snarky retort when his lawyer held him back. 'No comment.'

Ah, finally. Seeing the gap in Langdon's armour, Callan pushed. 'These are the medical reports of the tests carried out on Mr West. He tested positive for a dose of potassium cyanide. We think the poison might have been sprinkled on the scones after they'd been baked,' he lied.

'Ha! Didn't think you sods were so empty up here.' Langdon tapped the side of his head, smirking at Callan. 'The baker would have twenty poisoned customers that way.'

Callan burst out laughing. 'Funny you've given it such thought, Mr Langdon. I never mentioned *twenty* scones.'

Langdon pushed away from the table. 'You're putting words in my mouth! I never said anything about paper bags or twenty scones—'

Paper bags?

He rambled on as the tape recorder recorded the entire interview.

Callan and Walsh had caught the bastard for poisoning a random man. But for two murders?

'He coerced me. Threatened to fire me,' Langdon continued, his eyebrows knitted into a plea, his voice whiny. 'You have to believe me.'

After all the times he'd lied? Fat chance!

Walsh gestured for Langdon to stop. 'Tell us who, where, why?'

The lawyer leaned in, hands palms down on the table. 'My client would request your protection against the injustices his employer has inflicted on him.'

'Who, where, why?' Walsh repeated.

Langdon's eyes darted to his lawyer's tired ones. 'Mr Reid said I had to keep Ms Mackinnon away. He said if she nosed about the business, it would all go belly up.'

Callan pulled out his notepad. 'And?'

'So he asked me to speak to her. She didn't listen. I tried – twice. And then... I offered monetary help, knowing she's struggling with the inn.'

Callan gritted his teeth and stopped himself from lashing out at the man. He didn't want to comment on Aileen's circumstances given the conflict of interest.

Walsh rode to his rescue. 'How would you know about Ms Mackinnon's financial situation?'

Langdon pursed his lips. 'My boss told me. Mr Reid told me.'

His eyes didn't meet either of theirs and he wrung his fingers.

'We'd appreciate the truth,' Walsh snapped.

'Er... I called the bank. On Mr Reid's orders, I swear!'

That swine!

'And you threatened Ms Aileen Mackinnon?'

Langdon shook his head. 'No, I merely suggested she take another path out of pure goodwill.'

Callan growled out, 'And what about almost running her over?'

Eyes bulging out of their sockets, Langdon shook his mane of hair. 'I did no such thing! I am not a murderer.'

'That remains to be seen.' Callan pulled out the complaint Aileen had launched and the voice recording.

He played it in the room. They questioned Langdon again, but he stayed firm.

'I planted the poison as per Mr Reid's instructions and visited Ms Aileen Mackinnon at the inn, which, as far as I know, is legal. However, I didn't kill anyone and I certainly didn't attempt to run her down.'

A knock sounded at the door and Robert peered in. 'A minute?'

Callan shut the door a little too forcefully behind him. 'What?'

'Langdon doesn't own anything major in the UK. He's got some properties in Germany and a house in the south of France. There's a flat in London but it's rented out.'

Callan huffed. 'To whom?'

'A decent couple – I checked. They look clean. We called them up too. They said Langdon's agent handles their rent issues, if they have any.'

'Blast! This leads us nowhere.'

Robert's shoulders drooped. 'What can we do next?'

Not much. Where he'd hoped for a clue, he'd just found another dead end.

'Let's run through our data again. Maybe there's something we missed?'

They had done it countless times already and Callan knew they'd missed nothing. Andrew had vanished off the face of this earth. Just like Blaine.

CHAPTER EIGHTEEN

Aileen sipped at the hot chocolate Isla had made for them. The bakery was empty at this time of night. Darkness crept in through the glass windows, the heater barely keeping the freezing temperatures at bay.

Dr Macdonald had prescribed her some painkillers and a sleeping pill since she hadn't slept well in days. He'd also asked her to seek counselling and assured her that her PTSD was a natural response to what she'd been through. Apart from a few scrapes, Langdon hadn't caused much damage, but inside, anxiety ate her up.

Callan hadn't allowed them to stay for the interview, but he had told them the gist of what Langdon had said.

The slimeball had firmly denied having killed anyone. He had confessed to poisoning Mr West out of compulsion. But they had no evidence to connect Langdon with the murders. Aged two at the time, he certainly couldn't have murdered Lucas Fraser.

Aileen pushed the cup away. 'Sitting here wallowing is useless!'

Isla stared at the steam rising into the cold air from the cup. 'If Langdon doesn't have him, who does? Oh, where is that lad?'

They joined hands, seeking strength from the other. 'Maybe they'll find him—' Aileen tried to sound convincing and failed.

'He isn't at Langdon's house!' Isla teared up. 'Where could he have gone? Who else is there?'

Despair settled in with anxiety, fraying her nerves. Maybe she should go home and take the sleeping pill. Her brain had fried into lightweight popcorn.

'Let's just call it a night,' she whispered, hoping to convince herself.

Isla tightened her hold on Aileen. 'Take out your yellow notepad,' she urged.

A protest sat on the tip of Aileen's tongue, but she gulped it down at the insistence in Isla's voice and took out her notepad, making space for it on the table. 'What are we looking for?'

Isla flipped to an empty page and proffered a hand for the pencil. Then she drew two circles with Anvit and Lucas written in the centre. The circles overlapped to form a common area. Pointing at it, Isla asked, 'Who's a common link between both?'

Aileen narrowed her eyes. 'Er, Douglas Reid.'

'No one else?'

'Nope.' Aileen leaned in.

'Okay, now what about Lucas Fraser?' Isla listed down the Murray sisters, Mr Winters, Lucas's brother and his wife in the right-hand circle.

'Even if Mrs Fraser didn't know Lucas, let's keep her on there,' Aileen said. 'Now, for Anvit Nair.'

Here, they listed Langdon, Andrew and his friends, plus Anvit's teachers, namely Professor Moira Robertson.

Aileen flipped a few pages back. 'I remember Zay saying they didn't see eye to eye.'

That woman had seemed upset by Anvit's death when Aileen had run into her at the crime scene.

They took a minute to study each name on the small chart, then Aileen plucked the pencil from Isla and ticked each one off. 'We don't know much about the sisters. Callan's spoken to Reid, Langdon and the Frasers. I've spoken with Andrew and his friends. They were up to something, a plan to derail Gammit Inc. That's what Anvit was doing too.'

Isla caught on quick. 'But we don't know if he died because of it.'

One name on the list glared at her. An unturned stone. 'Moira Robertson. She's the only one on our list who I haven't looked into. She's Andrew's teacher as well, isn't she?'

Isla curled her lip. 'He hates her. Keeps complaining when she gives an assignment. But the police said they spoke to the college and she's away on a conference. They cross-checked it too and confirmed she's in London.'

She might be in Timbuktu, but Aileen would speak with her. 'Why don't we go to her place?'

Isla's eyes lit up with purpose. 'A stakeout?'

STAKEOUT IT WAS. ALL THEY HAD TO DO FIRST WAS FIND where she lived. Since the college sat in the next town, Isla didn't know any details about that area.

Tasked with a goal, Aileen focused on what she had to do to achieve it, like a horse with blinders on. She parked her car in the lay-by and texted Finlay.

'Where does Robertson stay?'

Being a typical teen, the answer came at once.

'Is he always online?' Isla exclaimed.

They rolled their eyes at the energies of youth and pulled out onto the road.

Half an hour later, Aileen passed by Andrew's house, which had all the lights on, and turned down several other lanes leading close to the dark abyss of the woods. She couldn't begin to guess where the tops of the trees ended and the sky began.

Most cottages sat in silence, their owners tucked in their beds. Sleep escaped the women inside the car though.

'There!' Isla exclaimed a few moments later, pointing out the window. 'That's her.'

Moira Robertson lived well. Each of the spacious houses in this neighbourhood had a front garden with well pruned bushes next to a small driveway that fitted one car, and Moira's was no different. Either she liked gardening or she hired someone to do it. All in all, her house looked well cared for.

But Aileen couldn't say the same for her car, which was coated in mud – it was all over the number plate and tyres and had even sprayed up onto the body.

Isla pointed at the car. 'Do you think she's just lazy or…?'

'It's the Highlands – there's bound to be grime on the roads. Besides, she's old – I wouldn't expect her to clean her car every other day.'

Contrasting the grimy vehicle, the rest of the stone structure pulled at Aileen's domestic side. Not a single speck of green moss or ivy clung to the beautiful stonework. A wilted flower sat on the windowsill on the first floor, reminding every passer-by that the owner wasn't home.

Aileen reached for the door to get out and sneak around.

'Are you crazy?' Isla stopped her. She pointed to the houses around them. 'It's almost eleven at night and in such a tight community, it's best not to show your face.'

A neighbour, who, like them, struggled with insomnia might get suspicious and call the police.

Aileen frowned. 'So what, we just sit here?'

'No! Why don't we come back tomorrow? Maybe speak to the neighbours.'

She didn't want to wait, wanted to do *something*, but sitting here wouldn't accomplish anything, and Aileen could hardly travel to London just to ask Moira a few questions. Maybe Isla was right and the neighbours might know more about her – like whether she hailed from Loch Fuar. If she didn't, it seemed unlikely she'd have killed Lucas Fraser.

What they had learned from Moira's home had been what they'd already known. She worked, earned well, and maintained a good house, but there was no ostentatious display of wealth, no obvious reason she would be disliked by her students.

Aileen started up her car just as a pair of headlights turned onto their street. At once, she and Isla ducked to hide from any spying eyes.

To Aileen's horror, the car halted beside her, engine still rumbling.

She heard the door open and shut. A pair of heels clicked on the tarmac – loud smacks in the dead night.

Isla gave in to the seduction of curiosity and peeked out the window. 'Oh! It's an old lady.'

Unable to bear it any longer, Aileen too looked up and saw Moira Robertson emerging from a taxi. She held her breath as the driver hefted a suitcase and a duffle bag out the boot, all matching the bottle green of her car, then drove off, leaving Moira on the road.

For a moment, Aileen considered getting out the car and helping the delicate old lady. But Moira, walking on stilettos, lugged her suitcase off the road, the duffle swinging from the crook of her arm.

A solitaire on her finger caught the streetlight, glistening. Maybe she was married.

Aileen sat up in her seat, eyes trained on the chic woman. The small iron gate creaked open in welcome, and Moira stepped inside. She kicked it shut behind her and turned, perhaps to lock it in place.

Instead of bending though, her eyes cut straight through the cool air and mild fog, latching onto Aileen's.

Aileen gasped, sure Moira had read her entire soul.

The professor's mouth tightened and she swished around, walking into her home and clicking the door shut.

Hands trembling, Aileen started up her car and sped away, thoroughly spooked.

CALLAN'S CAR BOBBED OVER THE STONE BRIDGE.

Exhaustion had finally set into his bones. He had contemplated heading towards his flat, but his heart wouldn't let him.

Here he was heading straight to Dachaigh, hoping for he didn't know what.

This investigation seemed to be leading nowhere. It seemed like eons had gone by, though it had only been a few days. He felt stuck in a vortex of listlessness and restlessness, his mind and gut telling him the clues he'd found led him all back to square one.

Putting Langdon behind bars had been somewhat of a

reprieve because he had found justice for Isla's Bakery at least. But he still didn't know who had tried to almost kill Aileen by running her off the road. Walsh had taken Langdon's car to an expert to analyse. Would there be a match with the skid marks?

As for Andrew… Callan just didn't want to think those thoughts anymore. They'd been stuck in his head, repeating on a loop like an unwanted song.

Daniel had called again, his husky voice woven with worry.

And Blaine… Callan ran a hand through his hair. That was another case he just didn't want to think about.

The whitewashed stone inn emerged from the darkness, bringing a smile to his lips. Aileen had left all the lights on, which meant she was still up.

He missed her, especially now he knew she'd been trying to solve Andrew's case. All those months ago in spring, he'd considered the new innkeeper a thorn in his side. And now, he wanted to bounce ideas off her, knowing she'd have a lot to add.

Callan brought his car to a halt in the car park and hiked to the back door.

Aileen had wrenched it open before he knocked. She leaned against the doorframe, brown hair loose, billowing in the slight breeze.

'Callan!' She hugged him tight.

Shutting eyes that stung with tiredness, Callan took a long breath.

Aileen gestured for him to enter and asked, 'Hungry?'

His stomach growled, answering for him, though, he was more ravenous for her company.

'I haven't eaten either,' she confessed.

Five minutes later, both sat side by side at the table, stuffing their faces with food, not uttering a word.

Callan shoved it all down with water. 'How are ye?'

Aileen swallowed the last bite and intertwined her fingers with Callan's. Her soft skin against his gave him some respite. 'As good as I can be in this situation, Callan.' She traced patterns on the back of his hand. 'Isla's working hard but, well, it feels like we're running into one brick wall after the other.'

Callan squeezed her fingers. 'At least we got Langdon in for poisoning Isla's customer.'

Aileen raised her hands, palms up. 'What about the other things? Who's the connection between Lucas and Anvit? Who is that old and connected to both?'

She reached for her satchel and pulled out her notepad. 'Isla came up with this brilliant idea.' She showed him the drawing of the two circles with Lucas and Anvit's names.

'Isla drew these. The only link we know for sure is Douglas Reid.'

Studying the diagram, Callan gave it some thought. Then he asked for a pencil and drew a third circle, labelling it 'Andrew'. 'Whichever way you look at it, Aileen, there is no connection between Andrew and Douglas Reid except for Anvit, and we haven't really checked that connection.'

Aileen nodded with understanding. 'You mean you haven't really checked why Andrew would keep secrets for his murdered friend.'

Callan nodded. 'He would speak with you, at least, wouldn't he? He trusts ye.'

Aileen thought back to the last conversation she'd had with Andrew just before Mr West had dropped by and bought his poisoned scone. 'I tried. He wasn't really telling me much though. He spoke in riddles.'

Callan clicked his fingers. 'The data. Anvit's data that

Leith had. What did he say to us that day, right here on the kitchen counter?'

'They were trying to find something about Douglas Reid, weren't they? That's one common element between Andrew, Anvit and the rest of their friends,' Aileen said excitedly. 'But Andrew and Anvit were the only two in the woods that night.'

'So they knew something more than the other three,' Callan completed her thought. 'That's why Andrew's missing.'

Aileen bobbed her head. 'That's why Anvit's killer has *kidnapped* Andrew.'

It all made sense now, the pieces falling into place. But where was Andrew now? Who had killed Lucas Fraser and Anvit Nair?

'Why do you think they wouldn't involve their friends in whatever they were doing in those woods that night? Why was it a secret between them?' Aileen wondered out loud.

Callan scratched his head, not sure how to answer that. 'Maybe Anvit and Andrew were close? We don't know.'

Aileen rifled through the pages and asked, 'What about Anvit's devices? Who has them now?'

'They're in evidence, of course.' Callan shrugged. 'But I think ye have a backup of the data, don't ye?'

Aileen grinned. 'I certainly do. And so do Leith and the rest of them. They had access to those devices even after Anvit's death.'

'And they were being careful,' Callan added. 'They set up tracking apps on each other's devices for their own safety.'

Aileen held up a finger. 'What if the tracking app wasn't just to protect them but also to protect their data?'

Callan's forehead wrinkled into a frown. 'Ye mean the

data is important?'

Aileen nodded. 'But why would they steal Anvit's devices then? If they were as savvy as they seem to be, they would have backups of Anvit's data.'

Callan understood what she was trying to get at. 'They didn't want the data to fall into police's hands.'

She clicked her fingers. 'Exactly! What did Leith say about going to the police with the data? Can you remember what he said?'

'Right.' Callan's sharp memory recalled Leith's exact words. He condensed them for Aileen. 'He said Douglas Reid had friends in influential places.'

Aileen dashed away from the table, heading for her chambers.

Callan shook his head at her impatience. This woman was too much when on a mission.

She returned, running down the stairs at breakneck speed with a slick laptop in her hand. The device clattered onto the table and she shoved it open, fervently tapping at the keys. 'It has to be something in the data here – it has to,' she said, eyes trained on the screen.

Callan swivelled his chair closer to hers until his shoulder brushed hers, staring as she scrolled and clicked. Her pace seemed dizzying to him.

They went through all of Anvit's documents, then checked his emails and his calendar entries. Finally, they landed on his messages.

'There!' Aileen exclaimed. 'Look at that!'

They had stumbled upon text messages Andrew had sent Anvit. The last one was on the night he died.

'This confirms they had plans!' Aileen clapped her hands. 'We're getting somewhere!'

Anvit had sent the first message to Andrew. *Are you there?'*

He'd answered in a minute. *'Nope. You?'*

'Yup.'

Then there was a difference of five minutes when Andrew had written again. *'Left from the library. Sorry got late.'*

He'd followed it up with. *'Ten to get to you.'*

That had been the end of their conversation.

Callan frowned at the screen. 'Maybe Anvit wanted to tell Andrew a secret?'

'Half past seven's when I got there, I think.' Aileen placed her chin on her palm. 'If it took him ten minutes to get to the woods, Anvit had to be loitering there for longer, perhaps fifteen to twenty minutes.'

Callan pursed his lips. 'These messages confirm Andrew had been in the library like Zay said.'

They each lapsed into silence, wondering if Andrew had saved his life by running late. Or had he mistakenly assured Anvit's murder?

Callan stared at the screen, hands on the table. He wasn't sure whether he should suggest anything about technology, but he ventured, mumbling, 'What about search history?'

Aileen turned to him, gaping. 'Search history?' she repeated.

Callan opened his mouth to deny what he'd suggested but swallowed his words when Aileen flung her arms around him to pull him closer. 'You have learned a thing or two!' she whispered in his ears, smacking her lips against his. 'You're brilliant, you know that? Sometimes,' she added as an afterthought.

Aileen clicked through to the search history.

The list went on and on, like Callan's when he'd procrastinated before heading to the grocer's. They scrolled and scrolled, Aileen's gaze zipping across the screen.

At that speed, Callan couldn't catch every word, but his eyes latched on to the common themes Anvit had searched for. He'd gone through Douglas Reid's background. And surprisingly, he'd also done a lot of research on Moira Robertson, scouring for data on her educational background and where she'd taught before joining the college.

Aileen then toggled to the data Anvit had compiled from Reid's app – the same app which compiled data of all its users unethically. She typed in Moira Robertson and found her details at once. 'So she uses this app.'

Callan made a note of it.

Aileen pointed at a map. 'Look – she's been logging in almost every day from this weird spot.'

The spot appeared to be in the middle of nowhere, the map covered entirely in green.

'Maybe there's an issue with the data?' Callan asked.

'Maybe. Besides, the only search Anvit has done about her is regarding her educational background and career. It's nothing incriminating, and it doesn't seem like she had anything to do with Lucas Fraser.'

Callan believed they had the same killer on their hands, and they couldn't place Moira Robertson in Loch Fuar forty years ago – she'd apparently been busy studying for her degree, graduating with honours from Oxford in 1985.

Aileen sat back, shoulders slumped, completely dejected. She slammed her laptop closed and faced Callan. 'Now what?'

He didn't know, but it felt good brainstorming with his partner. If tech didn't help, good old paper might. He pointed to Aileen's yellow notepad. 'What've ye got in there?'

Aileen flipped to the page where she had penned the chronology of events the day Andrew went missing.

They studied the data, heads pressed together, trying to

find anything: a loophole in the timeline, missed information or an unusual situation. Their eyes darted back and forth as they flipped through the pages.

Fifteen minutes later, they were right back where they'd started. Callan dropped his head in his hands and considered resting his throbbing head on the cool wood of the table and just sleeping the night away.

Aileen's soft hands gripped his shoulders and squeezed in urgency. 'The library, Callan! Look here.' She stabbed a finger at the timeline. 'The day I found him – I mean, the day I found Anvit and Andrew in the woods, Zay said Andrew had been in the library. His messages just confirmed it. And look what it says here!'

Callan too had read the page. He finished Aileen's thought. 'The night he said goodbye to his friends after dinner and later went missing, he'd been to the library.'

A string of hope and alertness wound through all the fatigue. 'We haven't really checked the library, simply because it's a place where there are so many students every single day. Where would you hide in there?'

Aileen narrowed her eyes, fingers drumming away on the table. 'He might not be *hiding* there,' she said slowly. 'But he might have left a clue there.'

It made sense to at least check the place out. It was the only place they hadn't searched thoroughly.

Collectively Aileen and Callan stared at each other and spoke at once. 'Let's go to the library!'

The library couldn't possibly be open this late in the night. But they had to try, given it was their last hope. Callan might have to flash his badge.

Together, they rushed out of Dachaigh, heading for Callan's car.

Would they find Andrew that very night?

CHAPTER NINETEEN

Fatigue forgotten, Aileen and Callan raced to Loch Heaven.

The car's headlights hardly illuminated the roads, but Aileen caught sight of a feral eye or two from deep within the woods. There were no other cars on the road. It was just them in the middle of nowhere, armed with purpose.

Aileen's heart thudded with anticipation. Real hope blossomed this time. They would find Andrew.

They'd called Walsh, who'd promised to send a police constable and find the librarian. He'd been unable to come himself, preoccupied with another case.

The poor visibility didn't hinder Callan's pace. He pressed down hard on the accelerator, his car hugging the curves of the road, and they arrived at the library in thirty minutes rather than the usual forty-five.

There a police officer, dressed in uniform, stood next to a lean woman with a bunch of keys in her hand and a scowl on her face. The light from Callan's car played with her features, deepening the wrinkles on her pale skin.

Aileen and Callan approached her. She curled her lip. 'What is the meaning of this? Waking me up this late?'

Callan flashed his badge and thanked her. 'We think there's a clue to finding Andrew Mackay in the library.'

The woman had been ready to spit fire at them. Now she sighed, shoulders loosening. 'Why didn't you say so before? I'm Mrs Carpenter, Head Librarian. Come on.' She waved them towards the building.

Andrew was definitely in her good books.

Carpenter inserted a long thick key into the wooden door of the library and it creaked open with the sound that only old doors possessed. The timber had seen its share of history; scrapes and bruises littered its plane.

Inside a click echoed – the press of a button – and the entire library illuminated in radiant gold.

Shelf after shelf lined the walls, right from the ceiling to the floor, all of them brimming with books.

The entire library was resplendent in beautiful rich browns, from the shelves to the antique desks to the numerous mismatched chairs placed around them. Artistic Victorian lamps sat in the centre of each table, while above loomed bright, practical lights.

Aileen and Callan entered side by side, the police constable trailing behind them. Aileen gaped at the books and Callan scowled. This was a wonderland for Aileen, for sure. If only she'd had such a library when she'd gone to college. She sighed.

Callan gestured to Carpenter. 'Do you know where Andrew sat the night he disappeared?'

She held up one bony finger. 'Andrew is a creature of habit – he always chooses the same seat. Follow me.'

Their boots echoed off the wooden floorboards. Carpenter's practical pumps made no noise – perfect for walking in a library – as she took them to the last table in the long room and pointed at a chair in the corner. 'This is where he sat, every single time. He says it's the quietest place in the library.'

Aileen noticed it was a corner from where he could see the rest of the room clearly.

Callan approached the long desk, slipping on gloves. 'I'll have a look at this.' He crouched next to the chair and pressed his hand to the underside of the desk.

Poking and probing, his hand travelled around, looking for any sign Andrew had hid something there. He beckoned for the police constable and they together began to assess the underside of the base.

Aileen made a face when they found a couple of pieces of chewing gum plastered underneath. But apart from that and a few scrapes, they found nothing. Aileen peered at the maze of markings on the desk. People had drawn on it, scribbling their names – a desk full of history.

Nothing stood out to her as pertaining to Andrew, Anvit or Lucas Fraser. Nothing pointed to the killer either.

Carpenter stood to one side, arms crossed, eyeing the two police officers. Though she didn't hurry them along.

Finally, they approach the chair Andrew sat at. Callan asked, 'Do you move these chairs around?'

Carpenter shook her head. 'It's been here ever since Andrew last sat on it.'

Callan and the police officer flipped the chair over to study its underside, then its legs, the armrest, the backrest, the seat and found nothing. It was just a normal chair. Were they barking up the wrong tree again?

Hope deflated like air oozing out of a pricked balloon.

They rested the chair back on the floor.

Aileen crossed her arms and looked around her. Books – so many books. Books that held secrets, stories and possibilities. An idea struck her. 'What about the books he took out that night? Do you remember what they were?'

Carpenter tilted her head, thinking. 'Not off the top of my head, but I could find out for you.'

'That would be great, thank you.'

They followed Carpenter back to the check-out counter. Behind the desk sat an ancient computer. She tapped a few keys, pulled up Andrew's file and scrolled. 'He didn't take out any book the night he was last here.'

Callan leaned his arms on the counter. 'Do ye remember what he was doing while he was here?'

Drawing in a wrinkled lower lip, she gnawed on it. 'Not many students were in that night. Andrew was, of course, and I shushed a few sniggers and whispers pointed at him. He sat aloof in that corner. And I didn't have the heart to disturb him. I don't believe he would have hurt Anvit. I…' She rested her face in her palm. 'I can't remember. I'm sorry,' she said, still not looking at them.

Aileen wondered where he could have hidden the data. A desk or a chair was too obvious and glaringly easy to find. 'Was there someone with Andrew that night?' she asked. 'Did he speak with anyone else?'

Carpenter shook her head. 'No one that I'm aware of.'

Callan straightened. 'What about the night Anvit Nair died? Wednesday. Do ye have a log for that night?'

She swivelled to the computer screen again, squinting and typing.

Callan walked round to her side, peering over her shoulder at the screen. 'There. What is that?' He pointed.

'That's the book he was issued on Wednesday. He returned it the night he last came here.'

Aileen clicked her fingers. 'Where is that book?'

Again, their brigade followed Carpenter, marching

across the floorboards. The police constable's thick shoes smacked the hardest in the silent room.

Carpenter led them through the maze of aisles, walking for what seemed like miles, until they reached the far end of the library again. This time they circumvented the massive bookcase that cordoned off this side of the library from the back. Here were several dusty old shelves, with equally smudged glass doors. Inside, Aileen made out tattered books with missing spines and torn covers. Some still had their hardcovers on but with dog-eared edges.

Carpenter frowned. 'Strange,' she muttered.

'Strange?' Aileen echoed.

Carpenter tugged at a string. A dull light flickered to life, humming overhead.

'These are old books – old in the sense that we don't need them anymore.' Carpenter picked up one from beside her. 'This one, for example – not only is it damaged, but it's an older edition of the Companies Act which no one would actually need. We keep these titles here until they're collected for recycling.'

'So they're still technically a part of the library?' Aileen asked rhetorically.

When Carpenter placed the book back, a cloud of dust rose.

What would Andrew need with tattered old books unless he was using them to hide a clue? And why hadn't the police found it on him after Anvit's death? Could he have hidden it somewhere in the woods on his way to their meeting?

Carpenter led them round the front shelf and Aileen gasped. Five more long bookcases stood one behind the other – each of them filled to the brim.

They walked to a shady corner, then came the jangle

of keys as Carpenter sorted through her set, looking for the right one.

Aileen felt like she was in the forbidden part of the library – the sort of place where books would be chained to the shelves, as they once had been back in the day.

They watched the older woman try one key after another until, finally, one clicked and the glass frame opened with a puff of dust. Beside them, the police constable, who had been quiet all this time, let out a loud sneeze.

A row of books, most with missing spines, stood in a row, lined up like soldiers on parade. Studying the chit in her hand, Carpenter pulled out the fourth book. 'This is what he took out.'

It was an old telephone directory – of little use in the twenty-first century.

Callan picked up the book with his gloved hands. 'Why don't we take it back to the desk and study it there?'

They returned to the library where Callan placed it gently down on the table, without disturbing a speck of dust on it. Then he extracted another pair of gloves from his pocket and handed them to Aileen. 'If there's a clue in there, I need it as evidence, and I don't want ye to leave any fingerprints behind.'

Carpenter pushed a book stand towards her. 'Use this. It's what we use for older manuscripts.'

Placing the book on the right side, she opened the flap. Despite her gloves, Aileen felt the coarseness of the paper underneath her fingers.

She turned the page, a thin fluttery leaf, as carefully as she might stroke a butterfly. Just like a butterfly's wings, Aileen worried that the paper would crumple and tear.

The book, a doorstopper, was easily a thousand pages long. Aileen flipped through one page and then the next, studying every margin and space between the lines.

A few lines were highlighted, some marks scrawled in the margin. She deduced they didn't belong to Andrew but someone who'd used this directory decades earlier.

Could there be a connection between Lucas Fraser and this book? Aileen shrugged. That seemed too far-fetched.

She studied the date on the directory – *1970*.

When she fluttered to page twenty, Callan made a noise. 'This will take ye all night!'

He jostled her aside and shut the book. Tilting it on its side, he placed the spine onto the flat desk and studied the pages squashed between the front and back covers.

Aileen raised her eyebrows at him and he smirked, lifting the left side of his lips in a way she'd once found annoying. 'I never liked to study much. And, well, I'd stick notes into my books, so I'd know what part was important. I'd read it before the day of the exam.'

Aileen rolled her eyes at his laziness while he ran his finger against the bumpy cluster of pages then stopped right in the centre.

'Ah!' He settled the book down on the table open at that page, dusting a crumble of mud. 'There you go.'

Aileen studied the book. Neatly inserted between the tight binding was a sheet of paper. It hadn't turned brown or spotty; nor was it coarse like the rest of the book. The smooth paper shone under the overhead light.

A collective gasp rose from their small group.

Callan picked it up. Aileen too wanted to read the scribble on the chit – her eager eyes found the lettering and—

'What the hell is this?'

Callan stared at the chit, eyes running over the jumble of numbers and letters on repeat. Fifteen sets of characters stared back at him, written in bold black. On his tenth attempt at deciphering the code, Aileen poked his side. 'Show me!'

He handed the sheet over to Aileen, whose eyes scanned the inconspicuous paper. She held it up to the light and frowned. 'Does anyone have a lighter? Perhaps there's something written in invisible ink.'

'That's a last resort. I don't think Andrew would go to such lengths to write in invisible ink.' Callan turned to Carpenter. 'Does it make sense to you?'

Plucking the sheet from Aileen's hand, the old woman knitted her eyebrows. 'No.'

The police constable read the note and shook his head. 'Sorry.'

'This makes absolutely no sense!' Aileen pulled up a chair and sat on it, rubbing her eyes. 'Maybe someone else put that chit in there and completely forgot about it.'

Callan read the digits once again, really focusing on each of the letters and numbers.

J00F25DIR6Z1981.

His fingers caressed his chin, scraping against his prickly beard. Callan's mind wandered to all the possibilities and combinations this number might represent.

Something about it looked awfully familiar. What?

'J00F25DIR6Z1981,' he muttered to no one in particular.

All of a sudden, shards of knowledge pierced his mind. Callan clicked his fingers, almost jumping with accomplishment. 'Could ye please hand me that sheet of paper, Mrs Carpenter?'

Unsure, she handed him the chit where she'd penned the serial number for the directory.

Callan laid both those sheets side by side and read them again. A pattern formed in his mind.

Both codes had fifteen characters. They each started with a letter or two.

Callan used his forefinger to trace each number and letter. They had the same combination of a letter or two letters followed by one or two zeroes and then a letter, two numbers, three letters, number, letter and then ending with four numbers.

Excitement made his fingers tremble. Callan tapped at the paper furiously, then he swivelled to face an astonished Carpenter. 'How do ye read this, Mrs Carpenter?'

Carpenter read the paper again. 'I don't follow. I don't understand what that number means.'

Callan shook his head. 'No, no. How do you read this serial number?' He pointed to the other sheet she'd used to locate the directory. 'It must mean something in your filing system, the way the aisles are, where the books are placed… something.'

She rounded her lips, understanding blooming in her eyes. 'Yes, the first letter tells me which aisle, then which bookshelf, and so on and so forth.'

'So how would you interpret this number?' Callan held up the chit they'd found in the directory.

Carpenter took a chair beside Aileen, placing the two sheets next to each other, then pulled out a small notepad and pen and tried to make sense of it, her lips tracing every single number or letter.

When the three of them hovered over her shoulder, she waved them away. 'You're blocking the light. Don't breathe down my neck!'

The wait Callan considered as nerve-racking as family members waiting outside an operating theatre. Deciphering this code meant they would either be reunited with Andrew or never see his face again.

After a long while, the librarian sat back. 'I'm sorry, but this makes no sense. We don't have anything with this number at all.'

Aileen walked over to Carpenter and pointed at the sheet they'd found in the directory. 'Why don't you lead us to this aisle and we'll see where the problem lies?'

Carpenter, being very cordial, nodded.

The clock had just struck 1.45 a.m. and judging by the long yawns the police constable couldn't hold in, he was exhausted.

At this point, Callan's body was functioning on fumes of hope. He turned to the constable. 'You can call it a night, ye ken.'

The constable shook his head. 'DI Walsh wanted me to support you any way I could.'

Their brigade once again left in search of a book. This time, instead of walking to the back, they headed to the front, almost towards the librarian's desk.

As they marched down the long room, Callan realised what the 'J' stood for. Every aisle had a letter or two assigned to it, and each aisle consisted of several bookshelves lined up like an army ready for battle.

Carpenter led them down the 'J' aisle, right up to the wall, then from the bottom up, she located the twenty-fifth row, her finger tracing the number tags on each book.

She mouthed the number she searched for as she went. 'DIR6Z1981.'

Two minutes later, she turned to Callan and gestured at the last book. 'I'm sorry, this is where the numbers end.'

She showed them the serial number written on the chit. They'd got to DIR6Z1980. The series ended there.

'The next set of combinations are Z2000,' she explained.

Aileen tilted her head, running her fingers against the numbers on the books. 'What happened to the books between these two serial numbers?'

Carpenter narrowed her eyes, resting her chin on her fingers. 'I reckon the library either removed those books, or… they simply didn't exist. I've been here for a good ten years and I believe we have never had 1981 in this series at all.'

Aileen tapped on the rest of the DIR series. 'What about these books? What does "DIR" mean?'

'Oh, DIR just means it's part of this series. For example, we have directories in here, indexes, not the sort that are accessed by students very often though.'

They perused the titles of the thick books. Just like the directory, these set of books stood tall and thick, and were surely heavy. Dust had gathered on most of the spines except… Callan leaned so close his nose almost stuck to the shelf. 'What's this?' He used his gloved hands to tap on the wood.

Callan tapped the wood again. 'See this? There's dust on all of these books, but nothing on the spines of these two.' Pointing to the wooden shelving, he added, 'Here ye can see marks in the dust consistent with a book being pulled out recently.'

Turning around, Callan waved the police constable over. 'Let's get this out.'

Taking great care, he hefted out one book. Aileen reached over to grab the rest before they could topple like a row of dominoes, then they took them all out one after the other.

Despite the light illuminating the library, the dark

wooden furniture made it difficult for them to see inside the shelf. After taking off six books, an abyss gaped back.

Callan stuck his hand inside and felt around the wood on the bottom, then the top of the shelf, before checking the side plank to see if someone had plastered something on there. Perhaps Andrew had left behind an object or a letter… anything.

He found nothing.

Callan diverted his attention back to the other books, the ones coated with a thin layer of dust. Surely no one could have touched them in the last few days.

He pointed to the books the police constable had placed on the floor. 'Go through them like I've shown ye. We're looking for any letters or chits in there.'

The four of them lifted a book each and Callan came back for the other two. He checked their pages just like he had before and found a note. Excitedly, he opened it up.

'Eejit!' Someone had left a crude joke on a chit as a prank.

Callan looked up at the others. They too shook their heads, implying their search had led them nowhere. Just like every other clue in this case, they'd found bloody nothing.

Irritation and frustration, along with the fatigue he had shrugged off earlier, threatened to break through the walls and drown him. But he couldn't back down now. There was still one place left they hadn't checked.

His footsteps thudded like smacks of a hammer as he strolled back with purpose to the shelves they'd just left behind. Alone in that aisle, his height just right for the shelf, he took out his phone and flashed it into the hole the books had created.

There, reflecting back at him, in gold foil, were two letters – DD.

Callan reached inside and felt for the edges, then he wrapped his hands around a small leather-bound diary, stuck to the back of the shelf, and pulled it out.

This black hardbound cover shone, unlike the rest of the books.

Callan opened the first page.

CHAPTER TWENTY

All four heads loomed over the diary. The leather casing gleamed a beautiful glossy black. Aileen's fingers trembled to touch it, just to feel the softness under her skin.

The gold letters 'DD' cut through the fabric, stark against the backdrop.

'How old do you reckon it is?' she whispered.

Carpenter waved her hands. 'In my experience, I would say not more than fifty years.'

It mightn't be an original version of the Magna Carta, but Aileen still gasped in awe. 'It's so thrilling!'

Callan placed the diary gently on the stand, displacing the directory that had led them to it. With deft fingers, he opened the cover and they all leaned in, until their heads blocked the light.

Inside, where they'd thought there would be a name, they found the same letters – 'DD' – written in beautiful calligraphy.

Aileen rubbed a finger over the paper, unable to hold back. It felt rough and thick, almost handmade.

'Whoever owned this had to be rich,' the police constable breathed.

'Definitely,' Carpenter agreed.

Callan reached to flip over to the next page. They all held their breath.

The spine creaked as the thick paper moved.

'Is it dusty?' Aileen asked Callan.

He touched his forefinger to the page and swiped it. 'Nope.' He showed his gloved finger to the group.

Aileen frowned. The next page started with a letter. 'It's a personal diary!'

The police constable had taken his notepad out, scribbling down notes. 'Whose is it?'

Callan shrugged. 'That's what's odd. There's no name on the front page.' He turned the pages to the end of that diary entry.

No name, not even an initial.

'Why would someone be so cautious?' Aileen wondered aloud.

Carpenter sat on the chair on the opposite side of the desk. 'Well…' She gestured to the shelves. 'Mr Mackay took great pains to hide it from us. If we hadn't gone looking, we wouldn't have found it. That aisle – especially that bookcase – is almost redundant – no one ever takes anything from it.'

Callan looked at her over the rim of the diary. 'Ye mean to say there's something important in here about the case—'

'And Andrew's location,' Aileen finished.

They dug in, like ravenous children after a long day at school. Callan skipped back to the first entry, and together, they read each one, word by word. The entries started off obscure, almost bordering on senseless, waxing lyrical about the wind, the sun and the moon before abruptly talking about blood and grime.

The diary entries didn't have dates on them nor any inkling as to what year they'd been written. The handwriting sometimes turned too erratic to comprehend, while at other times the words ran as if written with great care.

'I'm not sure I follow any of this,' Carpenter said, setting her glasses on the table.

Callan, though, narrowed his eyes in concentration. 'I am. I think the owner of this diary is female. Look here, for example, she writes, "The curse of womanhood is plentiful in its nature. We must suffer such limitations. Women are known to be someone's wives, mothers, daughters, sisters but never as an independent entity with a voice which is heard." These are strong sentiments.'

Aileen drummed her fingers on the desk. 'But the phrasing sounds quite old-fashioned.'

Callan ran his finger down the page and tapped another sentence. 'Here – she writes about Margaret Thatcher being Prime Minister.'

That certainly narrowed down their timeline.

'Thatcher was Prime Minister between 1979 and 1990.' The police constable had his phone out and was reading from the internet. 'Lucas Fraser was murdered in 1981, right?'

'Aye.' Callan kept reading. Aileen followed his example.

As they read on, they found more proof the writer was female. She'd written of boring tea parties paired with a note on how sordid the host's family history was. Then she'd written about vengeance in the wind and the rain, talking about floods and their devastation as a wrath of the mother goddess. She'd written, 'A woman's vengeance leads to annihilation.'

The entries turned sadder as they went on, often veering towards tragic.

Heartbreak, disease and destruction – she wrote about it all but in no certain terms. The words read ambiguously. They hadn't come across any name or detail to identify the writer.

And then it happened – they struck gold.

The writer had written 'Loch Fuar' above an entry, along with the time, then proceeded to write in detail about a *crime*. It would've sounded like a story if it weren't all true, supported by forensic evidence. Such gruesome details like heavy heartbeats, her breath mixed with *his* and then the 'satisfying smell of blood'. This was followed by such a vivid description of her feelings, Aileen felt vomit rising in her throat.

Callan set the book down, rubbing his palms over his face. 'Goodness me!'

'This is just…' Carpenter had turned a shade of green.

This woman had admitted to a murder, murder in cold blood. She'd started off explaining her feelings of sadness and anticipation, before ending with peace and calmness. She sounded like a psychopath.

But would this woman be alive now?

Callan flipped through the pages and then they saw the last entry, barely two-thirds of the way through.

'She knew – she knew it all and told that little brat. What does she know? There is love and then it splinters with death, with betrayal and greed. I've seen it all.'

Gasping with horror, they read each word – the description of a river of blood and destruction. Another murder.

Finally, the diary ended with the words 'tears on my tongue', leaving them all in stunned silence.

Aileen didn't know what to think, let alone say.

Andrew had found the diary of a murderer, a serial killer.

Who owned this diary? They still didn't know. But they'd found the motives, the explanation of how the crimes were committed, though they didn't know who the victims were. And the killer had left no timeline to follow.

'I think this person's kidnapped Andrew,' Aileen only dared to whisper.

Callan turned to her, frowning. 'It's possible, but where did Andrew find this diary? Who'd leave it here in the library? Surely the killer wouldn't be this careless.'

Aileen pointed at the book. 'But it's almost written in code, isn't it? What do these entries really tell us? There are no names in there.'

Pulling out his notepad, Callan aligned it next to the diary. 'We know the writer is likely female and right-handed, just like our killer.'

Aileen sat almost at the edge of her seat. 'I agree.' She turned the pages back to where the owner had written about the first murder.

'It says here that love can turn to hurt, and betrayal mustn't be allowed to live. "When promises are broken, it's no longer an affirmative but an *I won't*. I won't obey, and I shan't honour, and I'll strike you down until death." These words sounded awfully similar to wedding vows, just turned negative.'

Callan tapped on the next page. 'Here it talks about breaking up a family. "She set a curtain on fire; set a home on fire." Sounds like vandalism.'

'And…' Aileen flipped two pages. 'Here she writes about "burying it all, friends and foe, dishonoured maids".'

Callan typed into his phone, then he held out another picture, barely visible through his cracked phone screen. 'Read this.'

Aileen read the letter in its entirety. The writer promised to marry the sender after talking about missing him. She frowned as her eyes darted to the flourished Fs and the curvy legs of the Gs. 'This handwriting looks the same as the diary's.'

Callan then scrolled to the bottom of the picture and zoomed in on the signature at the end.

Aileen smacked her palm over her mouth. 'Lucas Fraser received this from Isobel Murray?'

Callan confirmed what she thought. 'Isobel Murray killed Lucas Fraser.'

'I DON'T UNDERSTAND,' THE POLICE CONSTABLE SAID, dropping into a chair. 'Why would she kill her own fiancé?' He blushed. 'I've been following the case, sir, and they seemed so in love.'

Not to Callan though. He'd read this letter only once and forgotten about it. But now, he remembered the words and saw them in a new light.

A person in love didn't write like that, only talking about themselves and not asking about their loved one. This letter was written by someone self-absorbed, narcissistic.

He wrote down the findings in his own notepad. 'She was jealous to put it plainly. Here she'd written, using butterflies and nature as metaphors, about how Lucas Fraser behaved. "Like a butterfly fluttering from one flower to the next. It fails to realise some flowers give sweeter nectar and comfort that only stability finds."'

'She killed him out of jealousy?' Carpenter folded her spectacles to place them on the desk. 'What about the second murder?'

Aileen jumped in. 'The missing servant – Millie Baines! Read this bit about burying dishonoured maids. Millie Baines was a servant, wasn't she? I bet Millie found out. Perhaps there was blood on Isobel's clothes or something.

And then the sister had run off, as Isobel put it.

Intertwining her fingers, Aileen bit her lip. 'What I can't understand is, what about Anvit Nair? What's Isobel's connection with him? She hasn't written about his murder in here.'

And that's where they came up against a wall. Where was Isobel Murray? Had she indeed killed Anvit? How were she and Andrew connected?

As far as Callan was concerned, Isobel had committed two murders and confessed to them in here. And the DNA evidence connected Lucas's and Anvit's killer, meaning she was responsible for all three.

Why then wouldn't she write about Anvit? The diary seemed to be some sort of confessional and she had enough space.

Callan asked this question to the room only to receive unsure shakes of the head.

Aileen pulled out her trusty yellow notepad, staring at her notes as if they'd give her the answers.

Carpenter let out a loud yawn.

Callan pushed off the table. 'I'm sorry for dragging you out here in the cold night. You've helped a lot.'

She shrugged. 'But we still didn't find Mr Mackay, so my help wasn't good enough.'

Aileen didn't let go of her notepad, clutching it to her bosom when Callan led her outside.

The lights clicked off, blinding them.

A cold gust of wind rustled Callan's hair, making him want to crawl under a warm blanket and sleep the week away. Mist hung low, allowing fears and ghosts to wander.

The police constable pointed to his cruiser. 'Let me drop you home, Mrs Carpenter.'

They waved the old woman off after Callan thanked her again profusely. If it weren't for her, they certainly wouldn't have found the identity of the killer. Now if only they could find Isobel Murray and match her DNA to the two crime scenes.

Thinking of DNA, Callan realised Dr Brown hadn't called him back about the analysis of whether the blood belonged to a man or a woman. Now though, they knew it was a woman's.

When they sat back in the car and Callan started it up, Aileen shivered. 'It's so cold.'

Checking the time on his watch, he realised it was half past three. Isla should be at the bakery by four. He started up the car, heading out into the misty night.

Their ride back went by quicker, each lost in their own musings. Callan's brain tried to figure out how Anvit or Andrew could know Isobel. It seemed like the dead lad and his friends were more interested in Douglas Reid. Could he have framed a defenceless Isobel Murray?

And why would a woman lost for so long return to haunt them now?

He entered Loch Fuar, foot flooring the accelerator. No one in town wandered about this late… or early. The market square, which always brimmed with people, lay deserted. Not a soul lingered outside the grocer's, the butcher's or the bakery. Only one car – belonging to Isla – was parked.

Aileen blinked up at Callan. He'd wondered if she'd fallen asleep, but no – she'd been staring at her notes in the darkness of the car.

'Coffee?'

'Isla'll skewer us alive if we go in there without Andrew.'

Callan rolled his eyes at her dramatics and urged her out of her seat. 'We need coffee.'

Isla had left the door leading to the kitchen and her office open. Hearing the door open, she raced up to the counter looking like hell.

Callan winced at the dark circles under her reddened eyes. 'What happened to ye?'

She wagged a finger. 'Have babies and then you'll know, especially when the man you married is afraid of bloody tears. And a missing nephew—'

Aileen rounded the counter. 'Isla…'

Isla leaned in and sniffed. 'Seems like you haven't even been to bed. Up working?' Before Aileen responded, she pulled her into a hug. 'You're the best friend anyone could ask for.'

Callan saw Aileen swipe a tear. 'Come on you! It's too early in the day to be sentimental. We need coffee.'

Five minutes later, Isla sat two steaming coffees on the table. 'My first customers for the day. Give me a shout if you need anything.' She bustled away. 'I have a feeling today'll dawn beautifully.'

It felt nice to see Isla in a better mood.

After she left them, Aileen pulled out her notepad again and turned the pages till she got to the one with three circles.

'We're looking for a woman. Who is she?' she mumbled to herself. On her list were Charlotte Fraser, Moira Robertson, Isobel Murray and Leana Murray.

Callan tapped Isobel's name. 'We ken it's her.'

'Aye, but if it's not her, then who is *she*?' Aileen chewed on her pencil, eyes trained on the page. 'What I'm trying to get at is you searched for Isobel and Leana, but you couldn't locate them. What if that's because they no longer use those names?'

'Ye mean Moira and Charlotte are sisters? That sounds ludicrous.'

Aileen sighed with exasperation. 'I mean one of them is Isobel. The younger sister ran away, remember?'

Callan scratched his chin, thinking about the possibility. 'If one of them is, she'd need guts to come back to Loch Fuar after what she did.'

Aileen pulled out her phone. 'Whoever it is, Anvit needs to be connected with her to know about her past. How did he find out?'

She tapped the phone screen and then typed something in. 'I'm looking at Anvit's data. It's on the cloud, shared via my laptop.'

Five minutes later, Aileen shook her head. 'No mention of Isobel or Leana.'

Callan narrowed his eyes. 'Is there anything about Lucas Fraser?'

'Nope. No matches for Fraser.'

Now his mind worked into a frenzy. 'Anvit Nair didn't know about Lucas Fraser or his connection with Douglas Reid. Nor did he know about the Murray sisters. He never searched for them.'

'Oh my God, Callan!' Aileen slapped the desk. 'He did search for—'

She held out her phone, pointing at the screen.

Callan nodded. 'Anvit wasn't only interested in bringing Reid down, he hated Moira Robertson too. That's why he was looking into her. He was trying to find dirt on her but—'

'She doesn't have any history before the degree in London thirty-five years ago. There's no record of Moira Robertson before 1985.'

'Because Moira Robertson was Isobel Murray,' Callan finished then frowned. 'What about the location Reid's app captured from her phone. Where is it?'

Aileen pulled up the map. 'It still makes no sense – it's in the middle of the woods.'

Callan cupped his chin. He whispered, not wanting Isla to overhear, 'Perhaps that's where Andrew is?'

Aileen frowned, looking at the picture. 'But the image's got no markers. How... Hold on,' she spluttered then. 'The diary. Open it!'

Callan pulled it out from his pocket, removed it from the evidence bag, slipped on gloves and cracked the spine open.

'First page.'

He followed Aileen's instructions. Once there, his memory clicked to the words Isobel Murray had scrawled. *All roads lead to Violet's Rose.'*

Callan pushed off the table. 'Andrew's at Violet's Rose.'

Aileen joined him, turning to the door leading to the kitchen. 'Isla?'

'Not yet. She's too close to this. It's dangerous and anyone could get hurt. The woman's a loony, remember?'

So they hurried out of the sweet-scented bakery and into the cold night, hoping to find a killer along with a breathing Andrew.

CHAPTER TWENTY-ONE

The thin woollen jacket she wore offered little protection against the cold, her teeth chattering. Her exposed fingers didn't tingle as they clutched the icy metallic torch – frozen. She might have come ill-prepared to face the sub-zero temperatures but thanks to her previous adventures, Aileen had now resolved to always carry a torch. She kept a spare and extra batteries in the glovebox of her car too.

Callan crouched next to her, his breath mingling with hers as they blended into the trees.

The sprawling Victorian mansion loomed before them, its broken windows gaping ravenous jaws. The chimney sat still, as it had for decades. The only sign of life was the thick ivy wrapped around the red bricks – like staunch enemies at each other's throats.

The ostentatious front door made from intricately carved wood was shut tight. It couldn't mute the scampering of rats inside. Haunted this place certainly was, with no sign of human life.

Had they been wrong? Perhaps Moira Robertson

wasn't Isobel Murray. Maybe they were grasping at straws. Perhaps Andrew was just gone, vanished like Blaine.

Fear found its way into her veins.

Aileen pressed the palm of her right hand onto the coarse tree trunk she huddled against. The night, almost moonless, made everything creepy.

Stars littered the sky like solitaires, their luminance hindered by dark grey clouds. A bad omen?

A flutter caught Aileen's attention — the dark silhouette of a bat bursting from within the house and making for the woods.

Once again, nature settled around her.

Aileen shivered and pulled her jacket closer.

Callan moved beside her, then — 'Argh!' he yelped, then gritted his teeth. 'Shit!' he whispered-yelled.

Eyes spewing fire, Aileen turned to glare at the man. 'What's wrong with you?'

He didn't have to reply. Behind her, she found him sprawled at an awkward angle. His foot must've slipped and he'd now landed in a ditch covered by thicker foliage. Neither had been able to see it in the dark.

Callan tried to move but just hissed.

Aileen faced him. 'Does it hurt?'

He gave her a glare that told her just how he felt.

Aileen reached for her phone to dial for help when she groaned. 'No reception!'

Was this another stupid move?

No, she wouldn't think about it that way. She was here to save a life. Callan's injury would just have to wait.

'Are you bleeding?' she asked with urgency.

Callan shook his head. 'I just tumbled down. My foot's caught in these roots. I can't get it out and you won't be able to reach over without falling in.'

Aileen nodded. 'Stay here. I'll get Andrew out.'

'No way are ye heading in there alone!'

Aileen clenched her teeth, throwing daggers at him with her eyes. 'Watch me, DI Callan Cameron. I promised my best friend I'd do this so I will get her nephew to safety.'

Chewing the inside of her lip, Aileen breathed once, twice and then crouch-walked, circling the house, still sticking to the woods.

As she went around the bend and came to what must be a side entrance, Aileen almost tripped over a twig. *Crap!*

Her palm scratched against something, drawing a long red gash. Aileen exhaled, pushing the pain to the back of her mind as scores of swordsmen had in centuries past. She had important things to focus on, like the green sedan parked next to the house. She had seen that bottle-green shade before.

Moira Robertson, aka Isobel Murray, was here. As well as a bike – Andrew's bike surely – leaning against the space between the mansion's wall and her car.

Aileen waited, the two sides of her brain warring, hoping she didn't freeze. Should she barge in?

Five minutes turned to ten and now she shivered. Should she turn back and get reinforcements.

What if Isobel had left by the time they arrived? What if she killed Andrew?

Something flickered causing Aileen to think she was seeing things. She rubbed her eyes, hissing at her stinging palm. There – a soft glow lit up the broken window on the first floor.

It swayed as a light breeze rustled the ghostly leaves and then the light stretched across the room and lit up a blob of darkness.

'A head?'

Aileen slapped a hand over her mouth. Her eyes flittered over the windows, trying to find a way to get in. There were several windows with broken glass. Her footsteps, though, would alert Isobel.

Aileen considered. If she was with Andrew up there, would it be a bad thing?

If – Aileen swallowed – if he was still alive.

Moira was here with Andrew, the place where all roads led. She was here to do drastic things, things like murder.

Once again, Aileen crouch-walked through the woods, eyes on the uneven ground and fallen leaves.

Aileen then stealthily jogged to a bottom window, finding one that had entirely caved in. She peered in, studying the large room. Ghostly moth-eaten sheets had been draped over furniture, while the once flamboyant wallpaper had stains of leakage, peeling off at the top. And the entire thing stank of damp moss.

Sticking to the dark ivy, Aileen found her way to the other room, which had large enough windows to step through.

Against her better judgement, she took off her coat, knowing now she'd be freezing soon, wrapped it around her arm and—*Slam!*

The glass tinkled, breaking away like the shell of a cracked egg. The sound echoed through the house and Aileen leaned into the shadows again.

Finally, she tiptoed to the last window in the room and saw *her*.

Moira's outfit was precise – a pearl necklace and turtleneck with woollen trousers. Her hair though was in disarray, and her wrinkles resembled lines drawn in charcoal. She looked like a skeleton with skin.

Aileen wasted no time in stepping through the window in the other room. But she hadn't accounted for the creaky floorboards.

Crap!

She sank behind a piece of furniture.

Moira still tinkered in the other room, her boots smacking as she treaded back and forth.

Aileen peeked from behind the dusty sheet and gasped when her white bob peered into the room.

Moira left it and went to the next.

Carefully, Aileen made for the door. She would've taken off her boots, but this damned place had no heating and lots of debris littering the floor.

Plastered to the flaky wallpaper, Aileen peered round the wooden doorframe and saw Moira disappearing behind a doorway. Then she looked at the foyer.

A large door, the back of the grand entrance, stood to the right. The stairway, sweeping as it curved to a bottleneck like a woman's waist, faced it. More doorways, some with doors and some without like hers, led to the base of the stairs.

Andrew had to be on the first floor.

A dark carpet ran over the staircase, held together by rusted brass rods. Would it muffle her footsteps?

Aileen waited for Moira to leave the room she'd entered, but she didn't.

It was now or never.

Aileen took a deep breath and immediately regretted it as it filled her nose with damp moss.

One, two, three—

She tiptoed forward, her heart thudding. A couple of months ago she wouldn't have dared this hare-brained scheme.

She got to the middle of the stairs, still pressed against the balustrade, when a click struck her ears.

'One more move, Ms Aileen Mackinnon, and a bullet

will lodge itself into that pretty forehead. I'm a good shot. I *know*.'

The cold voice made her freeze as her gaze met eyes bright with madness. Standing right below the stairs was Isobel Murray, cradling a well-polished hunting rifle. And the steely look on her face assured Aileen she wasn't joking.

CALLAN STARED AFTER HIS OBNOXIOUS GIRLFRIEND. What the hell did he like about her?

He reached for his phone and remembered there was no reception here.

The day refused to dawn, letting the cold mist rein free. It hurt to breathe, and the jacket he wore didn't keep the wind at bay.

Gulping in oxygen, he tried to pull his leg free. His breath misted as he huffed, tugging at his leg with all his might, his lungs catching fire.

Callan twiddled with his phone and switched on the torch.

Damn Moira! He needed to get to Aileen.

He had only just flashed the torch when a loud bang rang out, followed by the sound of glass splintering.

Fear gripped his heart and his arms trembled. Thinking quickly, he reached over, moaning at the shards of pain piercing his back, grasped hold of a root and tugged. The long vines were decades old and didn't budge.

If he'd got in, he'd get out.

Callan tried again and something around his ankle loosened. His palms turned muddy and his skin scraped. A stone pricked him near the elbow.

'Bloody hell!'

He tugged at his leg again, trying again and again until

his chest felt like it was bleeding with each inhale. One last pull at and— 'Ump!' He crashed to the soggy ground, landing on his right side.

At least he was free.

He tried standing upright, putting weight on his foot and realised he'd sprained it. So he began to crawl on his forearms. His black shirt and jeans nicked the twigs and branches, but he didn't stop.

No way could he get into the mansion and cause a hinderance to Aileen. But he would call a team. He might look like a maniac, but he was on a mission.

Blood pounded in his head, heart bursting out of his ribs and then a single sound pierced the sky. The sound of a bullet.

Callan involuntarily ducked until his forehead scraped the ground.

Nothing happened. He continued into the woods, the romantic notions of pines and petrichor forgotten. The chilled air froze his bones but the pre-dawn crawl warmed his arm muscles.

Callan had rounded one corner and swivelled towards the house. He hadn't seen the actual mansion last time. Broken bricks of what used to be a tower appeared from between the dense foliage. A carpet of stars illuminated the sordid structure. Violet's Rose had wilted into a shell of mayhem and murder.

And now his girlfriend was in there.

He reached for his phone and thanked the one weak bar of reception.

All at once, piercing pops banged loud in the night, oozing blood through his heart. Bullets – the sound reverberating through the walls of the old mansion. Fear turning his blood to ice, Callan could only lie there, forced to listen as a killer fired at his *banlaoch*.

At that moment, Aileen had two choices. Die or die while doing something stupid.

She stuck to her mantra.

Her feet swivelled and, still crouched, she raced up the stairs.

Moira, clearly shocked by her move, fumbled with her rifle. But Aileen wasn't quick enough – the first shot wedged itself in the wood near her feet. The next grazed the top of the balustrade, sending up an explosion of splinters.

Scared she was, but experienced with criminals too. Aileen didn't stop and was at the top step when a bullet whizzed past her ear.

She bit back a cry.

No – adventurous! Come on!

She almost fell onto the landing but scampered away before a bullet found her.

Racing along a corridor, she ran through doorways that led into other doorways. Then she realised that if Moira couldn't find her, she'd find Andrew and finish him instead. The thought almost paralysed Aileen.

'Andrew!' she screamed at the top of her lungs. 'Andrew! It's Aileen!'

A groan sounded from within one room. Aileen followed it, relief propelling her. What if Moira got to him before her?

An angry woman didn't think straight though.

Moira was still pursuing her, shooting like a maniac. Aileen realised she'd taken a wrong turn then, a turn closer to the she-devil. Footsteps thundered closer instead of away.

There was no time for regret. 'Andrew!'

Another muffled groan drew her attention to the next room. She ran into it and saw him, finally saw him, unmoving but breathing.

A trickle of blood ran down his forehead and he sat slumped in a chair, wrists tied and mouth gagged.

Aileen raced to him, wishing she had a knife. But the faint light of the stars caught on a broken fragment of glass and she snatched it up. She winced when it dug into the soft skin of her already injured palm, but she set to work on the thick rope.

Footsteps neared; Aileen's heart didn't slow down.

Moira entered the room when her fingers touched Andrew's. Aileen gasped. He burned with fever. No wonder he was so out of it.

'Get away from him, you bitch!'

Aileen cocked her head, still working on the rope. 'Why? You're out of shots, aren't you?'

Moira curled her lips into a nasty smirk. 'I don't kill with bullets. A good stick or' – she raised her rifle – 'a hunting rifle is much better.'

Aileen gritted her teeth, biding her time. 'You killed a teenager.'

She shrugged as if they spoke about an ice-cream scoop she'd dropped. 'Threatened to expose me. Then this idiot came here to do the same. I'd be rid of him already if it weren't for that stupid conference; I couldn't kill him before I'd had a chance to find out who else knew about me. And I'd have killed you if that detective's car hadn't interrupted us the other night. Now you're here. You'll meet the same fate!'

She lunged for Aileen, her scream echoing through the silent house, startling some nestling birds.

The shard of glass dropped to the floor and crunched

under Aileen's feet as she ducked, crossing her arms in front of her to protect her head.

The gun cracked across her side, and pain almost doubled her over, but Aileen wasn't going to be a helpless victim. Not again, never again. She wasn't that woman anymore.

Aileen used what she knew – before Moira could attack her again, she slammed her entire weight into the thin yet tall woman.

Moira's back slammed into the ground with such force Aileen worried the old floor would give out. Her elbow cracked against the wooden boards and the gun went flying to the other corner of the room.

Red mist descended – Aileen could see the change in Moira – blinding the older woman to the limitations of her power, and she sent her fist flying at Aileen. But Aileen ducked, so it only nicked her ear.

'Oof!' She battled the next punch, the burning in her side hindering her movement. Using her other arm, she landed her own response squarely on the older woman's jaw.

They grappled for dominance, kicking and punching. Moira, despite her age, knew her way through a fist fight.

Aileen was unstoppable when on a mission though.

Roaring, an engine gathering its strength, she punched once, hard and soundly on the woman's face and Moira's head banged on the floor, knocking her unconscious.

Aileen checked her breathing, ensuring she hadn't killed her, then scrambled over to Andrew, loosening the ropes tying him to the chair, before scampering back to Moira. She tied her wrists and ankles together then went to Andrew. He had barely moved – he just sagged in his chair, eyes tightly shut and shivering slightly.

She made out a backpack in the corner, a laptop

sticking out the top. He must've come here alone to challenge the murderer. Eejit! Aileen huffed. Callan would call her the same.

She leaned in to try to rouse him when the wail of sirens flooded through the night. Soon the dark night shone with red and blue lights.

Aileen smirked. 'Guess someone's fashionably late.'

The great door gave out easily – she heard a battering ram slam into it – and footsteps ran through the house.

Moira stirred beside her. Aileen lifted her head and banged it against the floor again. 'In here!' her holler echoed. Response came soon when a single pair of light steps raced to where they were.

DI Walsh rushed to Aileen, his trench coat off shoulder and hat missing. 'Callan called.' He gestured to the paramedics to get to Andrew. 'I could barely hear him, so I traced his phone. Where is he?'

Aileen didn't know.

They handcuffed Moira, and Walsh instructed the uniformed officers to take her away. 'Get her some medical help then get her into an interview room.'

He turned to Aileen. 'Are you hurt?'

Aileen shook her head. 'Thanks for coming.'

'You didn't seem to need my help – again.' He grinned. 'I didn't know you had a degree in amateur sleuthing with honours in combat.'

Aileen's laugh reverberated off the old walls. She winced when her side ached. 'Yeah, I single-handedly defeated Moira. It feels so good to say that.'

Side by side, they walked downstairs and into the dawning day. 'Let's go find my boyfriend. He's bound to be a little grumpy seeing as he had to sit this one out.'

EPILOGUE

Callan wasn't grumpy because he'd missed out on the action at Violet's Rose. But when Aileen had dragged him to the hospital, he'd gone kicking and screaming, threatening to arrest her.

He had indeed sprained his 'bloody left leg'. He'd even cursed his right prosthetic one, as he often did.

The day had indeed dawned beautifully – bringing Andrew back to them – just like Isla had predicted.

Walsh had arrested Moira, though she'd spent the past week at the hospital being looked at for her injuries. But she'd confessed to the crimes, even Anvit's murder, once she'd been told her DNA had been found at both crime scenes.

Aileen sat at the kitchen counter, smiling at a grumbling Callan, their daily ritual for the last week. Her injuries had healed already, much to her satisfaction.

'Ice it, you!'

He scowled. 'What do you think I'm bloody doing?'

She reached over to touch his ice-cold hand. 'Stop being grumpy.'

The back door opened, and Isla, Daniel and Carly bustled in with a smiling Andrew, walking on crutches. An injury to his foot had festered, giving him a fever, but he was looking much better now.

Carly nestled in her mother's arms. She smiled at Aileen so radiantly it put the sun to shame. Aileen went to her, cooing and awing. Carly blew her a raspberry then gave her a sloppy kiss on the cheek.

'Aw, you sweet girl.'

Isla crushed Aileen and her daughter against her. 'The doctor said Andrew'll be alright. Oh! I can't thank you enough! Andrew.' She beckoned to her nephew.

The lanky lad blushed the same colour as his hair. 'Er, Aileen, er, Ms Mackinnon, thank ye.'

Aileen grinned at him and drew him into a hug. 'I'm glad you're okay. Next time though, stay out of trouble.'

Sniffles and smiles rose up in the air.

'How did ye do it?' Callan raised an eyebrow. 'How did ye find the diary?'

Andrew took a seat at the dining table. 'Anvit said Moira Robertson had something to hide. They were always arguing, so when he had his doubts about her, we laughed it off. But the day before he died, he said she had something to hide. His voice – I can still hear it – sounded so sure. I believed him. He wanted to search her office but we knew she'd point the blame at him.'

Andrew stared out at the beautiful autumnal day. 'We decided I would get into her office when she was in class teaching Anvit, so he had an alibi. I pretended to go meet another teacher and slipped into her office. I searched and couldn't find anything and then Anvit texted saying she'd left the class. I panicked and hid in a nook.'

He breathed deeply. 'She walked in and tucked a book in her desk drawer. That was the diary. Right then, someone called, and she walked out, so I plucked it and went in search of Anvit.

'Later I heard they'd had a massive argument where he'd said, "I know all about your secrets." And threatened to expose her. Anvit read the diary that afternoon and then passed it to me. He asked me to hide it for him. Said Moira was suspicious of him.'

Aileen sighed. 'The threat — that's what got him killed.'

'Looks like it.' Andrew ran a hand through his hair. 'So I made a plan to hide it. That's why I was in the library that night, the night that…'

He didn't need to say any more. Isla patted him on the back. 'It's alright, dear.'

Daniel had taken a seat next to Callan. 'We're glad you're back safe, Andrew.' He watched Callan ice his leg. 'What did you find about Blaine?'

Callan dropped the frozen peas on the counter and faced them. 'Dr Brown's looking for him, but we've got nothing.'

'It's almost become a dream at this point. There are no clues about where he might be. Those peatlands are so vast, finding him is like trying to paint the Great Wall of China with a liner brush.'

Aileen's heart reached out to Callan but there was nothing they could do.

Daniel sighed and patted his leg. 'Something will turn up. If Blaine wants us to find him. On that note…' He straightened. 'Isla and I have decided to head out for a day trip. We'll be leaving this one with her grandparents though.'

'And me.' Andrew tickled the toddler's bare feet. 'She loves spending time with me.'

Carly giggled, and Isla kissed her chubby cheek. 'It's

going to be hard leaving her alone for an entire day. We've never done it before.'

Daniel rubbed his tired eyes. 'Aye, we'll miss her.'

Callan patted Daniel's back. 'With your driving skills, I'm not sure ye'd get further than the next town.'

'Shut up!'

Aileen hushed the two friends and gestured to herself. 'Hey, if you ever need a babysitter.'

Isla grinned deviously at Aileen, then spoke with a stronger burr. 'Siobhan says, "Push a baby into ma grandwean's arms. That'll make her and that eejit detective of hers get a move on!"'

Aileen hooted. 'She's incorrigible, Gran.'

Callan leaned in to press a tender kiss to Aileen's forehead. 'Just like a *banlaoch* I ken.'

PLEASE WRITE A REVIEW

Thank you so much for reading this novel. Please write an honest review for this book. Your review helps me as an independent author reach new readers. If you've never written a review before, don't worry. It doesn't need to be a long literary essay, just a sentence or two is perfect. And if you have the time, leave one on Goodreads and/or Bookbub as well.

THANK YOU!

The end? Nope. Aileen and Callan are up against the toughest odds
When Old Fires Ignite is coming soon…

READ AN EXCLUSIVE NOVELLA

When a storm cuts off the tiny town of Loch Fuar from the rest of the world, a murderer strikes. And it's someone among them.

Download your free copy on www.shanafrost.com/exclusivenovella

AUTHOR'S NOTE

Dear Reader Friend,

Thank you so much for taking another journey with Aileen and Callan. This story had been cooking in my mind for a while. I really like Andrew and wondered how he would react in a crisis like the one he goes through in this book. And to add to it, it was also a test of Aileen and Isla's friendship. Personally, I felt a sense of pride when Aileen not only stuck to per promise but, despite her fears, saved a teenager's life.

I must confess, this case was a tough nut to crack. There were definitely times when I was certain we weren't going to solve this mystery. But finally it all came together. I guess all's well that ends well, eh?

This story wouldn't be as succinct as it is without these incredible people.

Thanks to my amazing cheerleader and friend, Janae Rogers, for her help and encouragement for getting this book just right. Thank you for having the patience to read this story not once, but twice!

Leonise van Reenen and Jean Soderquist, thank you as

always for your feedback. You guys are the best beta readers I could ask for.

Special thanks to Shilpa Wagh for taking the time to brainstorm the story with me when things seemed stuck. Your inputs definitely made the story so much clearer.

Thank you to my amazing copyeditor, Laura Kincaid. Only you can catch errors that many others missed!

A very huge thank you to my proofreader, Charlotte Kane, for taking the time to read and edit this novel despite everything.

As you read this, I'm plotting away at the next book in Aileen and Callan's world. I promise it'll be out soon. Until then, I hope you enjoy the other novels and, if you like, you can try out the first book in my other series Smokes of Death Beer. It's a mystery with a twist!

See ye soon,
Shana

ABOUT THE AUTHOR

Are you looking to solve murders? Perfect, Shana loves plotting them.

As a debut writer, Shana Frost is in her secret den hatching murders and having a blast with Aileen and the gang. It's crazy in there...

When not in the den, Shana always has her nose buried between the pages of a fiction novel. After all, the tantalising aroma of a story is far more enticing, especially for a sensitive nose like hers.

Shana's powerful sense of smell has helped her sniff out murder mysteries and a wide variety of characters.

Occasionally, she finds herself wandering ancient hallways of a castle, or a museum trying to smell the tales these walls effuse.

The traveller Ibn Battuta wasn't wrong when he wrote, "Travelling - It leaves you speechless, then turns you into a storyteller"

Visit the website for more: https://shanafrost.com

www.ingramcontent.com/pod-product-compliance
Lightning Source LLC
LaVergne TN
LVHW030318070526
838199LV00069B/6493